ACC

# HEAVEN

What if Heaven were a real,
*physical* place…right now?

*Michael McKinsey*

DENVER, COLORADO

Outskirts Press, Inc.
http://www.outskirtspress.com

ISBN: 978-1-4327-9629-7

Outskirts Press and the "OP" logo are trademarks belonging to Outskirts Press, Inc.

PRINTED IN THE UNITED STATES OF AMERICA

*"In my Father's house are many mansions...and one of them is Mine!"*

*Michael McKinsey*

# Foreword

**I am not** a writer. I'm just a boring, middle-aged guy who has a fascination with Heaven! I was inspired to write this book after having had a near-death experience while attending my son's wedding in Southern California. After that, Heaven became as real a place as I could ever imagine. I have always believed in Heaven, but as a child I was taught that Heaven was merely a "spiritual" place. After all, the Bible says God is "spirit," and that's where He lives! But that spiritual Heaven is not our permanent home; it's only temporary. And that's a good thing, because we are spiritual *and* physical creatures.

The Bible teaches us that God will remake Earth, and that it will become our new home forever. That's perfect for us, because we need a physical place to live! While I don't confess to having all the answers regarding Heaven (and I doubt anyone on Earth does), I do believe that Heaven will one day be a physical place, right here on this very planet! I have studied what the Bible says about the "intermediate Heaven," and "paradise restored," or our permanent home here on Earth. Those studies have led me to the only logical conclusion; Earth will become our permanent home, free from sin, where we will live with God, sometime in the near future.

The Bible also teaches us that Heaven is a real, physical place. For example, in Revelation 15:8, the Bible says, "The temple was filled with smoke from God's glory and power." The book of Revelation also mentions scrolls in Heaven, elders who have faces sitting on thrones, martyrs who wear clothes and even people with palm branches in their hands. These are all physical attributes describing Heaven.

But we are also told in Acts 7:55, when Stephen is stoned to death that "he gazed steadily into heaven and saw the glory of God, and he saw Jesus standing in the place of honor at God's right hand." Some Biblical scholars believe that Stephen didn't just see an illusion, but rather that his eyes were opened to a spiritual dimension of reality, which God has hidden from us in this modern age.

It's quite possible that this is what happened to me during my near-death experience in 2005. In this book, I tell of a dream I had while very ill in the hospital. But what I have always referred to as a dream could have been much more. If God allowed Stephen to see Heaven, couldn't He show me as well?

As a child, I used to pray that God would show me Heaven, to give me the proof my simple human mind needed. I've always been the type of person who needs physical evidence; I need to take apart a watch and see the gears and springs to figure out how it works!

When Jesus held His hand out to me in my hospital room, He said, "I want to answer your prayer." He took me by the hand to a mountain top, where I looked at Heaven with Him standing at my side. The wonder and indescribable nature of what I saw was all the proof I needed! I have always wondered where I went that night with Jesus.

That leads me to the premise for this book; a book I told God I would write. What if Heaven were a real, physical place *right now* – somewhere out there in the vastness of the universe; a universe created by God ... couldn't He have put Heaven some*where*? Wouldn't he have to?

# Chapter 1

**"Do you believe** in God?"

"What kind of question is that?"

"The kind of question a believer in God asks the new guy!"

Except the new guy wasn't exactly new. Dane had worked for Sem-Con for about a year. Sem-Con was the largest defense contractor in the United States. The company headquarters were located in San Diego, California, but they also had offices in Saudi Arabia, Turkey, Germany, Australia, and — most recently — Iraq. The company also had satellite offices in others parts of the globe, including a small office in Antarctica. They employed over thirty thousand people, and had been listed on the New York Stock Exchange for over fifty years. Sem-Con always turned a healthy profit, and a few key associations in the United States Senate made sure that this would continue indefinitely.

Until last Monday, Dane Robinson had been an intern, but a twist of fate had landed him a full-time job as an assistant to Michael Owens. Michael was head of research and development for Sem-Con, and had been for the past twenty six years.

Michael asked again, "So, do you?"

Dane got quiet and obviously uncomfortable. This was unfamiliar territory for him. He had been voted the most outgoing personality in high school, along with most athletic. An all-star pitcher in college, he'd had his sights set on a career in the major leagues, but an injury had put an end to that dream. He'd never been the kind of guy that stopped to think about God … and why should he? He never really had a need for God. He'd always gotten by on his good looks, athletic talents, and charming personality. He was the guy who everyone wanted to know. He had over one thousand friends on Facebook, and he knew them all!

But for some reason, Michael's question stopped Dane dead in his tracks. He squirmed as he answered. "I never really thought about it. But since you ask, I guess no, I don't believe in God. I mean come on, Mr. Owens, some giant wizard of Oz behind the big curtain in the sky, inventing stuff, making galaxies and solar systems out of nothing at all? And where did this God come from? Who made him?" Dane rolled his eyes and slowly shook his head from side to side. "No, I don't believe in God. I mean, I always considered even the thought of God to be a cop-out, you know, a crutch for weak-minded people."

Dane could see that he was sucking the life out of his new boss, and realized that he had probably said way too much. He looked down and shuffled his feet nervously for what seemed like hours, then looked back up at Michael, who was still staring at him in disbelief.

"What?" Dane asked.

Michael looked perplexed. He cleared his throat and said, "I just never get how people can say they don't believe in God. Where else would all this come from?" He motioned around the room, as if to say, God made all this. As Michael looked around at all the beakers, Bunsen burners, and computers, he said, "Well maybe not this, but you know what I mean ... all that." He pointed to the window at the far end of the room.

"Where did all the flowers come from, and the bees, and sunsets, and mountains, and on and on? And why does it all work so perfectly?" Michael paused, scratched the top of his head, and continued. "Dane, did you know there are over forty thousand nerves in your eye? And there are over six hundred muscles in your body? And none of that even matters if your brain doesn't tell them what to do, and your brain won't work without oxygen from your lungs, circulated by blood flowing from a heart supported by the brain? That's a pretty good plan, orchestrated by a being with intelligence that I can't even begin to understand. I just can't believe people don't see things the way I see them. Dane, I see God in *everything* ... every day."

Michael had been a believer all his life. It all made perfect sense to him. God created everything, Heaven and Earth, and it was perfect. He never even questioned the existence of God. He was raised in a Christian home, where every Sunday morning his mom had packed him and his two sisters into the station wagon and gone to the Presbyterian Church downtown. Although as a kid, church was just something his mom made him do; Michael still knew why he went. It gave him a purpose in life and also planted in him the need to worship.

Michael's relationship with God had its ups and downs. But a few years earlier, things had become very clear to him. An unexpected illness had brought him to death's door, and God had given him a new lease on life. He was incredibly grateful for that, and it had changed his life.

Michael could see, though, that Dane was uneasy talking about this stuff, and thought again about getting so personal so soon in their relationship.

"Well, now that we've got that out of the way, why don't you tell me about your family?" he said, changing the subject.

Dane smiled again, relieved. "I don't really have a 'family,' unless you call two beagles and a parakeet a family."

Michael laughed and asked, "No significant other?'

"No," Dane said. "I don't even have any brothers or sisters. I was an only child, and my dad died about ten years ago. It was just my mom and me until she died last year, right about the time I got this gig with Sem-Con. After she passed away, there was nothing holding me back on the east coast, so I sold all their stuff and moved out here. Thought a fresh start might be just what the doctor ordered."

Michael continued the questioning. "So how do you like it? San Diego, I mean?"

"Oh I love it. It's a lot warmer than back home – it doesn't snow here, after all. It's been really nice, a good break. Besides, I always wanted to learn how to surf, and this is the perfect place for that. I think I might just stay here a while! What about you? You have a family, right?"

Michael smiled. "Yea, married with four kids, although the kids are all grown up. But we still have two that live with us. We'll keep them as long as they want to stay. Our family's really close. We've always been that way."

"Sort of a modern-day *Leave it to Beaver*?" Dane asked with a smile.

"I guess so." Michael chuckled as he thought about that. As the analogy sunk in, he agreed again, sounding a little more convinced. "Yeah, I guess so."

Michael walked into his spacious home, which overlooked the Pacific Ocean, and threw his briefcase on the chair just inside the front door. Duke, his black lab, lumbered in, as if to say hello.

"Well hi Duke, how's my boy?" Michael asked as he bent over and scratched Duke's back.

Duke just pranced around, his huge tail crashing into the walls with repeated thuds.

A woman's voice called down from the second floor. "Honey, is that you?"

"Yea, where are you?"

"In the bedroom."

Michael looked down at Duke, who was now standing in front of him with a ragged tennis ball in his mouth. "Give me a minute boy!" he laughed.

He raced upstairs like a man half his age. He was an avid runner, and was in excellent shape. He'd been running since he was a kid, and had entered his first race, a 5K, when he was just twelve years old. He still spent a couple hours in the gym three or four times a week, and at fifty years old still had the body of a teenager; at least that was what his doctor always told him.

He reached the top of the stairs in seconds and turned into the master bedroom, where he found his wife. "Hi sweetie, how was your day?" As she turned, he realized that she had been crying. "What's wrong?"

"I just miss the kids." Michael's wife Ruth had a heart as big as Texas. She still had bouts of 'kid depression,' though the second of their four kids had moved out almost three years earlier.

"Honey, we still have two at home! Let's not write them off already." Michael was confused. "I miss Brandon and Hunter, but I think Tyler and Haley might be here for a while. Let's try to focus on the two we have left, and be happy with that. I'm in no hurry to become an empty nest!"

"Oh, I know," Ruth lamented. "I was just thinking of when we dropped Hunter off at school, how proud he was, and how it all worked out. It was really a miracle. But I just miss him. I miss them all! I wish they could live with us forever."

Hunter was their third child, now twenty-one years old. He was attending CBU, a Christian university in Riverside, about 70 miles north of their home in San Diego, as a nursing student. In that, he had followed her wishes. Ruth had always preached to their kids about getting into medicine in some capacity. She knew very well the opportunities in the medical field, and wanted the kids to have the best options available. She worked for Tri City Medical Center in Oceanside, as an Administrative assistant to the CEO. She saw first-hand the monetary rewards and advancement opportunities for the people working in a hospital every day. Their oldest son had taken her advice as well, and was now a nuclear medicine technologist, working in Irvine.

Ruth had worked for years to get Hunter into nursing. She had always said that Hunter would be a great nurse. He had a soft, compassionate side, while still remaining very competitive, and both qualities would help in the life and career of nursing. But Hunter had always dreamt of becoming a major league baseball player. He had played organized baseball since he was six years old, and was well on his way to becoming one of the area's top recruits. But that all changed his senior year of high school, when it became obvious that God had other plans for Hunter. A nagging injury that dogged Hunter for years finally ended his quest for the big leagues.

So he decided on CBU, and settled on nursing as his future just one week before leaving for his freshman year. Until that day, his major had still been undecided. Michael and Ruth had been excited for Hunter. Ruth was especially encouraging, since she had been urging Hunter to get into nursing for a while.

There was a small problem however; CBU didn't offer a nursing program. The three of them had figured that Hunter could attend his first year or two of college at CBU, and get the basic classes out of the way, while applying to schools that offered nursing programs. It would be a challenge, but they had faith, and asked God to take Hunter down the right path. God had done just that. The first thing that greeted them when they dropped Hunter off at freshman orientation was a very large banner hanging on one of the school buildings, which read, "Cal Baptist is proud to announce the brand new Bachelor of Nursing program." This was extremely unexpected, and such an answer to their prayers, that they could hardly believe their good luck.

Michael read the sign and asked Hunter, "So, do you think God wants you to be here?" It was obvious to them that God was in control of their lives, and leading Hunter by the hand.

Michael smiled at the memory and looked back at Ruth. "I miss them too. But they have their own lives now. Besides, you're going to see them pretty soon. Thanksgiving is next Thursday!"

"I know," said Ruth. She had spent the afternoon looking through old photographs of the kids, and knew she had only herself to blame for the mood she was in. "Don't you ever wonder where the time went? It seems like just yesterday that they were all here, playing baseball, playing football, or playing with the dog."

Michael smiled at his wife, put his arms around her, and squeezed. "I think about it all the time. I mean, it just goes by in the blink of an eye! It's really crazy … and I sound like a walking cliché!" Michael sat down, Ruth's words echoing in his head. He was dealing with it better than she was, but she was right. *Time really does fly*, he thought.

"Michael, our lives are a cliché. *We* are walking clichés! And it certainly doesn't help things when you guys do that movie speak thing!" Ruth looked at Michael and smiled. That dialogue always amused Ruth. Michael and the kids could have a complete conversation just by quoting movies. It wasn't unusual for Ruth to hear a conversation around the dinner table that went something like this: "Dad, fetch me that pitcher!" (One of the kids would say in a very bad impression of a female voice). Michael would answer, "As you wish."

Another one of the kids would chime in and say, "That day, she was amazed to discover that when he was saying 'As you wish,' what he meant was, 'I love you.' And even more amazing was the day she realized she truly loved him back," to finish off the line from the movie, *The Princess Bride*. Ruth would always give them the look and ask, "How do you guys remember all that stuff?" After a few more lines from *The Princess Bride*, the dinner table would erupt in laughter.

Ruth, still thinking about the photographs, wiped a tear from the corner of her eye and asked Michael, "How was your day, Mike?"

"Not bad," Michael said. "I got my new assistant. But he's not a believer."

Ruth looked surprised. "Wow, you don't waste any time, do you?"

"Actually it was the first thing out of my mouth. I think I might have scared him a little! Oh, and if it's alright with you, I'm going to ask him over for Thanksgiving dinner. He doesn't have a family."

"That would be very nice. I'm sure he would be grateful, and there's always plenty of food." Ruth turned and thought for a minute. "Michael, you're not turning into one of those guys we saw yelling in the streets in Denver are you?" She was referring to a recent trip they had taken to Denver, Colorado. One night, while walking downtown, they passed by a man standing in the middle of the street, yelling at everyone who walked by to turn to Jesus, that the end was near! His favorite line had been 'repent or die!'

Michael laughed. "No, of course not. That guy *scared* me!"

Ruth continued, "You know, God wants you to be a good witness for Him. But you also need to be an *effective* witness; otherwise you're no good at all."

"Well what can I say, it's the ABC's of me, baby!" Michael exclaimed, doing his best Cuba Gooding, Junior impersonation from the movie *Jerry McGuire*.

Ruth's demeanor turned sarcastic. "OK, Mr. Movie Speak! I'm going downstairs. Hurry up and get changed. Duke missed you."

Ruth walked out of the room and stopped halfway down the stairs, to turn and yell back at Michael. "Would you turn out the light when you come down? Dinner should be just about ready."

In the room, Michael whispered to himself, "As you wish."

# Chapter 2

**Michael stood up** with the rest of the congregation, and began singing the first hymn of Sunday morning worship. He loved his church; he and his family had been attending Redwood Heights Baptist Church for eight years now. He looked around, silently thanking God for all the new friends in his life. He thought back to when he had first started going there, how he had no real friends, and certainly no one he could call a best friend. Now, thanks to God's grace, he had many.

He had shared good times and bad times with this congregation. These people had been there for Michael and his family through it all. They had provided dinners while Michael battled that life-threatening illness a few years ago. They were also supportive through Hunter's injuries, offering prayer and words of wisdom. His friends in the congregation kept Michael focused on God and what was right with the world, instead of what was going wrong with his. Their children had also made friendships that would last a lifetime in this church.

As they sang, the wife and young family of the youth pastor quietly snuck in and sat in the empty row in front of Michael. That's when he first heard the voice.

"Help them," someone whispered in Michael's ear. It was quiet and at first, he ignored it. He didn't recognize the voice, but after a moment those words were whispered again. "Help them."

Michael heard it several more times before he finally looked around and asked, "Help *who?*"

The voice gained clarity, and now Michael heard it as if someone were standing right next to him, urging him. It said, "There is a need in this family, and I want you to help them." The congregation kept singing, but Michael sat down and prayed silently. "God, are You talking to me? I think I may be just hallucinating, or making this up in my mind, but if this is You, You know I will do whatever you ask, but You've got to be specific. Am I supposed to give them money?"

The voice said, "Yes."

Michael was floored. He took a deep breath and asked, "How much?"

The voice was silent. Michael thought to himself, *great*, thinking that he'd been left alone again. But he knew that he had to do something. Was this really the voice of God?

He'd heard of things like this happening. Most of the time he didn't believe it was real, but it would be hard not to believe in what had just happened. He'd actually *heard* a voice!

The church had a picnic scheduled later that afternoon, he knew. He decided to go home, ask God to be a little more specific, get some money, and give it to the family at the fellowship. As church was dismissed, Michael walked out, praying. He grabbed Ruth by the hand and hurried across the parking lot, toward the car.

As they rushed to the car, Ruth asked, "Michael, what's going on? Are you in some kind of hurry? Is there a game on or something?" Michael just kept walking, and Ruth asked again, "Michael, are you okay?"

When they reached the car, Michael sat down in the driver seat, started the engine, and looked at Ruth. With tears slowly forming in his eyes, he tried to put the words together to explain.

"God just told me to give Pastor Chase's family some money. Apparently there is some sort of need," he whispered.

Ruth sat in stunned silence. Michael didn't speak again, but pulled out of the parking lot and headed home, trying not to cry. Michael was a very emotional guy, though he tried his best to hide it. Showing emotion to anyone, especially tears, was not something he was used to. He had grown up in a house where his father always told him to 'be tough' and 'act like a man.' Crying was not something his father would consider 'manly.' He didn't like feeling this vulnerable, but things like this didn't happen all the time. In fact, this had *never* happened! Michael had talked to God plenty of times, but God had never actually talked to *Michael*.

When they got home, Michael headed upstairs to his bedroom, closed the door, and knelt next to his bed. He folded his hands, closed his eyes, and rested his forehead on his mattress. Then he tried to decide what to say.

"Lord, thank you for talking to me today." Michael thought about those words. God had actually spoken to him, and he didn't know how to take it. "I feel overwhelmed that You would do that, and I'm amazed that I could hear You! I always knew You were real, but this was really cool! I'm going to do what You ask, but I need help … I need to know how much to give them. I can't just give them a blank check, or hand them a few bucks and say it's from You! It has to be the *right* amount! So if you would, please, tell me how much! If there's a need, I have to be sure to cover it."

He paused; reflecting on what he had just asked, and finished. "Amen."

He lifted his head off the bed and thought for a moment, then quickly bowed his head again and said, "Oh and Lord, thanks again for caring enough to ask me to do this for You. I promise I'll do the best I can. Amen."

With that little task checked off his list, Michael went back downstairs. Ruth was in the kitchen, packing their lunch for the picnic.

She asked, "Do you know how much you're supposed to give them?"

"Well not exactly. You can only get so much from an ATM at once, so I hope it's not going to be *too* much. I'm just going to have to wait and see. I prayed about it, but I haven't heard yet. I'm really afraid that if I don't know, and I make something up, that it will be the wrong amount."

"Michael," Ruth said, "this is God you're talking about. He will let you know."

"I sure hope so!"

"Well either way, we'd better get going. We need to stop by and pick up my mom. I told her that it would be good for her to go with us; get her out of the house for a bit."

Ruth's Mother, Edna, lived a few miles away, in a retirement community. She was eighty-five years old and had symptoms of Alzheimer's disease, although no official diagnosis had been made yet. They both knew, though, that it was only a matter of time.

Mental disease was prevalent on Ruth's side of the family. Her aunt had died a few years before from Alzheimer's. Her sister and cousin had been institutionalized because of mental disorders. Michael knew that they needed to spend as much time as they could with Edna now, because it wouldn't be long before they had to move her into a home with full-time nursing care. If she had Alzheimer's, it wouldn't be too long before she stopped recognizing them at all. With that in mind, he was happy to take her places whenever they could.

They grabbed the lunch basket, blanket, and a few folding chairs, and were off. While Michael drove, he began to pray again. "Lord, I'm on my way to the picnic and I haven't heard from You yet... I'm a little scared."

Dane opened his eyes, yawned, and rolled over in bed. He reached for the book next to his head, which he had been reading the night before, and pulled it toward him. Before he could find his place on the page, though, his two dogs, Bella and Lucy, jumped up and started licking his face. Dane laughed and tried unsuccessfully to push them away.

"Come on, you guys!" The dogs could sense he wasn't serious, and kept licking. "Alright you two, how about we let Sunday morning open its eyes slowly, that's what weekends are for!"

The sun had just started peering through the tiny openings in the mini blinds covering the window in Dane's bedroom. Although the sun was up, he thought, it was still too early to get out of bed, especially on a Sunday morning. But the dogs had business to take care of, Sunday morning or not!

Bella jumped off the bed and started barking. Dane was very familiar with this morning ritual, and knew that they both needed to go outside. Lucy was the older of the two, and was happy to let Bella do the talking for her.

Dane stretched and rolled out of bed. "Is it true that you dogs can small fear? Because I'm afraid I'm not awake enough yet to find the back door." He picked up a small pillow and gently tossed it at them. Both dogs were barking now, and leading Dane down the hall. He opened the door and they both bounded outside, ecstatic to be free of the apartment. "If you're good, maybe we'll go to the dog park today," he shouted. He certainly didn't have anything else to do, and it would do the dogs good to get out and do something different.

As Edna came walking out toward the car, Michael considered the coming scene; things would go one of two ways, he knew. She would either climb in with a familiar hello, or get in the car and sit down quietly, looking around for something familiar.

Michael got out and opened the car door for his mother in law. "Hello, Michael," she said with a smile.

Michael, feeling somewhat relieved, replied, "Hi Edna, ready for a picnic?" He was happy when he realized that today was a good day for her. She was well aware of her surroundings, which meant that they might just have a fun time at the picnic.

She nodded and he helped her into the back seat, buckled her belt, and closed the door. He backed slowly out of the driveway and the three of them made their way through Edna's neighborhood into town. He made a quick stop at a grocery store around the corner from church, and walked up to the ATM inside the front door. He was still unsure of how much he was supposed to give. Was he missing something? What if God had already told him how much money to give to Pastor Chase's family and he just hadn't heard it? Doubt started creeping into Michael's mind.

*This is stupid*, he thought. *Maybe I should forget the whole thing. Maybe I didn't really hear that voice this morning. Maybe I just imagined it.*

He put his ATM card into the machine, though, and said out loud, "Come on, Lord!" Suddenly he was under attack. Those voices of doubt were back, and they echoed in his mind. He imagined a spiritual battle, good versus evil, being waged in the heavens above, via his mind, but tried to control himself.

Of course he had heard the voice! And he was going to do this, no matter how stupid he felt. He suddenly felt compelled to withdraw $200, all the time hoping that this was pleasing to God. Before he left, he walked to the greeting card section and picked up a card. It simply said 'Friends' on the front. *This should work*, he thought.

Once back in the car, he wrote inside the card. 'Chase, God asked me to give this to you. I'm not sure why, but there must be a need. And just in case there's not, keep it as a thank you for all you've done for my kids. We love you.'

As he was writing in the card, Ruth was telling her mom about the voice Michael had heard in church that morning. Edna grabbed her purse, reached into her wallet, and pulled out a $20, which she held up to Michael.

"I want to help too!" she said, smiling.

Michael smiled, but insisted that this was between him and God. "You keep your money, Edna. If God wants you to give it away, He'll tell you!"

"Well," Edna said with excitement in her voice, "how do you know He didn't?"

Michael was a little perplexed at the clarity of her thought process. He had always heard God worked in mysterious ways, but this would be more than mysterious. This would just be weird!

Reluctantly, Michael said, "OK, I'll add your $20 to mine. It will be a kind of strange amount, but ... whatever!" He was in no mood to argue. Besides, what if God really *did* want that extra $20 in there?

With that, he stuffed the money into the card and sealed it up.

"Two hundred and twenty dollars," Michael chuckled to himself. "It *is* a crazy amount."

When Dane pulled up to the dog park, he was glad to see that it didn't look too busy for a Sunday. There was only one other car in the parking lot. The dogs got restless the minute they recognized where they were, regardless of how many other dogs were there; they loved dog parks, and this one was no exception.

Dane used to take his dogs to a park back home three or four times a week. For a dog, this was heaven! This particular dog park was no more than a very large field surrounded by a chain link fence, with a few picnic tables. His dogs could run and play with the other dogs until they dropped. As Dane opened the car door, Bella and Lucy jumped out and ran toward the gate, tugging on their leashes. Bella turned around and looked at Dane as if to say, "Come on, open the gate, we've got some running to do!"

Dane locked the car and got to the gate as soon as he could. "OK guys, sit and just chill!" Dane always talked to his dogs like they were his kids instead of his pets. And a small part of him wanted to believe that they could understand him. Since his mother had passed away, they were the only family he had. They sat immediately as he asked, their tongues hanging out of their mouths with excitement.

He laughed and reached for the gate while looking back at his dogs. As he grabbed the latch to open the gate, his hand covered another hand; someone had reached for the latch at the same time. Dane looked up to see a very pretty young woman. She was as startled as Dane.

"Oh," Dane said. "Excuse me, I'm so sorry. I wasn't paying attention!"

She said, "I'm sorry too. I wasn't paying attention either."

She giggled and added, "My dog has her eyes on the traffic out there."

They opened the gate together, and Dane let his dogs off the leash to run. The young woman had a beautiful white German Sheppard on a pink leash. She was walking her dog calmly along the track inside the park fence. Now her dog sat and looked up at her, and she bent to unhook the leash. The three dogs ran to the far end of the field and began sniffing each other.

"They *are* dogs, what can I say?" Dane laughed. "My name is Dane."

"I'm Diana, it's very nice to meet you."

Dane thought that it must be his lucky day; Diana was a slender, good-looking brunette woman, and appeared to be about Dane's age.

"Do you come here often?" Dane realized how corny that sounded as soon as he said it. Diana must have realized as well, because she glanced at him quickly. They both laughed.

"I know that didn't sound too good, but you know what I mean, right?" he amended quickly. "I haven't been here that many times. In fact, I moved out here almost a year ago, but I just found this dog park a few months ago."

The two sat down at one of the picnic benches while their dogs played in the distance.

"Yes I've been coming here for a long time; probably about ten years. I bring Sasha here a few times a week. I was born and raised here, actually about a mile from this very spot! I couldn't imagine living anywhere else. I just love it." Diana's dog started running back toward the two, with Dane's dogs in hot pursuit. Diana loved dogs, she told him. She'd owned dogs all her life, as far back as she could remember.

Her mother had bought Diana her first dog as a birthday

present when she was just five years old. She was a little white poodle, and Diana had named her Hubble. Her parents had no idea where that name came from, but it stuck. Diana was also very athletic, and had loved living by the ocean. She had been surfing since she was ten years old, and taught her little poodle how to ride on the end of the board. She and Hubble had been quite a hit at the beach. Sasha, on the other hand, didn't care for the ocean at all.

"She's a beautiful dog, though," Dane said when Diana finished her story.

"Yours are cute too." Diana smiled back at Dane.

The two sat on the bench and talked for about half an hour more, the conversation coming easily between the two of them. Although he had just met her, Dane felt very comfortable talking with Diana. She told Dane about all of the great dinner spots, coffee shops, and even the best dry cleaner in the neighborhood.

"We should meet again sometime for coffee, at the Bean and Leaf," she said finally. "I'll introduce you to my favorite barista!"

"I would love that," said Dane, excited at the prospect.

"Dane," Diana said finally, "I have to get going. I would love to sit and talk longer, but the weekend is quickly coming to an end and I still have some work that *must* get done before tomorrow morning. This was really fun, though!"

"It's alright, I understand," Dane said. "I'd hate to be the cause of stress! I'm so glad to have met you. If you're serious about that cup of coffee, I better get your number."

Diana pulled out a business card and handed it to Dane, calling for Sasha at the same time.

He looked down at the card in his hand, then glanced back up at Diana. "You're in real estate? It's funny, we were so busy talking about the dogs that I didn't even think to ask!"

She laughed. "You're right. Yes, I've had my license for about five years now. I work for my dad – he's a developer and I sell the homes for him. I sell other properties too, but Dad keeps me pretty busy."

With that, Diana turned and put the leash back on her dog, and started walking toward the gate. As she loaded Sasha into her car, she turned and yelled back at Dane. "You'd *better* call me!"

"Don't worry, I will!" Dane shouted back. He turned and called his dogs then, thinking that if Diana was leaving, he would leave as well. "Come on girls, time to go!"

As soon as Dane had his dogs back in the car, he reached for his phone. He entered Dianna's number in his contact list and texted her. 'So happy to have met you. I'll call you soon … I love coffee!'

He got the reply he was hoping for almost immediately. 'Me too, looking forward to it.' Dane smiled and drove away.

# Chapter 3

**"Hello?" Michael didn't** usually answer the telephone. He would rather let the machine answer his calls. But since he was anxiously awaiting a call from Pastor Chase, he picked up. He had given the card with the money inside it to Pastor Chase's wife just before leaving the picnic. Now he was really curious to see if he had followed God's command, and Chase was the only one who could answer that question.

"Michael, its Chase." He sounded out of breath. "My wife gave me the card a few minutes ago. She said to tell you she was sorry, she completely forgot about it until just now."

Michael looked at his wristwatch. Nine o'clock. It was a little late for Chase to be calling.

"I don't know what to say." There was a long, silent pause.

Michael let doubt creep back in, and began to feel like a complete idiot again.

While he was busy feeling stupid and allowing all those negative thoughts to enter his mind, Chase kept talking.

"Michael…" Chase's voice cracked, and he paused. "Michael, it's unbelievable." Chase paused again, as if to collect his thoughts. "We had a flat tire today, and my wife brought the van to the tire shop. They told us we needed four new tires immediately. They also told us not to drive the van anymore, until the tires were replaced. They are so badly worn that it made driving dangerous! But Michael, we didn't have the money, and we didn't know what we were going to do. And then tonight I opened your card and almost fainted. Do you know how much the tires are going to be, Michael?"

Michael was tearing up again, and felt very uncomfortable. "How much?" he asked.

"Two hundred and twenty dollars, Michael…" Chase paused again, and Michael could hear him taking a deep breath. "That's exactly how much you gave us. I just can't believe it. What a blessing! Thank you, Michael, thank you. I love you, brother!"

Michael was stunned. While he was telling Chase that he was welcome, he was thinking *thank you, Jesus!*

He was also thinking about that strange amount of money. Michael had been almost embarrassed when Edna had added that extra $20. Now it seemed as if God knew just how much the family was going to need. This was certainly confirmation from God that Michael had not only done the right thing, but that it really was God who had been talking that day. Michael couldn't believe it. God had really spoken to him! He was overwhelmed by the whole experience.

He hung up, dazed, and walked into his office, Duke right by his side.

"What a day!" He sat down on the small sofa across from his desk, and looked around at all the sports memorabilia and trophies on his shelves. His office walls were filled with pictures of his kids playing some type of sport.

That made him think about his life, and he closed his eyes and began to pray again. "Lord, this is why I love You so much. I look around this room and know it all comes from You. All this stuff brings back such great memories. Every one of them reminds me of a point in time that brought me joy. But this thing You did today for Chase was amazing. I had my doubts, serious doubts, but You came through in a really big way. Thank You."

He laid his head back on the soft leather couch, and Duke

jumped up and laid his head on his master's lap. As Michael softly stroked Duke's head, the two drifted off to sleep.

Dane pulled into the large parking garage outside Sem-Con. It was a beautiful day. He looked across the hundreds of cars to see a bright blue sky, not a cloud to be seen. As he walked from the parking structure to the lobby of the building, he could hear hundreds of birds chirping in the trees. He walked through the glass hallway leading to the main entrance, rounded the corner, and stepped into Michael's office just before 8am. He was wearing blue jeans and a Tommy Bahama tee shirt, and still wearing his sun glasses as he approached his boss. He could feel himself adapting to the Southern California lifestyle.

"Good morning, sir," Dane said, lifting his glasses up and perching them on top of his head. "What's on tap for today?"

"Sit down, Dane, I need to talk to you."

Dane's face fell. "That doesn't sound good. What did I do?"

"You haven't done anything wrong, Dane! And please, call me Michael. I wanted to apologize to you about my introduction the other day. I'm not normally that forward, you know, with my religion."

Dane smiled. "No problem, Mr. Owens – I mean Michael. I totally get it!"

"But I just want to make sure that you understand where I'm coming from, Dane. God is very important to me and my family. I wouldn't be here, living this great life I have, if it weren't for Jesus. And I make sure that everyone around me knows it. But I think I came on a little too strong."

"I actually admire that, Michael. I mean, I think it's pretty cool. I didn't really mean what I said about the crutch. I mean, maybe that works for some people that — you know — if they need a crutch, but I don't think that's you."

Michael stood up and held out his hand to Dane, laughing at his assistant's obvious discomfort.

The two men shook hands, and he said, "Thank you, Dane, now let's see if we can turn this beautiful day into a productive day. We need to get some more paperwork out of the way this morning, so follow me."

# Chapter 4

**Michael walked through** his front door after work, and found Duke there – as usual – waiting to greet him. Just like he had done every day for the past eight years or so.

"Hi, buddy."

He felt bad that he hadn't had much time to spend with his best friend lately. Michael had been so busy with work that he hadn't spent much time playing. He kept hearing about layoffs and things slowing down because of budget cuts, though he hoped that the rumors were in regard to other departments, not his. With the amount of work they had in his department, he couldn't imagine them facing any layoffs. And the weapon delivery system he was working on was too important. It was what he called a "game changer," and he assumed that his boss knew that.

Michael slowly made his way from the front door to his office, while thumbing through the day's mail. He came across an envelope that he had all but forgotten about. Michael had done some consulting work for a friend's company almost a year ago, though it had slipped his mind that the invoice had never been paid. He opened the envelope and slowly pulled out a check. It was for the full amount he had billed – $2200.

"Almost forgot about this," Michael said to himself. He remembered back when he was younger, how he would be happy to find a couple bucks in his pocket after washing his jeans. The stakes had gotten higher, and the amount of money had grown, but it was just as much fun to receive unexpected money now. To Michael, that was the best kind.

"This will buy a nice little getaway somewhere for me and my beautiful bride."

As Michael thought about the amount, though, he froze. It was for $2200. He said it over a few times in his head, trying to figure out why it had struck his attention and then suddenly remembered the money God had told him to give to Pastor Chase. That odd amount of $220. Michael's knees got weak, and he sat down on the couch behind him. Duke had already climbed up and started licking Michael's hand as he sat down.

He realized now that the amount he had given to Chase was exactly 10 percent of the check he just received, to the penny! Was this God's way of saying thank you? Or was it God's way of acknowledging that he had done the right thing?

Michael started crying. Of course it was. It was both of those things, and more! Michael had confirmation from God. He had tithed on an amount he had not even received yet! He had done the right thing, and he knew for certain that the message ... that voice he had heard in church ... had come from God himself. It was as if God was thanking Michael for trusting Him. He grabbed the Bible from the table next to the sofa, and turned to a passage in Deuteronomy that said, 'All these blessings shall come upon you and overtake you, if you obey the voice of the Lord your God.' Michael was sure that God had sent this check as a blessing for listening and obeying. He looked up through his tears, and whispered, "Thank You, Lord. Thank You."

It wasn't the first time the Lord has showed him the way. This made him remember a road trip they'd taken several years earlier.

# Chapter 5

*Five years earlier*

Michael had driven his family to his oldest son Brandon's wedding in Ventura, California. They arrived the Thursday before the wedding, which was scheduled for Saturday, so they had time to do some visiting before the big day. Michael pulled into the hotel parking lot with great anticipation. They had just completed a journey that would unite family and friends, and when they left in four days, Michael and Ruth would have a new daughter-in-law.

"This is going to be so fun," said Ruth.

"I know I can't wait!" Michael agreed. "The hotel looks nice."

Ruth nodded, glancing at the building in front of them. "Heather recommended it. They came up a few months ago and checked it out. Just about the entire wedding party is staying here. It should be a blast." She could hardly contain her excitement.

Heather was Brandon's fiancée. They had met at church a year before, and fallen in love. She was a beautiful young woman, with red hair and bright blue eyes. She was also a mountain climber and very athletic – a perfect match for Brandon. Her parents had lived in Ventura for about ten years; they had a beautiful home at the top of a hill, overlooking the city and the Pacific Ocean. The couple had decided to have their wedding here, close to the bride's family, and Michael and Ruth had happily agreed.

Michael checked in, and, after a few trips to the car, had all their bags up in the room. Suddenly Hunter came running in, yelling for his father.

"Hey Dad, there's a sweet park right next to the hotel! We're setting up a game of whiffle ball home run derby. You want to come play with us?"

Michael looked out the window and saw a large park just outside their room.

"Come on, Dad, it will be fun!" Hunter looked at his father with great anticipation, and Michael laughed. Most of his favorite memories had something to do with baseball and his boys, and he was drawn toward the idea of a game with them, even after a long drive.

"Okay," he finally said. "Give me a few minutes, and I'll be right down."

"They still love playing baseball don't they?" asked Ruth as Hunter ran out of the room.

"It's who we are," laughed Michael. He grabbed his camera and headed for the door. "Are you coming, sweetie?"

Ruth said, "I wouldn't miss it for the world."

When Michael and Ruth got to the park, the kids all started clapping. They had already decided what imaginary line was going to be the home run 'fence.' All the rules were in place, and all Michael had to do was join in. That was just the way he liked it, and he dropped his bag to start doing some stretches.

"Hey Dad, you're up!" shouted Hunter.

Michael grabbed the big yellow plastic bat and stepped into the imaginary batter's box. "What's a home run again?" he asked.

Brandon yelled from about 100 feet away. "Just over my head, past these two trees!" He spread his arms apart and pointed at a couple of trees on each side of him.

"That seems kind of far doesn't it?" Michael was looking for some small advantage in this game. After all, he was playing with kids twenty years his junior, and he hadn't swung a baseball bat in quite a while. It was only a plastic bat, but Michael figured it was worth getting some sort of consolation.

"It's not *that* far!" Brandon shouted back, laughing.

Hunter didn't give his dad any time to reply; he wound up and threw the little plastic ball. It whistled past Michael's face.

"Strike," came the call from Tyler, who was playing catcher and umpire.

"You call that a strike? That ball was 2 feet outside!" Michael knew he didn't have a chance at getting a strike call overturned, but he wanted to at least let them all know that he was taking this little 'game' very seriously. Deep down, he knew it was all in good fun, but that shouldn't mean that they could cheat.

"Come on, Dad, everyone gets ten swings. You can't strike out! What's the point in arguing?" Tyler laughed.

"Okay, okay," Michael said, digging his feet into the grass and raising his elbows for the next swing. "That's more like it!"

Michael swung at the next pitch, and sent the ball sailing over Brandon's head for a home run.

Brandon turned and yelled back as he ran toward the ball, "I told you it wasn't that far!"

Michael laughed as he watched Brandon run to retrieve the ball, realizing that the game wouldn't be as hard as he thought.

The game went on for about an hour. All the boys had fun swinging the bat and chasing balls, and Ruth sat and watched from a blanket in the shade. Every once in a while she would shoot a few pictures of the kids. Finally, Michael called all the boys together.

"Guys, this was a lot of fun, but we better clean up and go

pick up the tuxes. Let's shower and meet in the hotel lobby in an hour."

They all scattered and went back to their rooms.

Ruth gave Michael a hug. "You did great. I'm proud of you, keeping up with those youngsters."

"Yeah, that was fun. You should call Heather and have her meet you in the bar. Haley has been with her since we checked in. You guys can hang out while we get fitted. It would give all you girls a chance to bond! This tuxedo thing shouldn't take more than an hour or so, then we can all go get some dinner."

"Sounds good, sweetie, I think I'll do that. I'll see you in a bit"

Michael kissed his wife and they went off in separate directions. As Michael walked back to his room, he thought about how lucky he was. He had a terrific family, who he loved very much.

Michael got out of the shower and dried off. He reached into the closet for the suit he'd brought for the rehearsal and dinner, and glanced at the neatly pressed black tux and stark white shirt he and the boys had picked up yesterday. As he looked at the tux, he pictured himself and his kids standing in front of all their loved ones for his oldest son's wedding, and felt himself welling up with emotion. A tear formed in his eye and slowly trickled down his cheek. It was going to be difficult watching his son take the plunge, and he hoped he could keep it together.

Michael was the kind of person who took marriage vows very seriously. It was, after all, a covenant with God. But he also knew that it would be an emotional time. Michael had cried at every wedding he'd ever witnessed. He even cried — secretly — at Princess Diana's wedding, and that was only on

TV! He threw his towel on the floor, laughing at himself, and came around the corner to find Ruth sitting on the bed, looking at her camera and scanning through the pictures she had taken so far.

Michael began rubbing his stomach, and groaned slightly. "I'm not feeling so good."

"Oh no, not now! Was it the baseball yesterday? You're not as young as you used to be, you know!" Ruth looked up at him, obviously concerned. "Our son is getting married tomorrow, Mike, and the rehearsal dinner is happening in a few hours. You've got a lot to do. Do you think you'll be alright?"

Michael shrugged his shoulders and held the back of his hand up to his forehead. "I don't know. I think I have a fever, too." He suddenly felt awful, but knew that he had to keep it together for one more day. "I'm sure I can take something and I'll be fine. I'll just put off being sick until we get home." He buttoned up his shirt and grabbed his tie off the hangar. "Did we bring any Tylenol?"

Brandon tapped his knife on the side of his glass of water. 'Ting, ting, ting, ting.' He stood up and looked around at all his family and close friends. He had their full attention; everyone in the room looked at him, anticipating a speech.

"Marriage!" he said in his best impression of *The Princess Bride*'s priest. Suddenly the quiet room was filled with laughter. Brandon always knew how to entertain a large group of people. Ever since he was a little boy, barely able to walk, he had been the entertainer of the family. It wasn't unusual for Brandon, while running around in his diapers, to put food on his head or summersault clumsily and wait for a reaction. He usually got the response he was looking for.

But it hadn't always been fun and games. Once, when Brandon was a little over a year old, Michael and Ruth had been eating dinner with Edna. It was just the three of them and baby Brandon, in his high chair, sitting around Edna's kitchen table. During a lull in the conversation Brandon yelled out, "fudge!" only just like Ralphie in *A Christmas Story*, he didn't say fudge! He blurted out the *real* "F" word! Michael, Ruth, and Edna collectively gasped, which caused Brandon to drop his head onto the high chair tray and start to cry. Michael couldn't help but laugh, which had brought a few jeers from Ruth.

Today, though, he was pleasing the crowd. He looked around the room again with a big smile, and laughed right along with all the dinner guests.

"I told my dad I was going to have the preacher start the ceremony tomorrow by saying that. As you may or may not know, that's a line from the movie *Princess Bride*. It's one of our favorite movies, well everyone except my mom! She hates it when we quote movies, but we all get a kick out of it. But seriously, it *is* marriage that brings us together today."

Hunter, who was sitting next to Brandon, was shaking his head and giggling. He said quietly, "I can't believe you said that."

Brandon looked at his younger brother and winked, then looked back out at the crowd. Some of them were still chuckling and shaking their heads. "This rehearsal dinner is just the tip of the iceberg for us in beginning our celebration. I wanted to say thank you to everyone for coming all this way to see us get hitched. Believe it or not, we take this very seriously. Tomorrow is going to be the most important day in our lives. Heather and I are so happy you all found a way to share this day with us. We love you all. I would like to ask my dad to lead us in prayer before we eat." Brandon looked toward his father as a few waiters entered the room carrying the entrées. They stopped when they saw the crowd was about to pray.

"Dad, would you mind?" Brandon tried to catch Michael's eye from across the room, but paled when he saw his father's face. "Dad, are you okay? You don't look so good."

Michael agreed; he was, in fact, feeling worse by the minute, but he struggled to keep it together. Now wasn't the time to let his family down.

"I'm okay, Brandon; that game of home run derby yesterday killed me, that's all! Actually, I think I might be coming down with the flu. Maybe I can have the preacher lay hands on me tomorrow before the ceremony!" Everyone in the banquet room laughed, including the waiters.

Michael waited for the laughter to die down, then started. "Let's bow our heads and pray." He led his family in a prayer, and asked for blessings on the family and on Brandon's new marriage. As he did, he could feel his stomach churning and growling. He was sure that everyone in the room could hear it, but tried to put it to the side. He didn't have time to get sick right now.

Later that night, everyone went back to the hotel. Michael and Brandon sat in the hotel bar; Brandon sipping a martini, Michael clutching a glass of water. They spent the last few minutes of the evening alone talking about how much fun tomorrow would bring. It was Brandon's last evening as a single man, and he relished spending it with his father.

"You better get up to bed, Brandon," Michael finally said. "You have a really big day ahead of you."

"That's a good idea, Dad. Thanks for everything. I hope you

feel better in the morning." Brandon hugged his father, and turned and walked to the elevator. Michael sat back down and wondered if a good night's sleep was all he needed. Maybe the stress of having his first son get married was making him ill. His stomach churned, though, disagreeing with this easy diagnosis. Michael had always handled stress pretty well; his job was extremely stressful, but it never made him sick, and he couldn't remember ever having felt this bad before. His stomach physically hurt, and he was starting to sweat. He was sure he had a fever. *It's got to be the flu, but this is a nasty one,* he thought. He walked up the stairs to his room and was surprised to find Ruth still awake, sitting in front of her laptop. The light from the screen cast an eerie glow in the otherwise dark room.

"Everything ok, sweetie?" Michael asked.

Ruth closed the laptop abruptly and said, "Yes, fine. Just some work stuff."

"On a Friday night?"

"Yeah, just some emails I needed to respond to. I'm going to bed, how about you?"

Michael rubbed his stomach and frowned. "I guess I could try, but I doubt I'll sleep much, feeling like I do."

"Still feeling sick?"

Michael bent over to try and alleviate the pain that was now welling up inside his abdomen. "I feel terrible! This isn't good … maybe I'm just all backed up." Michael rubbed his eyes, grimacing in pain as he watched Ruth climb under the covers. "I think I'll go get some pink stuff. They have 7/11s up here, right?"

"Mike, maybe we should go get you checked out. There's bound to be a hospital around here somewhere. Something could be seriously wrong!"

Michael shook his head. "It's not that bad, I'm sure I'm fine. But I think I'm going to go find a store that sells something to soothe the stomach. If that doesn't work, we'll go to a hospital, but not until after the wedding. I'll be right back."

He kissed Ruth on the cheek, grabbed his car keys, and left.

Michael drove around downtown Ventura, looking for an all-night quick stop market. When he saw lights in the distance, he knew relief was nearly at hand, and sighed. He parked his car and looked around the tiny parking lot. To his surprise, it was bustling with action. There had to be twenty-five people just wandering around. Most of them didn't look out of place at all; they looked as though they knew exactly what they were doing there.

*This could be what they do every night, I suppose*, he thought. He began to wonder if this was such a good idea, though. Although it was only a few blocks from the hotel, it didn't look like the safest place in town, and the number of people in the parking lot made him nervous. But the pain in his gut was not letting up, and he needed to get some kind of relief. He got out, locked his car, and headed straight to the medicine aisle, where he grabbed some more Tylenol and a bottle of Pepto that promised relief within eight hours.

"Perfect," he said to himself.

When he got to the checkout, Michael was surprised again at how many people were waiting in line. To amuse himself and take his mind off his pain, he put scenarios together with each one of them. There were two guys in the front of the line buying beer. *No surprise there, probably going back to the party*, Michael thought. There was also a couple buying some ice cream. *Okay, maybe they were home watching a movie and got hungry!* Behind them were a group of six pretty drunk guys, all buying something to eat off the spinning oven; they chose hot dogs, *taquitos*, and other snack food that he couldn't readily identify. The *taquitos* looked like they had been spinning and heating up for several days. The edges of most of the flour tortillas were black and burned. Surprisingly for someone in Michael's condition, though, they smelled pretty good! The guy right in front of Michael just wanted a pack of cigarettes and a lottery ticket. He was covered in tattoos.

Michael finally got to the front of the line, paid for his two items, and quickly headed back to the car. As he walked outside he heard the tattooed guy yelling at a car full of young men who had just pulled up. They all jumped out, and the driver grabbed the tattooed guy, holding him against the side of the car as two of the other men started throwing punches. Michael watched in horror as they continued to pummel the guy, wondering what he should do. The group of six drunken guys came running back, then, and jumped in. A full brawl had broken out right there in front of the store. The parking lot started to clear as people sprinted away from the scene. Michael knew he wasn't safe, and that there was nothing he could do, so ran to his car. He jumped in, locked the door, and raced out of the parking lot. *Unbelievable*, he thought. *That's all I need is to get beat up, or thrown in jail the night before my son's wedding ... or worse!*

A few blocks down the road, he passed a Ventura cop. The cop was speeding toward the fight, lights blazing and siren blaring.

Michael was relieved when he finally reached the hotel. As he closed his car door, he could hear sirens wailing in the distance. He opened the door to his hotel room, expecting that he would need to wake Ruth and tell her about his close call. It was quite a surprise to find her out of bed again, sitting in front of her lap top.

He frowned at her. "I was sure you'd be sleeping by now. Didn't you get into bed when I left? Are you still working? You're not going to believe what just happened to me!"

"Yep, working, but that should do it." She slammed the cover down and jumped into bed. "What just happened?" she asked, yanking the covers to her chin.

Michael was preoccupied with the thought of Ruth and the computer, and paused for a moment. *What could be so important that she would have to work the night before her son's wedding?* Suddenly he realized that she was staring at him, waiting for his response.

"Oh, it can wait until morning," Michael mumbled, puzzled. *She sure seems distracted.*

After a moment, though, he decided that now was not the time for confrontation, and just let it go. They both had a big day coming up and needed to try and get some sleep. But he couldn't help but wonder what could be so important that she would get out of bed and back on the computer after he left. Was she so busy at work that it couldn't wait until Monday morning? She hadn't mentioned anything about doing work this weekend, so he was surprised that something was taking up this much of her time.

Shaking his head, he went to the bathroom and poured a glass of water. He took a few Tylenol and then swallowed some of the thick, pink medication for his stomach. He drank an entire glass of water to wash it down while reading the directions on the package. "Relief within eight hours or overnight; either one would be just fine," he murmured.

Michael walked out of the bathroom and quietly slipped

under the covers, whispering, "Good night sweetie." There was no response, and he glanced over at his wife to find that she was already asleep. Michael closed his eyes. He tossed and turned for hours, and finally glanced at the clock next to the bed. It was 4:15.

"Great," he muttered. His stomach hurt so much that he could barely stand it, and he certainly couldn't sleep. If he could just throw up, he thought, he would feel better. He got up and staggered to the bathroom, where he tried sticking his finger down his throat in a halfhearted attempt to gag himself. It didn't work. His son's wedding was in a few hours, and here he was, wide awake, burning up with a fever, and leaning over a hotel toilet trying to puke! He was sure it was just the flu, but Ruth's words were haunting him now. What if it was something more serious? He didn't know what it could be, but he was sure it wasn't going to be pleasant, not with this much pain. Still, there was nothing to be done; he *had* to get through Brandon's wedding tomorrow. Then he would go to the hospital. He washed his face and went and lay down in bed again.

It was an absolute beautiful day for a wedding. The sun was shining and the forecast called for temperatures in the 80s. Michael and Ruth arrived at Ventura Golf and Country Club before anyone else. Michael hadn't slept at all the night before, and was still feeling very sick. He was exhausted, but he was hoping that the tuxedo would at least mask some of his discomfort. He had taken so much Tylenol to try to get through the ceremony that he wasn't sure if that was helping him or making him feel worse. He was sure about one thing, though – he was definitely going to a hospital to get checked out as soon as the reception was over. His ears were ringing, which he attributed to all the Tylenol, and he finally felt that if he tried, he might actually be able to throw up. But today he needed to keep it together and put on a happy face. Today was all about the bride and groom. He didn't want to let any more people know how sick he was.

He walked out to the patio, which over looked the practice green, and watched a few golfers practice their putting. The aroma of freshly cut grass filled the air. A grounds crew was working on the eighteenth green in the distance.

*This place is gorgeous*, he thought. They were obviously very meticulous about their grooming. The fairways were bright green and looked to be in perfect condition. It was going to be tough for Michael to be this close to the game he loved, on such a splendid day, and not be able to play. He had started playing golf when he was eighteen years old, when he and his college buddies would go out and play almost every weekend. He got pretty good at it, but when Brandon was born, he just didn't have the time to commit to the game. They said if you don't play a minimum of twice a week, you wouldn't get any better, and they were right. Nowadays, Michael only had time to play once a month or so. The tradeoff was well worth it, although a hole in one was still unchecked on his bucket list!

Brandon came around the corner and saw his dad checking out the course. "Did you bring your clubs?" he asked, grinning.

Michael squinted as he looked back at his son. "Good morning, Brandon. No, unfortunately I didn't."

"Too bad, because we probably have time to play a round! Although I don't think Heather would appreciate that!" Brandon laughed at his own joke. "How are you feeling this morning, Dad?"

Michael forced a slight grin. "I'll be fine as long as the Tylenol lasts!"

Heather arrived a short time later with her mom and dad. She ran quickly into a small room near the entrance of the clubhouse, which had been set up just for the girls. She believed in the tradition of not letting the groom see the bride before the wedding. It was a tradition that had been around for centuries, although no one was certain of the origin. Ruth told Heather that she thought it had started during the times when marriages were arranged; the two people to be wed were never allowed to see each other. Marriages in the biblical times were like business deals between two families. A father wanted his daughter to be wed to a man from a rich, land-owning family, which spelled prosperity and fortune for his daughter. But if the groom met the bride before the wedding and saw that she wasn't attractive, the groom could back out and cancel the wedding. That was something the family of the bride wanted to avoid, especially if they wanted to secure marrying into a wealthy family. This was also the case for family members who were giving a dowry – they were paying the groom, in effect, to take the daughter as his wife.

While Heather doubted Brandon would back out, she did believe it just wouldn't have the same effect if he were to see her before the wedding. So much time and effort would go into her hair, make-up, and the dress that she felt it was a way of keeping the ceremony magical.

Ruth and the other bridesmaids filed into the clubhouse, giggling, as they attempted to keep Heather secluded. When Michael and Brandon walked past the door, Haley, Michael's daughter, came running out and gave him a hug.

"Hi, Dad, sorry I haven't been able to spend much time with you guys. All the girls are pretty busy keeping Heather calm."

"Is she nervous?" he asked, concerned.

"I think she'll be alright, but we're not taking any chances. Well, gotta go!" Haley turned and smiled at her big brother and added, "Are *you* nervous?"

Brandon laughed, "I'm fine. It's Dad you should be worried about."

Haley turned toward her father with a frown. "Still sick, Dad?"

Michael rubbed his stomach and said, "I'm afraid so. I'll go get checked out right after the wedding. Hey, there's the photographer, you better go." Michael pointed back to the door where a few bridesmaids were leaning out and yelling for Haley. The photographer appeared behind them, holding up his camera.

Soon after that, the makeup artist arrived, along with the hairstylist. Everything was finally under way.

As weddings go, it was perfect, and it was everything that Brandon and Heather could have hoped for. The weather was beautiful, the country club was absolutely gorgeous, and the food was fabulous. It lasted a little longer than Michael was hoping for, but he was torn. On one hand, he was hoping for a short ceremony due to the pain in his belly, and on the other hand he wanted it to last forever.

Michael realized that this was a huge event in his life. His firstborn son was getting married, and he couldn't be more proud. Here was his little boy, all grown up, and starting a family of his own. Michael choked back the tears as he watched Brandon and Heather recite their vows.

Soon there would be grandkids, which meant that he would officially be considered old! Michael would have a hard time calling himself Grandpa, and then wondered if his grandchildren would call him 'grandpa,' or if they would choose something else. When Brandon was little, he had started calling his grandmother 'Boppin,' so it wouldn't be out of character for his kids to find their own names too. No one really knew where that name had come from, but it stuck. She had been Boppin ever since! In fact, Michael's mother had a total of thirteen grandchildren, and each one called her Boppin.

*Funny how kids do that*, Michael thought to himself, watching his son.

He was really happy for his son and new daughter-in-law. Immediately after the reception, all of Michael's family was going to meet at Heather's parents' house to watch the newly married couple open presents. Their home was large enough to fit everyone who wanted to continue the celebration. It was an expansive tri-level home, built into the side of a mountain, with a beautiful view of Ventura and the Pacific Ocean. After the reception, Michael helped Brandon take the gifts to the car, and took Brandon aside.

"Brandon, I can't stay. I'm feeling so bad, I've got to get to a hospital and get checked out. I haven't slept in over twenty-four hours and I'm ready to drop! I'm really sorry, I'm afraid something might be seriously wrong."

Brandon looked concerned. "Dad, I understand. Thank you for everything. We're leaving for our honeymoon in the morning, but we'll only be a couple hours away. I'll call and check up on you tomorrow." Brandon was planning on spending two weeks in Palm Springs with Heather; he had booked a beautiful room and had reserved plenty of massage time for the two of them. It was supposed to be a very relaxing get-a-way, but Michael knew this little problem of his was going to be a distraction. He also knew that if he needed Brandon, the boy would come rushing home immediately.

"Please don't worry about me, Brandon. I'll be just fine. You have a great honeymoon, and I'll see you when you get back. Have a great time."

Brandon looked at his dad and grew even more concerned. He'd never seen his father in this kind of shape. Michael had always been the quintessential father – strong and able. He didn't like to show a vulnerable side to his kids. They all knew that he was sensitive, but they also knew that he didn't like to show it. Seeing him giving in to this sickness just proved how bad it was.

"OK, Dad, but just remember, I'm only a phone call away."

With tears forming in his eyes, Michael hugged his son, patted him on the shoulder, and said good bye.

# Chapter 6

**"Brandon says this** is the best hospital in Ventura." Ruth was doing her best to encourage Michael. "You have to get checked out, Michael."

"I know, I probably waited too long, but I wanted the wedding to be perfect. I hate being a distraction." Michael never wanted to be the center of attention. No matter what he was doing, he tried his best to blend in with the crowd. He always said that he was just a boring middle-aged guy!

Michael and Ruth walked through the Emergency Room doors, into a very crowded waiting room. It was almost 10 on Saturday night, and the room was still packed.

Michael looked around and sighed. "There must be fifty people here! It's going to take forever to be seen. You work in a hospital, is there any way to get moved to the front of the line?"

"Chest pains usually do the trick." Ruth quipped back. Her patience had finally run out.

Michael found an empty seat and sat down while Ruth checked him in. He rested his head on his hands, slumped over in his chair, and closed his eyes. An hour passed, with Michael drifting in and out of sleep and Ruth thumbing through several magazines, before it was finally his turn.

"Michael Owens." A nurse had come through the door and called his name. "Michael Owens!" she yelled again as she scanned the waiting room.

Ruth jumped up and waved at her. "Michael, let's go, you're next."

Michael got up slowly and walked toward the nurse, who was reaching out a hand to help. They made their way to a small room inside the ER.

"What seems to be the problem, Mr. Owens?" the nurse asked.

"I think I have the flu," Michael said softly.

Ruth interrupted him. She sighed and rolled her eyes, then looked at the nurse. "He's been sick since Thursday. He has a very high fever and pain in his stomach. He's sweating and wasn't able to sleep at all last night." Michael could tell by the tone of her voice that she was totally frustrated. He realized he had put this off far too long and not only had himself to blame for his circumstance, but was also the sole cause of her frustration. "We're here for our son's wedding. He got married today, so Michael didn't want to be an interruption."

While Ruth was describing his symptoms, the nurse handed Michael a gown. "Congratulations," she said, smiling back at Ruth. Then she motioned to Michael. "Everything off and slip this on, opening is in the back."

Michael changed into the gown and lay down on the examination table. The nurse started checking his vitals, and found that his blood pressure was slightly elevated. She went on to take his temperature, and looked closely at the thermometer in surprise.

"Yep, you have a fever alright – 103!" She grabbed a small rubber mallet from a table nearby, and tapped the bottom of Michael's left foot. "Does this hurt?"

Michael laughed. "No, of course not!" But when she tapped the bottom of his right foot, the pain in his abdomen made him scream. It was excruciating!

The nurse looked at Ruth and said, very businesslike, "It's his appendix. Judging by his fever, the chances are pretty good that it's ruptured already. If it hasn't ruptured, you'll have surgery and go home in a couple days. If it has, there will still be surgery and you could be here for up to five days. I'll be right back. We'll need a blood test to confirm my suspicion. I'm also going to call in a surgeon. The doctor on call tonight is Dr. Iwasiuk. He's the best."

An hour later, Dr. Iwasiuk walked in and introduced himself. He was a tall man, over 6 feet, and already wearing his green scrubs. He was soft spoken, with grey hair and glasses.

"Michael Owens, I'm Dr. Iwasiuk." The doctor was already glancing over Michael's chart when he entered the room. "Your white blood cell count is extremely high." He paused and walked around to Michael's side, laying his hand on Michael's belly. "That's a good thing, because it means that your body is fighting this infection. But it's also bad because it tells me that your appendix has more than likely ruptured, maybe as long as two or three days ago. Have you been feeling ill for a few days?"

Michael looked at Ruth and said, "Yeah, really sick the past few days. I thought it was just the flu."

"Well, it's not the flu! I'm going to assume that your appendix has ruptured, but I won't know until I get in there." The doctor gently pushed on Michael's abdomen. "Does this hurt?"

"No," Michael said.

Dr. Iwasiuk moved his hand around, feeling as he went. "What about this?"

Michael winced. "A little bit."

"OK, well let's get you into surgery and see what's going on in there. I'm going to try and go in through your belly button first. Since we aren't completely convinced that your appendix has ruptured, it's a good way to start. I can go in and look around before I decide how to get this thing fixed. Hopefully I can do everything from that first small incision. I hate to cut up your belly if I don't have to! Let's get you into surgery. I'll see you in a bit."

"Thanks, Doctor, sorry for calling you in so late."

The doctor smiled, "No problem."

Another nurse came in just after the doctor left, and told Michael that she would be taking him to surgery. Michael kissed Ruth and thought how quickly life could turn. A few hours ago he had been at his son's wedding, watching one of the most important and memorable days of his life; a day Michael had tried desperately to enjoy. Now he was heading for surgery!

It reminded him of a time when he was a teenager, hunting with his father. Michael's father had been a sheriff, and always took young Michael dove hunting. It was something Michael had always looked forward to, especially since the first day of dove season landed on or around Michael's birthday. This particular morning, Michael had watched a hawk circling in the sky. Suddenly the hawk dropped straight down to earth to swoop up a field mouse in his claws. It struck Michael at the time how ironic it was that one minute that poor little mouse was running along, unaware of any looming danger. Then the next minute, the mouse was gone, reduced to no more than hawk food. That made an impression on Michael. One he had never forgotten.

That's how life was for some people. One minute, you're happy, enjoying all that life has to offer, like attending your son's wedding. Then the next, it all ends. Michael hoped his life wouldn't end as abruptly as that little field mouse, but the tone in Dr. Iwasiuk's voice wasn't too comforting. It may have been Michael's imagination, but he didn't think that the doctor seemed too positive. Maybe it was the fact that Michael's emergency had called him in at nearly midnight on a Saturday night. Or maybe it was the fact that Michael had waited too long to seek medical attention. After all, if Michael had gotten checked out at the first sign of trouble, things would have been better by now. But he would have missed his son's wedding. Now Michael was stuck with the circumstance he had created. There was no other path to take than the one he was on. Besides, it could have just been all his imagination. Michael could only hope and pray that things would be just fine.

After a moment, the nurse wheeled Michael down the hall. As they passed a restroom, Michael asked the nurse to stop for a moment. She helped him to his feet and he walked into the restroom and closed the door. There he leaned on the sink and looked at himself in the mirror. "You don't look so good Mike." he said to himself, gazing at the big black circles under his eyes. "You already look dead!"

Michael sat down on the toilet seat, closed his eyes, and began to pray. "Lord, please be with me during surgery, and be with the doctor. Please guide his hands. Help me get through this and heal quickly. Lord, be with my family and give them peace."

Michael paused and thought about the last few days and how much fun they were. He loved having a big family, and loved spending time with them. He began to tear up suddenly, and swallowed hard. He felt very lucky to have lived such a fun life, surrounded by such a great family. That was what he should be focusing on, not the possibility of it all being over.

"Lord, I know I don't thank You enough for all the blessings … but thank You. You've been really good to me. I love You, Lord. In Jesus name I pray, amen."

Michael got up and walked back out to the hall, where the nurse waited with the gurney. He climbed back up and lay down. Ruth looked at Michael as if she were waiting for the details of what had just happened. Michael just rubbed his belly and smiled, thinking that she didn't need to know about his thoughts and fears. She would have enough of her own at the moment.

The nurse began pushing the gurney again, pushing him a little further down the hall. Then she turned to Ruth and said, "You two better say goodbye here. There's a waiting room at the end of this hall. The doctor will come find you when he has some news. Until then, make yourself comfortable, it will be a few hours."

Ruth leaned down and gave Michael a kiss. Michael smiled at her, and whispered, "Everything will be fine, you'll see."

"I'm really worried, sweetheart. You're really sick, and I hate to say it, but you don't look so good. I hate that the doctor said he has to get in there to find out what's going on. If we were home, you could go to my hospital and I would know the doctor. I don't even know this guy!" Ruth started to weep.

Michael again tried to reassure her. "Honey, they said he's a great doctor, remember? The nurse said he's the best! I know I don't look that great, but it's going to be ok, you'll see." He patted her arm. "I'll see you in a couple hours. I love you."

Ruth stood quietly sobbing as the nurse wheeled Michael and the gurney a few more feet down the hall and threw open the surgery doors. The room was cold, and Michael shivered as the temperature started to sink in. He closed his eyes as two attendants moved him from the gurney to the cold metal surgical table. All he could think was, *God don't let me be the field mouse today!*

Jesus held out his hand, gesturing for Michael to grab a hold. "I want to answer your prayer," he said.

Michael struggled to make sense of this situation. The last thing he remembered was talking with a doctor about surgery. "Wait a minute, did I already have the surgery? If not, I should be in surgery right *now*," he said aloud. "Or maybe I should be done by now." Michael didn't know what to think; Jesus was standing before him, dressed in a white robe, waiting for him to take his outstretched hand.

What was happening? Was Michael dead? If so, then what? Was Jesus here to escort him to Heaven? This didn't make any sense. He looked at Jesus, who stood right in front of him. This was real!

Michael wanted to reach out, grab Jesus' hand, and hang on, but something inside him said no. He wasn't sure what would happen if he did that, and he didn't want to make any permanent decisions or mistakes. He thought about Ruth and his kids. Would they be alright? If he took the hand of Jesus, what then? Was that it? He hadn't had a chance to say goodbye. Michael thought again about all the things he would leave behind. He would never meet his grandchildren. He would never see his dog again, play golf, walk on the beach, or drink coffee or wine! There were so many things he still wanted to do; things he needed to accomplish. What about the bucket list, the hole in one? He felt suddenly sad, lonely, and defeated at the thought that this might be the end. He remembered telling Ruth that everything would be alright. Now it looked like he'd been wrong. Then again … he'd always had a fascination with near-death experiences, and read every book he could get his hands on about the subject. He'd heard that most survivors of near-death experiences said that they floated away, looking down to see their bodies lying below them. Michael didn't see that, or experience anything like that, so maybe that meant that he wasn't *actually* dead.

What, then? Jesus was standing before him, and that must mean *something*. This didn't make any sense at all, but this was definitely Jesus! He looked just like Michael had thought He would, although His skin was a little darker, more olive in hue. His eyes were a vivid blue, and seemed to look right through Michael. His hair was light brown and shiny, hanging just past His shoulders. Of course, Michael was only comparing this Jesus to artist's renderings; no one had actually taken His picture! But Michael had seen hundreds of pictures of Jesus, and all of them looked similar. Something told Michael that this was the real deal. It might have been just a feeling, but that feeling came from deep within. In Michael's heart, there was no question that this was Jesus.

Whatever hesitation had caused Michael to pause before taking the hand of his savior suddenly vanished. He reached out to take Jesus by the hand.

As if by magic, he found himself standing on top of a mountain, surrounded by fog. He rubbed his eyes; the fog made it nearly impossible to see anything. He held his hand out in front of him and looked, but couldn't see it; the fog was too thick.

Then something caught Michael's eye. He noticed a very bright light, shimmering in the distance. He squinted and strained his eyes to see, and the light became stronger and brighter, until it was almost blinding him. But in a strange way, his eyes seemed to adjust to the light. He began to see, slowly at first, but with ever increasing clarity. He noticed trees on his right. Then he saw more trees … in fact, there were hundreds of them. The scene in front of them began to take shape.

Michael could see now that the trees were growing on the side of a mountain, and all around them. The tips of the trees were shimmering in the brilliance of the light, as if they had diamonds on the tips. Beams of tiny light shown through the tree tips and filled the space in front of him. It was breathtakingly beautiful.

As his eyes continued to adjust, the landscape became clearer. He was standing on the edge of a cliff, and the fog was starting to lift, as if it were a giant white curtain being pulled open from his right to his left. Straight ahead were more trees, the tips of their branches now bursting with tiny rays of light. The light seemed to go right through Michael, almost becoming a part of him.

"How can I ever explain this to Ruth?" he murmured to himself. The scenery around him was the most beautiful thing he'd ever seen, and his heart yearned to pass it along to his wife. It had to be a dream, but it seemed so real. Michael could feel the ground beneath his feet, and the cool mist on his face. He looked down and saw grass under his bare toes. He curled his toes and felt every blade. It was cool and damp, yet soothing.

*You can't feel things in your dreams can you?,* he wondered.

As the curtain of fog drifted away, he began to see colors.

*Do you dream in color?*

These weren't just colors, he realized; they were amazing colors. So vivid, so clear, and so brilliant. The sky was so clear and colorful that it rendered him speechless. He looked down and saw what he thought to be a city below him, but in the depth of the valley the layer of fog was still thick, so he couldn't clearly see the buildings. Still, something in him knew that it was a bustling city.

Now he could actually feel the light, warming him. As he struggled to see the city again, his eyes were drawn back to the light. He just couldn't take his eyes off it.

Just then Jesus said, "It is the glory of the Lord."

As He said that, Michael fell to his knees. He had always been captivated with the phrase, 'the Glory of the Lord.' As a child, he had watched the cartoon *A Charlie Brown Christmas* every year during the holidays. Linus had a part where he walked out on stage and said, "The glory of the Lord shown all around them." It had always brought tears to young Michael's eyes. As a child he had wondered, if this was the Lord God, creator of Heaven and Earth, what must His glory be like? He remembered praying to God as a child, asking Him to show him His glory. Now Jesus had miraculously taken Michael by the hand and was revealing to him, 'the Glory of the Lord!' Was that what Jesus meant when He said, "I want to answer your prayer?" Had Jesus waited all these years to answer Michael's prayer; something he asked God as a child?

Whatever it was, whatever he was witnessing, was beyond human description!

When Michael's knees hit the ground, he was jolted out of a deep sleep. He opened his eyes to see a young doctor standing over him. He was asking Michael questions. "Do you know your name? Do you know where we are?"

Michael answered each question in his mind and thought, *of course I do!* Then the doctor asked Michael to answer him.

Realizing he was only answering the doctor in his head, Michael parted his lips to speak. His mouth was dry and his lips chapped, though, and whispering was all he could manage.

"My name is Michael and I'm in Ventura," he replied in a hushed tone. Michael's body shivered as he spoke; he was freezing! His vision was blurred as he struggled to look around the room. He didn't recognize anyone. His teeth began to chatter and he asked quietly, "Where is Dr. Iwasiuk?"

The doctor looked around, relived. Apparently there were quite a few people in the room, all looking at Michael. He felt strange and out of place, as though something had gone quite wrong. He thought to himself, *where did Jesus go? What the heck is going on here?*

Then it hit him.

"I died!" he gasped.

# Chapter 7

**Michael lifted his** head off the pillow. It felt like it weighed a ton. He saw medical personnel, mostly nurses, walking out of the room. One young man wearing green scrubs touched Michael's foot and said, "You take care now, Michael." They all had such concern on their faces.

He laid his head back down. He was covered in sweat and freezing cold, both inside and out. Things certainly hadn't improved since he went to sleep.

The doctor beside him leaned over again and began speaking to Michael. "How are you feeling?

"Cold," Michael said. The doctor motioned to a nurse, who left quickly. Michael's eyes followed her as she walked out the door, hoping she would come back with a blanket.

"My name is Dr. Sweeney. Dr. Iwasiuk went home quite a while ago, right after your surgery."

The doctor looked at the last nurse left in the room and whispered something to her. It was obvious that he didn't want Michael to hear what he said.

"Doctor," Michael said finally, "what's going on? The last thing I remember was going into surgery." His voice still cracked but found it easier to speak.

"Well Michael," the doctor said, laying his hand on Michael's leg, "you crashed for a couple minutes there. Your surgery was over a few hours ago. Your appendix had ruptured, but we figure that happened at least two or three days ago, judging by the amount of toxins in your system. All those nasty germs were trying to finish the battle, and they almost won."

The doctor paused and patted Michael's leg gently. "Let's just say you're a very lucky man. This usually happens about twenty-four hours after a surgery like yours, but since your appendix had ruptured so long ago, you reached this critical point a little sooner than normal. Your immune system is so weak that your body couldn't fight off this attack. Your heart stopped for a little bit, and we had to shock you to get you back."

"So I *did* die?" Michael asked.

"Well, technically no, since you're still here. Your heart stopped for a little over four minutes, though." The doctor's tone of voice changed from clinical to concerned. He leaned a little closer to Michael and whispered, "It was really close, Mike. We're going to leave you in intensive care for a few days and keep an eye on you. Don't worry, you have one of the best medical teams in the state looking after you."

The doctor kept talking, but Michael didn't hear anything else. All he could think of was the dream that he'd just had. Jesus was there. If he'd died, did he go to Heaven? Why did he come back? *What if I'd taken Jesus' hand right away?* he wondered. *Did waiting somehow change my fate? Am I supposed to be dead?* Michael struggled to remember whether he'd made a choice to come back. Had he decided on this, or had Jesus sent him back?

Sadness gripped Michael suddenly, and he began to cry. He felt as if he should still be with Jesus ... and he wanted to be there. He felt so weak and so lost, having left that mountain top, where everything was so secure. He began to pray, seeking some confirmation that he had done the right thing.

"God, I don't know what this is all about, but You have your reasons, I'm sure. That dream, if that's all it was, made me realize that this life won't last forever. It bothers me, though, that maybe I did the wrong thing. Was I supposed to stay with Jesus? I don't remember having a choice, but the doctor said they shocked me. Did that bring me back before my time? I'm so confused now Lord, I just don't know! I guess You're not done with me yet. I know one thing though; I will never look at Your creation quite the same, knowing there is something more waiting for me. It makes me love You even more and yet, makes me humble to think You would show me. You are so amazing God, thank You. Thank You for loving me so much."

Early the next morning, Ruth came into the room with a big smile and said, "How are you feeling?"

Michael was still so weak that he was unable to lift his head off the pillow, but he knew that he needed to tell her what he'd seen. He gestured for her to come closer, and pulled her down next to him.

"I need to tell you what happened. I had a dream." He started to cry at the thought, and worked to choke back his tears. It was such a beautiful experience that he couldn't wait to share it with his wife.

She stroked his arm. "It's ok, take your time," she said.

Michael tried again, but couldn't get the words out. He just kept crying. Ruth tried her best to comfort Michael, but the thought of that dream, that place he'd been, was too fresh in his mind. He wanted to tell her all about this magnificent experience, but couldn't get the words out.

Just then Dr. Iwasiuk came in. "Good morning, Michael, I see you decided to stay with us through the night?"

Ruth looked at the doctor, puzzled. "What do you mean?" she asked.

Doctor Iwasiuk motioned for Ruth to follow him. "Let's take a walk to the nurses' station and I'll fill you in. We had a close call last night." He put his arm around Ruth and left the room.

Michael closed his eyes and imagined the dream again. He wanted so badly to go back, to feel the warmth of that light! Going back would mean giving up this life, though, and he wasn't sure that he wanted to do that. The conflict hurt his head, and he worked to clear his mind. Perhaps if he went back to sleep, it would erase some of the confusion…

As Michael closed his eyes, Dr. Iwasiuk and Ruth walked quietly down the hall. He tried his best to comfort Ruth and explain what happened the night before. "After surgery last night, as I told you, everything was fine and you left. But a few hours later, Dr. Sweeney who was on call for me was called to your husband's room. Michael's body came under attack from the E*coli* bacteria in his system, and things began to shut down. He arrested for a few minutes, and they had to shock him to bring him back."

Ruth gasped and covered her open mouth with her hand. The doctor took her hand and continued gently.

"Doctor Sweeney called me with an update a few minutes after he stabilized your husband, and I told him not to bother you since it was so late. We were comfortable that the worst was behind us and that Michael would be alright. There was really no sense in disturbing you after the long day you had yesterday. Anyway, with that said, he should be fine and ready to go home in about a week or so."

Ruth turned and ran back into Michael's room. She saw he was asleep already, so she leaned over and kissed his cheek. She walked out dialing her phone. She had to talk to the kids and let them know what had happened.

Michael spent two days in ICU. After Dr. Iwasiuk's morning visit on the third day, he told Michael that he was ready to be moved to a regular bed on the fourth floor. Michael lay in bed and watched as his nurse packed his possessions into a plastic bag. Just then a transporter came around the corner, wearing light blue scrubs and holding a clipboard.

"Michael Owens?" he asked.

"Yes," Michael replied.

"Looks like you're ready to go!"

"I guess," Michael said as he looked up at the IV bag hanging just above his head. "What about all this stuff, all these tubes?"

"It all goes with you, Mr. Owens."

Michael had two IVs in his hand, a tube connecting the lower portion of his abdomen to a bag hanging on the side of the bed, and a catheter ending in another bag. He watched the transporter gently gather up the two bags, lay them at Michael's feet, and cover them with a blanket. The nurse put the bag of his belongings on the other side of the bed and helped the transporter start the bed rolling.

Michael jumped, surprised. "The bed goes too?" he laughed. This was easier than he'd anticipated!

"The whole thing, Mr. Owens, you just relax and enjoy the ride. Next stop, fourth floor!"

When they got to the elevator the nurse leaned over, wished Michael good luck, and said goodbye. After a short elevator ride, Michael and his bed on wheels were pushed into his new room.

Within seconds of his arrival, he heard, "Hey how you doing, buddy? You look comfortable."

Michael's abdominals were still too weak for him to be able to lift his head, so he smiled at the ceiling instead. "Hello," he answered the mysterious voice.

"Looks like we're roomies," the voice said in a heavy New York accent.

*Sounds pretty friendly, at least*, Michael thought.

All of a sudden he heard a strange sound coming from the bed next to him. "Awt, awt, awt, awt, awt."

*What the heck was that?* he wondered.

The voice in the bed next to Michael's said, "Sorry man, I'm in a little pain here and burping helps me feel better."

Michael smiled and said, "Don't make me laugh, it hurts!" The tone of Michael's voice let his roommate know he wouldn't take it personally, but it was a little irritating.

"Sorry, buddy, what are you in here for?"

"Ruptured appendix." Michael turned his head in the direction of the voice, but was still unable to lift it off the pillow. "But I flat-lined a few days ago, and I've been under observation since then. I'm happy to get out of the ICU alive. Guess Heaven's not quite ready for me!"

"Wow." The tone of the mysterious voice suddenly changed from funny to anxious.

Michael looked up towards the ceiling and noticed a handle on the end of a chain, a few feet from his head. He had noticed it before, but only now realized why it was there. *It must be so I can pull myself up off the bed; they think of everything*, he thought. He reached up and grabbed the handle, then pulled with all his strength and lifted himself a few inches to turn and look at his new neighbor.

"I'm Michael, nice to meet you." He dropped back down onto the bed, exhausted from the small amount of movement. Lifting his body up had allowed some air circulation between him and the mattress, though, which had cooled him. He made a note to try it again a little bit later.

"I'm Terry, nice to meet you too." Terry looked like he was about Michael's age. He was a handsome man in his late fifties, slightly overweight, with jet black hair.

"It's been a few days since I had a roommate. The last guy was only here for a few hours before he croaked! Hope you stick around a little longer than that."

"Holy cow," Michael said. "Me too. What happened?"

"The guy was in bad shape. He had a heart attack, but I think they just stuck him in here to get him out of the hall until he died. It's been pretty busy around here, especially on this floor. Anyway, I don't think they expected him to make it. He was out the whole time he was here, poor guy."

"Well, I hope I bring you better luck. I already had my close call. And I had this weird dream. I guess you could say I had a near-death experience."

"No shit!" Terry sat up in his bed.

Michael was surprised at that response, and didn't know what to say.

"You've got to tell me about it man!" his roommate urged.

Michael thought about the dream, about Jesus holding his hand, and how they had flown to that mountain top. He thought about all the colors, those spectacular colors. It was so awesome, but how could he ever describe it and do it justice? He opened his mouth to tell Terry, but started crying again. He was so humbled by the experience that he was unable to speak. He tried again to tell Terry about his dream, but when he opened his mouth to speak, all that came out were sobs. All he could manage to say was, "Sorry."

*What was it about that dream that made it impossible to tell anyone?* he wondered. *I should be able to shout that experience from the mountain tops. It would be so good for everyone who hears it, if I could only tell people. I should at least be able to tell Terry; I just met him, for goodness sakes!*

Michael realized that he had to get past the sobbing part, and find the words to describe the dream. It was so magnificent, so wonderful, and he wanted to tell everyone!

Terry seemed sympathetic, though, and understood Michael's difficulty in speaking. "Hey, it's ok, I understand. It must have been really something to affect you that way."

Michael tried to respond, but once again all he could manage to say was, "Yeah, it was." He closed his eyes and dozed off, hoping and praying to have the same dream again.

# Chapter 8

**Michael awoke several** hours later to Terry trying desperately to get a nurse's attention. "Hello, Hello, anybody there?" he shouted into the intercom system that was supposed to ring directly to the nurses' station. "Is this thing working? Hello!" His voice became panicked with the long answering silence.

Finally a small voice on the other end answered. "Yes, what can I do for you?" It was a night nurse, answering Terry's page. She spoke in a very heavy accent. "Can I help you, sir?"

Terry answered, "Yeah, hey … I got a little problem here."

"Yes go ahead, what can I do for you?"

"Well…" Terry paused, embarrassed, and Michael squeezed his eyes shut. "I either just passed gas … or I crapped my pants." Terry let go of the intercom button and giggled, then spoke softly to himself. "I don't know how to say this delicately."

The tiny voice on the other end said, "Excuse me?"

Terry giggled again and pushed the call button. "I just passed gas or I crapped my pants. I'm really sorry."

The voice on the other end could not understand and asked one more time, "Excuse me sir, what is it you need?"

Terry, sounding desperate now, said in a loud voice, "I just farted or I *shit my pants!*"

After a long pause the nurse said, "I'll be right there."

Michael, now completely awake, started laughing after hearing that exchange. When Terry heard Michael laughing, he started laughing as well.

"Ouch," Michael finally said. "Stop, it hurts to laugh!"

This made Terry laugh even harder.

A few seconds later a nurse walked in and saw Terry smiling. "So what happened?" she asked.

Once again, Terry told her his dilemma. "I think I may have crapped my pants! I woke up coughing and, well, it was an accident."

"Well," said the nurse, "let's take a look."

Terry voluntarily rolled onto his side. The nurse leaned over and checked his backside. "Nope, everything is fine!"

Terry sighed, "That's a relief!"

Michael couldn't help chuckle at Terry's circumstance as the nurse left the room. The two men giggled quietly as Michael closed his eyes. Before he fell back asleep, two men walked in, approached Michael's bedside and spoke softly to him.

"Mr. Owens?"

Michael opened his eyes to see two young men standing over him. One was wearing green scrubs, the other a white lab coat. They both looked very young. *High school kids*, Michael thought.

"Yes?" he asked aloud.

"We need to draw some blood, sir."

"At this time of night?" he asked again, surprised and slightly cranky at the thought.

"Yes sir. I'm sorry; it should only take a minute," said the young man in white. He set a tray containing syringes and a few vials of blood samples down as the young man in the green scrubs grabbed Michaels left arm. He wrapped Michael's arm with a rubber hose and tied it, while the other man moved closer holding a syringe.

"Little stick," said the man in white as he plunged the syringe into Michaels arm.

"Ouch!" Michael let out a yell. "That's a *big* stick!"

"I'm sorry, Mr. Owens."

As he struggled to find the vein the man in green began giving instruction. "Try a little higher, right there," he said, pointing to Michael's arm. The other man jabbed him again, moving the needle around as he tried to get into the vein in question.

"Ouch!" Michael shouted again. This was getting out of hand. Should he call the nurses' station and ask them for help?

Michael leaned his head over expecting to see Terry watching in horror! He was surprised to see Terry resting peacefully, eyes closed. *I can't believe he can sleep through this,* he thought. *He must have already had his fill of excitement for one night, I guess.*

The man in green glanced at the other man, frowning. "You got it or do you want me to try?"

"No, no, I got it," said the syringe-wielding man in white. "I'm going to try right here!"

He withdrew the needle and tried another spot on Michael's arm. Once again Michael let out a yell when the needle broke the skin.

"Oh my gosh that hurts!" he muttered.

"I'm really sorry, Mr. Owens, it looks like your veins may have collapsed slightly. I'm going to try your hand." He pulled the needle out and started tapping the top of Michaels hand with his finger.

The man in green pointed, muttering, "There, right there!"

This time the needle wasn't as painful when it entered Michael's flesh, but he still let out a groan. When the young man in white pulled back on the syringe, he yelled even louder than before. "Guys, that burns like hell!"

Once again they started talking between themselves. The man in green scrubs instructed, "A little slower, that's too fast!"

"Ok, ok!"

Michael started panting as the burning sensation increased. "How much more, guys?" He winced in pain and closed his eyes.

After a few minutes, the man in white said, "That's all Mr. Owens." He removed the syringe and taped gauze over the wound, handing the last vial of blood to the man in green.

"OK, Mr. Owens, you can go back to sleep now."

The man in white picked up the tray of blood samples and the two walked out of the room. Michael could hear them talking in the quiet hallway as they left.

"Dude, that was rough!"

"You did alright for your first one!"

"First one," Michael muttered to himself. "With my luck, I'll get those same guys every time!"

Michael thought Terry was still asleep and was somewhat startled when he asked, "You ok over there?"

"Yeah," Michael exhaled. "I'm alright. I'll be fine as long as dumb and dumber don't come back. That was a little harsh, but they were terrible!"

Terry burst out in laughter. "Hey, don't worry about it – as soon as you fall asleep, they'll come back and wake you up to give you a sleeping pill!" He continued to laugh as he rolled over.

Michael laughed right along with him, while he clutched his belly. "Oh man, it still hurts to laugh!" Their laughter dwindled slowly and before long, Michael fell into a deep sleep.

Michael's eyes opened slowly. Terry was crunching on ice chips. 'Crunch, crunch, crunch.' Michael cringed at the annoying sound, and tried to think of a way to make him stop. "So Terry, you never told me why you're here. What's your story?" he finally asked.

Terry said, "Oh yeah, sorry Mike. I had colon cancer and had a bit of my colon removed. It's no fun, believe me. I mean it's nothing like what you went through, at least not yet! I actually feel pretty good. My doc says my prognosis is great. They expect me to make a full recovery."

"That's awesome, Terry. I'll keep you in my prayers! I'm sorry, I don't want to offend you, but are you a Christian?

"Yeah, I guess I am."

"If you are, you should know!"

"What are you, a preacher?" Terry asked, surprised at Michael's tone.

"No," Michael laughed. "I'm sorry Terry, I do that sometimes, you know, come on a little strong at first! But I take my relationship with Jesus pretty seriously. I have to admit, though, I might still be under the influence of that crazy dream I had the other night!"

"Well, you'll be happy to know that I have a relationship with the big guy myself, although I'm not sure He's crazy about it. I don't exactly live it every day. I know I'm not the best guy, but I try.

"That's all we can do, Terry." Michael smiled and silently thanked God for giving him this opportunity to witness to his new friend. Michael had always felt that God orchestrated people's lives enough to put them in situations that would test their faith in order to strengthen it, and push their limits of expressing that faith in order to make it easier. Michael wasn't always comfortable talking about his relationship with God, but after what he had just been through, he knew that God had kept him around for a reason. *Maybe that's what God was trying to do,* Michael thought, *keep me alive so I could become a better witness for Him!* Whatever the reason, Michael promised himself to keep an open mind.

"Hey Mike, when you said you'd pray for me, did you really mean it?" Terry asked suddenly.

"You bet," Michael answered. He took his prayers very seriously. He knew that there were lots of Christians who said, "I'll pray for you" and then never actually did. And if there was one thing in the world Michael hated, it was a hypocrite. He took prayer very seriously, as well as his promises, and if Michael said he was going to pray for someone, then he would do it. Sometimes he would stop the conversation and pray right there on the spot.

Terry was humbled, and knew by Michael's voice that he was serious. "Thank you," he said softly.

Just then a nurse came into the room, grabbed the chart from the end of Michael's bed, and said, "Mr. Owens?"

"Yes," Michael said.

The nurse was a very young Philippine man who also spoke with a heavy accent. "Mr. Owens, my name is Manolo, but you can call me Manny. I'll be taking care of you today. Mr. Owens, have you boided?"

Michael tried to sit up in bed and failed. He reached up to grab the bar hanging over him for help, and slowly pulled himself off the bed. Once again the air circulating under him felt wonderful. He grabbed the remote and raised the back of the bed, then gently lowered himself back onto the sheets.

"Did I what?" he asked as he shifted his body and stretched his legs.

The nurse repeated, "Have you boided?"

Terry laughed. "Now you see what I had to put up with!" He was referring to the heavy accent of the night nurse. "You can't understand the guy, can you?"

Michael smiled and looked at the nurse. "I don't know what you're asking me."

Manny raised his voice and said, "Have you peed? According to your chart your catheter was removed an hour ago; have you been able to pee yet?"

Michael laughed. "Well why didn't you just ask me that? No, I haven't been out of bed yet, but come to think of it, I've got to go right now!"

Michael heard Terry giggling in the bed next to him.

"Great, I'm glad to hear that, Mr. Owens. Let me help you up and over to the restroom. Remember, you need to pee into this." He held up a large cylindrical bucket that resembled a giant test tube. "We have to measure it," he continued, seeing Michael's surprised look.

Michael was floored. "Seriously, you measure my pee?"

Manny laughed. "Of course, we measure everything in a hospital!"

Michael put his arm around Manny and stood up. He felt surprisingly good. He got a little dizzy and light headed, but that quickly wore off. He took a few steps with Manny's help, and then asked Manny to let him go. He finished the last few steps to the restroom on his own. He walked slowly in, shut the door, and collapsed onto the toilet in relief.

After a few minutes Manny asked, "Doing alright Michael?"

"I'm good, Manny." Michael finished up and pushed the door open to find Manny still standing at the entrance.

"One step closer to normal," he told the nurse with a big grin as he held up the slightly filled plastic tube. His proud smile was replaced quickly by a curious smirk, "Hey, can you bring me a razor? I haven't shaved in three days and it's really bugging me!"

"Sure, Mr. Owens, I'll have someone bring you one." As he guided Michael back to bed, Manny said, "Remember that you must force yourself out of bed to walk. It's the most important thing for you right now."

Michael nodded, thinking that walking around would actually feel good. Once he was situated back on his bed, Manny turned and left. As he did he passed Dr. Iwasiuk, who was coming in to check on Michael.

"Mike, how you doing?"

"Not bad, Doc. I'm still pretty weak though."

Dr. Iwasiuk lifted the sheets and pulled back the bandages over Michael's incisions. "It's going to take some time to get your strength back. This is the worst case I've seen, and I've been practicing for over forty years! This was a major surgery you just went through. It looks like the stiches are healing alright, but you still have a fever, which concerns me. Could be an abscess, so we'll be doing some scans."

Michael interrupted the doctor and asked, "Abscess, what's that?"

"It's an infection." As the doctor spoke he clutched his hands together as if molding a ball of clay. "Sometimes all the germs that are left after surgery gather together in one area and fight to survive. That may be what's happening in your case, and why you still have a fever. We'll keep an eye on it. Anyway, keep walking as much as you can – it helps get everything back to normal. No solid food yet, okay? I'll come back tonight and check on you again. Get some rest, Mike."

The doctor walked out, then grabbed the door and pulled himself back into the room.

He looked at Michael and said in a low voice, "Michael, I said it was the worst case I've ever seen, but that's not completely correct." He paused and took a few steps back into the room toward Michael. "I've seen worse, but they didn't make it. You're a very lucky man, Mike."

Michael whispered, "Thank you for saving my life."

# Chapter 9

**Michael woke up** with a very strange feeling in his chest. He glanced at the clock on the wall: 2AM. He breathed in and out, feeling waves of vapor coat his lungs as he struggled to breathe. His lungs felt like a car radiator that had suddenly been plunged under several feet of water; each little opening held a small amount of air, fighting to enter and escape. As he breathed, his lungs quivered under the fluid that seemed to be building inside his chest. Each rise and fall of his chest only resulted in small choppy gasps, which scared him. He was battling to take even the slightest breath.

He reached for the call button to alert the nurses, but was so weak that he could barely move his arms. He managed to push the button and ask the nurse on the other end of the radio for help. Within seconds, a nurse was by his side. He explained that he could barely get a breath of air. The nurse immediately put a stethoscope to his chest. She listened intently for a few seconds, then looked Michael in the eye.

"Honey," she said, "you're developing pneumonia. You don't want pneumonia!"

She called for more nurses, who came in immediately. One took his temperature, which was a whopping 104.6. Another nurse came in wheeling an oxygen tank. She strapped a small tube under his nose, leading directly into his nostrils, and turned a knob on top of the tank. Immediately Michael felt the steady flow of pure oxygen enter his lungs. Still another nurse came in carrying an ice blanket and laid it on top of him, tucking in the sides close to his body.

Michael hadn't felt this scared since finding out he needed emergency surgery a few days ago. *I'm not getting better, I'm getting worse!* he realized. He looked over at Terry, who was sound asleep and snoring quietly. He was so peaceful, Michael thought. He was on his way up, while Michael was sliding into another emergency.

Michael was totally frustrated with the situation, and suddenly felt as though he couldn't take it anymore. He began kicking his legs violently, and let out a loud scream, followed by another. The nurse leaned over and placed her hands on top of his chest, urging him to stop.

"Michael," she said quietly, "calm down. You're going to be alright, please settle down!"

Terry was jolted awake by Michael's sudden outburst, and looked around at the action in the room, confused.

An impulsive outburst like that was out of character for Michael, and he stopped suddenly, ashamed of himself. That was no way to react to this situation, he knew. As he strained his eyes to focus on the nurse she continued speaking.

"Michael, you may be delirious from your fever, and you may be scared, but I promise that things will get better if you relax."

Exhausted, he closed his eyes, trying to follow her orders.

"That's better, Michael," the nurse said while she gently patted his chest. "Just relax, that blanket will help bring down the fever pretty quickly."

Some of the nurses left the room, but another batch entered. One of them approached Michael and handed him a hard, plastic tube on a small stand.

"Michael, I want you to start breathing into this. It's a spirometer. It will help clear your lungs. You have some fluid forming, and we need to get rid of it. We need to nip this pneumonia in the bud!"

There was that word again – pneumonia. He knew how weak he was, and how serious that illness could be. In his condition, if he developed pneumonia he might die. Is that why Jesus had showed him Heaven? Was Michael's death inevitable? He had waited a long time to go to the hospital and realized he only had himself to blame for the precarious situation he was in! Would it all come to an end now?

Michael thought back to the first time he felt like he was getting the flu. It had been right after he played home run derby with the boys in the park. Could that twisting from swinging the bat have put too much stress on his appendix? It was certainly possible, especially if his appendix was already swollen. Maybe it all came down to that one game with his boys. How ironic he thought; the one thing in life that brought so much joy could end up killing him!

He tried to hold the spirometer in front of him, but was so weak that he couldn't hang on. The nurse propped it up on his chest and placed his hands around the base, motioning for him to breathe into it.

"Do this ten times an hour," she said.

Michael tried breathing into the tube and moving the little marble like she had showed him, but could barely move enough air to get that marble to budge. He paused, exhausted, and looked up at the nurse.

"You want to breathe hard enough to hold that little marble right here." She pointed about halfway up the clear plastic tube. "Keep trying. It will get easier."

As he struggled to move the marble, the last nurse remaining in the room sat down. "I'm going to sit with you for a couple hours and make sure you're OK," she told him. Everyone else began filing out of the room, their jobs done.

Michael nodded gratefully. He would be glad to have one nurse left with him, even if she was only going to watch him. Still, he felt bad about being so much trouble.

"I'm sorry, that wasn't like me to do something like that," he whispered. "I didn't mean to make your job harder."

"I understand," she said. "You've been through a lot. Now try to rest."

Michael managed to get the little ball in the spirometer moving, and used it so much that night that his lungs had cleared in three hours. His fever had come down the next morning to nearly 100 degrees, but still spiked slightly every night.

He spent the next few days walking up and down the hall, stopping to rest in the waiting area and spending hours at a time gazing out the plate glass windows at the Pacific Ocean. He learned about the warm areas on his strolls around the nurses' station and figured out where the cool spots were. He would migrate to the proper region depending on his internal temperature. Most nights found Michael sitting in the cool area under the air conditioning vent.

Day by day he got stronger, but the persistent fever remained. Dr. Iwasiuk ordered scans every day, trying desperately to find the source of the elusive infection. Michael hated the process of going downstairs for a scan, though he realized that it was necessary. He'd already gone through the process three times, and now he was scheduled for another one. An hour before the scan he had to drink a quart of the most disgusting flavored chalky milk he had ever tasted. The concoction smelled like a mixture of rotten fruit and stinky feet. The aftertaste was even worse, with hints of copper and ammonia. Each time he chugged about half the quart, then stopped to catch his breath. It took at least half an hour to finish off the remainder.

Doctor Iwasiuk was convinced that he must have an abscess somewhere, although it hadn't shown up on any of the previous scans. The fact that they were unable to find it was frustrating to Michael. He desperately wanted to get back home.

One afternoon while Michael stared out the window, his frustration came to a boiling point again. He stood up, pounded his fists on the glass, and yelled, "Damn it! I need to get out of here and go home!" He hung his head in despair and slowly sat back down; shouting at the window hadn't made him feel any better. In fact it just made him feel stupid.

He closed his eyes slowly, realizing that he was looking for an answer that was right in front of his face. He needed to talk to God again.

"Lord," Michael whispered with his head bowed, "please bring this thing to an end. I need to get back home to my kids. I need to get healthy again. I need to go back to work! Please Lord, end this; I can't take just sitting around in this hospital anymore. I'm miserable and bored to tears. Please let them find the infection and get me better. Watch over my family, since I can't be with them right now. Thank You, Father. Amen."

Michael opened his eyes to find that another patient had sat down in the waiting area a few chairs away. He was an elderly gentleman, dressed in a hospital gown and clutching his IV stand.

"I heard you praying," the old man said. "What are you in here for?"

"Ruptured appendix," Michael answered. "How about you?"

The old man smiled and said, "I have a long list, but this time it's my heart. I had a little episode yesterday, so they checked me in and I'm having emergency surgery tomorrow morning. Turns out I got a bad valve. It will be my third heart operation in the last two years."

Michael sympathetically said, "Wow, good luck with that."

The old man continued to smile, and leaned over and stuck out his hand. "Name's Ed," he said.

As Michael shook his hand he was struck by the lack of strength in the old man's grip. *He must be really weak*, he thought. The two of them sat and chatted for a few minutes, though Ed did most of the talking, telling Michael all about his grandkids.

When Michael stood up to leave, he asked, "So Ed, what time is your surgery?"

"First thing in the morning, supposed to start at 7."

"Well good luck!" Michael encouraged him again. "I'll pray for you."

"Thanks," Ed replied.

As Michael pushed his IV stand slowly back to his room, he said a quick prayer for Ed. Listening to the old man talk about his grandchildren made Michael miss his kids even more. Haley, Hunter, and Tyler had all gone back to Michael's home in San Diego with Heather's mom. She volunteered to babysit as long as she was needed; the kids had to get back to school.

Now that he thought about it, he realized that he missed Ruth too. She hadn't been in to see him all day, although she had sent a few text messages. She planned on spending the day at Heather's parents' house, helping them clean and get things back to normal. The last of the wedding guests had finally gone home. Still, he thought, it seemed like she could have come to the hospital for at least a quick visit. This bothered him, though he tried to put it out of his mind as he walked back to his room.

He climbed back into bed and lay down, exhausted. Walking was helping build his strength, but still tired him out. He looked at the tray next to his bed and there, amongst his box of Kleenex, magazines, and phone, saw the empty jar from this morning's preparatory scan juice. The chalky substance left a streaky white film on the walls of the container. Michael could smell it, even from a few feet away. *That stuff is disgusting,* he thought. The unpleasant aroma brought back all the frustration of numerous scans leading to negative results. Day by day, Michael's frustration mounted and it was taking its toll on his daily outlook. He was sinking lower and lower every day.

Just then, nurse Manny walked in and, in his now familiar Philippine accent, told Michael the news he'd been waiting for since waking up after surgery. "Well Michael, your latest scan came back negative again, so your doctor is going to let you resume a normal diet!"

"But what about the fever?" Michael asked.

"Nothing is showing up on your scans or blood tests, so he's probably decided that it's a very slight infection. I'm sure he's convinced that antibiotics will kill the remainder of the *Ecoli.* It won't get any worse if you eat solid food. I've ordered your dinner. It should be here in a few minutes."

The thought of real food was very exciting to Michael. He had already lost almost 20 pounds in the week he'd been here, and lately when he finished a liquid meal he was still hungry. He couldn't wait to eat "real food" again, hospital food or not! His dinner was brought in as Manny left his room.

The orderly placed the tray down and Michael raised his bed to a sitting position. He couldn't believe his eyes as the young woman lifted the top of the tray. Meatloaf, mashed potatoes and gravy, a fresh banana, some pudding, and milk. Michael never thought such a lackluster meal could look so delicious!

He grabbed the banana and started peeling. As Michael took his first bite, he began to weep. Here he was in a hospital, having barely survived a brush with death, and now this banana – something grown hundreds of miles away, out of the dirt of the earth – was helping make him healthy. He was blown away by the simplicity, and complexity, of it all. It was all such a miracle. The thought of God's creation hit him like a ton of bricks.

He laid his head back on his pillow and closed his eyes, remembering a conversation he'd had with Dane, when Michael had told Dane that he saw God in everything. *How could anyone live on this earth and witness the sustainability of life and not believe in God?* Michael wondered.

The aroma of the meatloaf wafting just below his nostrils made his taste buds salivate. He opened his eyes and continued his meal, quickly piercing a hunk of meatloaf, swirling the loaded fork through the mashed potatoes and gravy, and stuffing it in his mouth. Michael moaned as he chewed. *Oh so good,* he thought. He took a few more bites of meatloaf and closed his eyes again, savoring every morsel.

Just then a nurse ran into the room and yelled at Michael, "Stop eating!"

"Huh?" Michael asked, his mouth still full of meatloaf and mashed potatoes.

"They found an abscess!"

Michael spit his food out onto the tray, deflated. After a week and four scans they had finally found the cause of the infection. And right in the middle of his first meal.

"How much did you eat?" asked the nurse.

"I ate the banana, a couple bites of the meatloaf, and some potatoes, not counting the bite I just spit out!"

"Don't eat anymore, I'll be right back."

Michael fell back on the bed, disappointed. That was the last thing he had expected to happen, and the timing couldn't have been worse! Still, he supposed he should count his blessings – if eating was going to make the abscess worse, it was better that the nurse had caught him before he ate too much. The last thing he needed was for the infection to cause another setback.

The nurse came back in a few minutes later. "Ok, I just spoke with the doctor. You're going to go NPO at midnight and then tomorrow morning they're going to go in and get the abscess, so you can finish your dinner."

"NPO?" Michael asked. "What's that?"

She smiled and said, "It's a Latin term; it means nothing by mouth!" Michael nodded and she waited for his response. "Aren't you happy? You're one giant step closer to being able to go home, and you get to finish your dinner!"

"I guess," said Michael. He nibbled on the remaining meatloaf. "Are you sure it's okay to finish?"

The nurse smiled and looked at Michael empathetically. "Sure."

Michael picked up the fork and scarfed up everything on his plate. As he ate his last bite, he saw two nurses run into the room across the hall. A few seconds later a doctor hurried in, followed by two more nurses.

"What the heck?" Michael asked.

Terry was resting in the bed next to his, and got up to walk swiftly to the doorway. He looked back at Michael and said, "This don't look good Mike. It's the old guy."

Michael got out of bed and stood behind Terry, watching

the commotion in their neighbor's room. He caught a glimpse of the patient lying in the bed; it was Ed, the elderly man Michael had just met in the waiting room a few hours before. He heard the doctor yell, "Clear!" Then he heard a loud thump.

Terry gasped. "Holy shit, Mike! I've seen that on TV, but never in person. That poor old guy."

Once again, they heard the doctor yell, "Clear!" followed by another thud. This time the room got eerily quiet. Michael and Terry waited in stunned silence.

The doctor in the other room finally said, "Let's call it. Time of death, 6:04."

Michael was shocked, but not surprised. Ed had seemed so frail, not that far away from death. He turned and crawled back into his bed, saying another quick prayer for Ed and his grandchildren. Then a sudden wave of disappointment flooded over him. He had just talked to Ed, and hadn't even thought to ask if the man was a Christian. *This must be what God is trying to teach me,* he thought. *I came on too strong with Terry, and then did a complete 180 and didn't even ask Ed about his relationship with Jesus! I've got to find an effective way to share my faith!*

Michael watched as the doctor came out of Ed's room, followed by a couple of nurses. A few more minutes went by, and the hallway emptied. Then Michael noticed two men in white lab coats pushing an empty gurney into Ed's room. They closed the door behind them.

# Chapter 10

**"Michael Owens?"**

"Yeah." Michael recognized the young man in the white coat, standing in front of the empty wheelchair. It was the transporter from x-ray, waiting to take him for his latest procedure.

"So what all is involved in getting an abscess?" Michael asked as he walked toward the wheelchair.

The transporter laughed. "Oh it's fun, Mike, you're going to love it!"

"Why do I detect a rather large amount of sarcasm?" Michael sat down in the wheelchair, grimacing; movement was still somewhat difficult for him.

As the transporter covered Michael's legs with a blanket, he smiled and said, "You'll see, Mr. Owens. It can't be *that* bad, although I don't remember anyone I've transported having this done!"

"Oh that's just perfect!"

The two men laughed as Michael began the long descent down the hall, then three floors down to the x-ray department.

He was wheeled into the scan room, where a nurse greeted him. She told him to lie down on his stomach this time, on a long, cold stainless steel bed, covered only by a thin sheet of white paper. Every other scan he had done while lying on his back, and he asked about the change.

The nurse began to explain the procedure. "Well Michael, here's the deal. The abscess is at the very bottom of your abdominal cavity. We can't go in through the front because you have too many organs in the way. We need a straight shot to the abscess, so we're going in through your back side."

"What do you mean by 'your back side?'" Michael asked, already a little scared.

"What I mean is, um, we go through your butt cheek."

"What?" Michael picked his head up and looked at her. "Are you serious?"

"It gives us a clear path directly to the abscess."

Just then a very tall, slender, dark-haired woman walked in. "Hi. Michael?"

"Yes."

"I'm Dr. Miller. I'll be performing your procedure today." Dr. Miller looked like she could double as a model. She had a dark complexion and long brown hair, straight and smooth as silk. She was a very striking woman, at least 6 feet tall, although from Michael's vantage point it was hard to tell. If he had to go through something like this, at least he was going to have attractive women to talk to, he supposed.

Michael smiled and tried to hide his discomfort. So far this procedure didn't sound like much fun, but it was his ticket out of the hospital. Michael had adopted the attitude of go along to get along. Don't fight it, just go along. It will be over soon.

Dr. Miller continued. "Here's the plan. We're going to insert a needle through your gluteus muscle, right here." She took a pen and drew a small dot on Michael's left butt cheek. "Once we penetrate the skin, we will slide you into the tube and take a picture. We'll probably have to do this several times, to make sure we're on target to hit the abscess. Once we're in, we will penetrate the abscess, drain it, and leave a drain in for about twenty-four hours. After that, I think you should be clear of all infections and you can go home."

"That's the best news I've heard all week," Michael said. He felt somewhat relieved, but some of the procedure Dr. Miller just described still made him nervous. What did she mean when she said they'd have to repeat this several times, and what did she mean by leaving the drain in? What drain? Oh well, he thought, just go along!

The doctor and nurse talked for a few more minutes as the nurse disconnected Michael's IV bag. She connected his IV tube to a new bag, which hovered just above his head. Hopefully filled with something to ease the pain he was about to endure.

"Now Michael, this will keep you from feeling some pain, but I can't let you have too much at first. Let me know if things get unbearable, and I can give you a little more. I can't give you as much as you'll want; protocol on this type of procedure says that you have to remain conscious, so you're going to feel some of it."

As Dr. Miller left the room the nurse said, "The first thing I'm going to ask you to do is roll over on your side." Michael slowly rolled over and she said, "My name is Janet. If things get unbearable, you call my name and let me know."

Michael, now laying on his side with his legs straight and his arms slightly bent in front of him, said, "Janet, that's the second time you've told me I'm going to be uncomfortable. Is that nurse code for 'this is going to hurt?'"

Janet sat down on a small stool, wheeled it over next to Michaels face, and smiled. "I'm not going to lie to you Michael, this procedure is no fun."

"Thanks for the honesty," Michael said somberly.

Janet wheeled back around to Michael's back side and said,

"Now the first thing we have to do is fill your rectum with water so it will show up better on the scan. We don't want to puncture anything on the way in." As she said this she inserted a small metal tube into Michael's rectum.

Michael was shocked. "You're kidding, right?"

"The water is warm, so it won't be too bad," Janet said with a hint of sarcasm in her voice.

Michael knew Janet was doing her best to comfort him. "You really think the fact that it's warm makes it better?" He tried to keep a sense of humor about what was happening back there, but was finding it more and more difficult. He said to Janet, "I feel like I'm being violated by R2D2!" He was not looking forward to this, and it was already well underway.

As Janet started the flow of water, Michael realized that the water *was* warm, but it was going to get worse. He told himself to go along, and that it would be over soon.

"Doing OK, Mike?" Janet asked.

"So far so good." Michael was feeling relaxed; *the drugs must be starting to take effect*, he thought.

Dr. Miller came back in the room then, holding a very large needle, the size of a pencil.

Michael panicked, despite the relaxing medication. "That's going in my ass?" he gasped.

Janet couldn't help but laugh, which drew a harsh look from the doctor. "This is what we use to drain that nasty abscess, Michael. We'll keep you as drugged up as we can, right Janet? And we'll be done before you know it. Hang in there!"

Dr. Miller positioned the needle over the dot they had drawn on Michael's rear end and began to push it into his skin. Michael let out a scream as the pain hit him.

"Oh my gosh that hurts!"

"We have a long way to go, Mike. Be tough."

Michael looked at Janet and asked if she could give him more pain medication. "I won't make it if it hurts this much," he pleaded.

Janet reached up and adjusted the drip. "That should help."

Michael could feel the relief instantly, although the pain was still intense. Dr. Miller walked out of the room as Janet held the needle, now protruding out of Michael's butt cheek. She gently let it go, which hurt Michael even more as it now dangled by its own weight.

"A quick trip into the tube for a picture," she said. "Don't move, Mike, I'll be right back."

After Janet slid Michael and the dangling needle into the tube, she ran around the corner, pushed a few buttons, and powered up the machine. Michael heard the familiar sound of the scanner snapping pictures and then Janet came running back into the room, slid him back out of the tube, and grabbed the needle. A few seconds later, Dr. Miller came back in and took the needle still protruding from Michael's butt cheek from Janet.

"We're right on target," she said. She pushed the needle in a little farther. "Time for another picture!"

Michael groaned again in pain. "Can I get another hit of that stuff?" He motioned up at the IV bag hanging above him.

"A little bit more should be alright, but we're near the limit Michael." Janet adjusted the drip again. It had the same effect, immediately easing the pain, and he sighed in relief. Janet slid Michael back into the tube, letting go of the needle.

"Be right back," she said as she quickly ran around the corner. Again Michael heard the machine taking its picture. And just like before, Janet and Dr. Miller came back in the room. This routine was repeated until Dr. Miller finally said, "Michael, we're in. I'm going to drain it now and get you back up to your room." Dr. Miller slowly pulled the plunger on the needle, draining the abscess. Then she attached the bag to the end of the plastic hose which had replaced the needle protruding from Michael's derriere.

All those doses of medication finally took full effect, and the next thing Michael remembered was waking up in his bed. The entire procedure now seeming like a bad dream. But when Michael reached around and felt the hose and drain bag, he remembered. That was no dream!

# Chapter 11

**Brandon and Heather** decided to come home early from their honeymoon. They had been staying in the honeymoon suite at the Marriot in Desert Hot Springs. Brandon had spared no expense when it came to pampering his new bride; their room overlooked a lake and included a poolside cabana. They had spent eleven days in total luxury. But the thought of his father lying in a hospital room was too much for Brandon. It didn't take much convincing when he asked Heather if she would mind going home a few days early.

When they first left for Desert Hot Springs, Michael had been through surgery and Ruth had let them both know that he would be fine. She didn't tell them all the details of how close it had been. When Brandon and Heather got to the hospital twelve days after their wedding and the surgery, it was a shock. Brandon gasped when he saw his dad. Michael had lost so much weight, it was too much for him to handle. He started to cry.

"Dad, I'm so sorry I wasn't here for you. You look like death warmed over."

Michael thought back to the past week. His experience with Jesus, going to Heaven, and finally telling Ruth after failing so many times. Then there was the whole abscess, which was a story all its own. The emotion started to get the best of him.

"There's so much I need to tell you, Brandon. But I wish you had stayed on your honeymoon for the full two weeks. There was no reason to come home early; the worst is behind me now."

He looked at his son, who was turning white at his father's depleted state, and held out his hands. Brandon strode over and laid his head on his father's lap.

"I'm so glad you're going to be alright. You must have been through a lot," Brandon mumbled through the tears.

"You have no idea, Brandon, this was rough. It was a pretty close call."

"You still have a tube hanging out of you there, Dad." Brandon grabbed it loosely and asked, "What's it for?"

"They had to drain an abscess, and that's to catch the leftovers!"

"Nice!" As Brandon said that, Dr. Miller came in. "Hello everyone, hello Michael," she said, looking around the room.

"Hi, Doc," Michael answered.

"I'm here to remove the drain. Dr. Iwasiuk says you'll probably be going home tomorrow. Once my tube is out, if your temperature stays normal, you should be good to go."

Brandon, Heather, and Ruth excused themselves as Dr. Miller pulled the curtain around to shield Michael's bed from the rest of the room. As soon as she did, she went to work. In just a few minutes, the tube was out and Michael had nothing more than a small bandage covering the incision.

"Sure comes out easier than it goes in, doesn't it Doc?"

"Sure does, Michael," Dr. Miller laughed. She wished Michael good luck and left.

Ruth and the kids came back in and sat down. Ruth pulled back the curtain and found Terry packing his bag. Terry's wife had come in to help him pack.

"You leaving?" Michael asked, glancing at his roommate.

"Yeah, buddy, I'm out of here!"

"Well good luck to you, I'm going to miss you. What's the prognosis?"

Terry shook his head. "You know, I'm just going to take things one day at a time. Doc says I should be fine, but I think he's going to have me go through some chemo."

"I'll keep you in my prayers, Terry. Thanks for making my stay here so much fun!"

The two of them laughed and Terry said, "Yeah, there are a few stories I'll never forget, Mike. You take care."

A transporter knocked on the door and Terry sat down in his wheelchair. He saluted Michael and said, "Later dude!"

After Terry was gone, Brandon said, "What a cool guy!"

"Yea he was great," said Michael. "So funny. That guy had me cracking up, even when it hurt to laugh!"

"So Dad, you want to take a quick walk up and down the hall before we get out of here?" Brandon asked suddenly.

Michael smiled; the doctors must have told him that his dad should be walking around. "Good idea, Brandon," he agreed. He got out of bed more easily without all of the cumbersome tubes — this was the first time he'd been without them in eleven days. A few days ago, he had joked that he had tubes hanging out of him in places he didn't know they could put tubes! Once he was out of bed he stretched, happy to have his body almost back to normal. They walked down the hall, past the nurses' station. Michael stopped and looked out the fourth floor window toward the ocean.

"I spent lots of time right here," he told them.

"Because of the view?" Brandon asked.

"No, because this is the warmest spot in the hall!" Michael laughed. "In a strange way, I'm going to miss this place." Michael led the small processional slowly back to his room. Just before he got back in bed Brandon asked, "Dad, before I leave, can we pray?"

"I'd love that, buddy," Michael said softly.

Brandon grabbed his father's hand, along with Ruth's and Heather's. They formed a small circle in the hospital room, and Brandon led the prayer. "Father, thank you for watching out for my dad while I was away. Thank you for protecting him and giving him a new chance at life. We love You, Lord. Keep him safe and get him out of here tomorrow. Amen."

Brandon opened his eyes and looked at the floor below Michael. Suddenly he screamed. "Dad, you're bleeding!"

Michael looked down and saw a small pool of blood below him. Before he could react, Brandon had grabbed him and pushed him onto the bed. He turned over and saw that the blood was coming from the incision in his butt cheek, where the drain had been.

"Call a nurse," Brandon shouted at his bride.

Heather grabbed the call button and frantically asked for help. Brandon forced Michael over onto his stomach and pressed his hand over the wound, applying pressure to stop the bleeding. While they waited for a nurse to arrive, Brandon tried to relief the obvious tension in the room. He chuckled and said , "You've got a nice ass dad!"

Michael just muttered, his face buried in the pillows. Heather and Ruth giggled.

A few seconds later, a nurse arrived to relieve Brandon. A few minutes more and Dr. Miller walked in. She relieved the nurse and looked at the wound, which had already stopped bleeding. As she taped on a new, larger bandage, she said, "That should do it, Mike. You should probably should stay in bed the rest of the night to keep the wound from opening up again. No more walking around until tomorrow!"

The date was May 18. Twenty-five years ago on this day, Michael and Ruth had been married. Today was a very happy day for Michael. Not only was it his twenty-fifth anniversary, but Dr. Iwasiuk had just cleared him to go home. His temperature was back to normal, and had been steady all night. He'd spent twelve days in the hospital, but now it was time to get home and return to a normal life; at least as normal as one can have after a near-death experience.

Michael made some promises to God before he left the hospital. For one, he was going to be sure to tell all his friends and family how much he loved them. He had realized how quickly this precious gift of life can be taken from him, and he didn't want to end up being the mouse in the hawk's claws, leaving this earth suddenly without everyone knowing how he truly felt about them. That would have a lasting impact on his entire family, and as far as Michael could tell, a lasting impact on God's kingdom

The other promise Michael made to God was to become the kind of man he knew God wanted him to be. Not that he had been a bad person, but Michael knew he needed to be a better person and a better Christian. Ruth reminded him all the time to be 'an effective witness.' At times he felt that he'd become somewhat of a hypocrite. And the one thing Michael hated was a hypocrite. He always figured they existed because the devil had found a way to become so effective in this lost world.

Michael was determined to go away from this experience with a renewed sense of what Jesus wanted from true believers. As Michael saw it, this was a fresh start. And now, with God's help, Michael had a story; a real story! He vowed to use this in a brand new way. Michael couldn't wait to get home and begin his "new" life.

# Chapter 12

*Present Day*

In Michael's house, it was tradition to begin the Thanksgiving meal after the Dallas Cowboys game had finished. Ruth was from Dallas, and with a little help from her siblings had converted Michael to a Cowboys fan shortly after they tied the knot. Michael had been a Rams fan since he was a kid, but Ruth's three brothers convinced him to make the switch. He had never regretted the change. They had all shared Cowboys glory, and a few tough defeats, but none were tougher than 'the catch,' when Joe Montana and Dwight Clark of the San Francisco Forty-Niners put an end to the Cowboys' season in dramatic fashion in 1982.

Since the game started at 1, Ruth planned on a 5 o'clock meal, in case of overtime. The game ended by 4:30, so her carefully planned scheduling worked. Now they had all sat down for the Thanksgiving feast.

"Pass the stuffing, please." Michael was starving.

"Michael we need to pray before we dig in; but first, does everyone know Dane?"

"You're right dear," Michael said. "Has everyone met Dane? He's my new assistant at work." Michael looked at Dane. "You've met everybody, right?"

Dane nodded, smiling at the family members around the table.

Michael nodded, and looked around as well. "Great, let's pray." Everyone around the table reached out and held hands as they bowed their heads.

"Father, we thank You for this awesome meal. I thank You for getting us all together safely and allowing Your spirit to fill this home. I pray that You comfort those who are hungry today, and give them hope for a better future. Please be with us in our day-to-day lives and help us see the world through your eyes. Keep molding us into the people You want us to be. And Lord, thanks for the Cowboy victory today. Amen!" He opened his eyes and grinned. "*Now* pass the stuffing!"

Michael stood up with his fork in hand, reached to the center of the table, and pierced a small hunk of turkey, a portion of stuffing, and cranberry sauce. He held his fork up for all to see and said, "There's nothing better than Thanksgiving turkey, stuffing, *and* cranberry sauce all together in one bite." With that he stuffed the loaded fork into his mouth.

Dane couldn't believe what he was witnessing. Michael had just shoved a huge bite of food into his mouth all at once. No one else had even loaded their plates with as much as one serving.

"Oh no," said Ruth, "here we go!"

"I don't know," said Tyler, Michael's youngest son. "I like turkey, mashed potatoes, corn, stuffing, cranberry sauce, and..." as he said this he was reaching over everyone and grabbing one small bite out of every dish on the table and holding it precariously with both hands on his fork. He jumped out of his seat and ran to the refrigerator as he continued to yell, "Pumpkin pie, all in one." He took a small portion of pie and stuffed it on his fork, then right into his mouth.

He turned to the table from the kitchen, stretched out his arms and yelled, "Tadaaa!" As he did, small bits of stuffing began falling out of his mouth. The whole table started laughing and pointing at Tyler.

Dane looked around, surprised.

"We do this every year," explained Ruth. "The boys see who can fit the most food in their mouths at once, until a winner is declared." This year Tyler had apparently gone for the jugular right away, since he took a bite of everything on the table *and* something from the fridge.

With that, Michael stood up and shouted, "Tyler is this year's Thanksgiving mouthful champion." Once again, those at the table laughed and applauded.

"It sounds like you guys really enjoy your time together," said Dane, laughing.

"We do Dane; we've always been a really close group. We have a lot of fun together," Michael said. "I bet you never saw the Cleavers do that!"

Dane said, "I can't say I ever did!"

"What was Thanksgiving like when you were a kid?" asked Tyler, still choking down the last bit of pumpkin pie.

Dane sat back and thought a minute. When he spoke, he did so slowly, but very deliberately. "When I was growing up, it was just my parents and I. Our Thanksgiving Day always began with me watching the parade on TV, by myself. I spent a lot of time by myself, not just on holidays." The entire table had become very quiet. Dane had captured the attention of everyone.

"Don't get me wrong, I enjoyed my childhood, but I've never experienced anything like this. It must be nice to be surrounded by so many people who really love you."

Ruth said, "Dane, I'm sure your parents loved you very much."

Dane nodded. "Yes, I'm sure they did. But they never showed it. I mean, my dad was always busy, as they say, 'off slaying the dragon.' And my mom was away from home a lot.

She had tons of social commitments. She played bridge, orga- nized events for an old folks' home, and did lots for our little community. She was a very loving and caring person. She just didn't have much time for me. But I turned out okay. I under- stand her more now. I appreciate the life that she and Dad gave me."

The following silence was deafening, and seemed to last forever. The mood of the table turned awkward.

"Well," Ruth finally said, "I'm certainly glad you could join us. Now pass those mashed potatoes!"

Dane picked up the dish of mashed potatoes and passed them to her, then glanced at the food spread before him. "My compliments to the chef, this is one fantastic dinner!" he said, enthusiastically. "I always love a good hearty meal!"

Ruth smiled and said, "Thank you, Dane. I love it when people appreciate my cooking."

"I appreciate your cooking, Mom!" Tyler said. "In fact, I'm ready to just skip on down to the pumpkin pie; that was fantas- tic!" He managed to get a few chuckles from his siblings.

Everyone's attention turned back to Dane, though, as he spent the next few minutes explaining to Michael's family a lit- tle more about his life growing up in Massachusetts. He shared his love for baseball, and got everyone's attention with that, especially Hunter's. They both talked about how their base- ball careers had ended and how much they each missed the game. Hunter proudly admitted to Dane that he knew God had other things planned for his life, and that baseball would pale in comparison.

Ruth interrupted, saying, "I hate to change the subject, but Dane, do you have a girlfriend? I'm just asking because I know a lovely young lady I would like to introduce you to from church. Are you interested?"

Tyler rolled his eyes and said, "Mom, golly, so personal!"

Ruth smiled and countered, "Well, you know my reputation!" Ruth was known as a match maker in her circle of friends. She had introduced two different couples to each other, and both had gotten married and been together for quite a while. It was a point of pride for her, and she was always looking for another chance.

"Sure Ruth, that would be really nice," Dane said, with a little apprehension. "But I actually met someone at the dog park the other day. We promised to get together for coffee soon. She seems really cool, and I think I'm going to give that a chance first."

Michael dropped his fork in surprise. "What? And you didn't bother to tell your boss?"

Dane looked back at Michael with astonishment and said, "I guess I'm just a little private about those sorts of things."

"I'm just giving you a hard time Dane," Michael replied. "But private doesn't get you too far around here!" Michael looked around at all his kids and winked at his daughter as he spoke. "Tell me about her."

"Well, she's in real estate and grew up here in San Diego. She's really sweet. She has a German Shepherd named Sasha, and she likes coffee!"

Ruth looked at Michael and said, "Dane you don't let Mike intimidate you. You just tell him what you want him to know. And I would keep it to a minimum, if you know what I mean! I'm glad you met someone, and she sounds very sweet. But it's always good to keep your options open. Let me know if you want to meet the girl from our church."

"Thank you, Ruth."

"Hey, I think that's great, Dane ... get it? Great *Dane*!" Michael interrupted. He looked around expectantly, and managed to get a few giggles from the kids.

"Come on, Dad," Hunter grumbled, unimpressed with his dad's attempt at humor.

Michael ignored him and turned back to Dane. "You just keep us posted, okay?" he said.

Dane looked around at everyone, rather embarrassed that his love life had now taken center stage. "I sure will Michael. But I think that's enough about me. Let's talk about someone else for a while."

Dane opened the door to the Bean and Leaf and immediately looked around for Diana. The smell of freshly ground coffee was intoxicating. *What a wonderful atmosphere*, he thought. He stood there holding the door open and just breathed. The place was done in gold oak and deep brown leather, and bustled with the muted business of a friendly establishment. Now this was a coffee shop!

He spotted Diana in line and walked toward her. As he walked, his mind started racing; should he kiss her hello, or would that be too forward? *This is California*, he thought. *People are a little more forward here than back home. But what if that's too forward for her?* He didn't want to blow it with Diana. He really liked her.

Diana turned when she heard the door open, and saw him walking toward her. "Dane!" she called, waving. As he walked over, she held her arms out, and hugged him and kissed his cheek.

*That puts an end to that little drama*, Dane thought.

"How are you?" he asked.

"I'm doing great. Another beautiful day in Southern California! How are you?"

They ordered their coffees and found a seat, still talking. The coffee shop had decorative tile floors, elegant tables, and a few soft couches. They chose a couch in the corner, to give them more privacy, and fell into the overstuffed cushions.

Once again, conversation between the two of them was easy. Dane knew that he'd found someone very special. He had never felt like this about anyone. He loved hearing her talk about her life and her family, and she seemed so interested in him.

"How is everything this morning? Coffee okay?" Dane looked up to see a very large man wearing a long white apron standing in front of them. His white hair was cut military style, and he looked like a body builder.

"It's fantastic as usual, Mitch," Diana said with a smile. "Mitch, this is my new friend Dane," she said, holding out her hand and gesturing toward Dane.

Dane stood up and shook his hand. "Nice to meet you, Mitch."

"Likewise, Dane. Let me know if I can get you two anything. Good to see you Diana, and nice to meet you Dane."

Dane smiled at Diana and sat back down. "He seems very nice."

"Yes, very nice. He's a good friend of my dad's. He was a detective for the San Diego Police Department for almost thirty years. Then about five years ago, he had a heart attack and couldn't work anymore. He got tired of just sitting at home, though, collecting his pension. It's funny; he said he'd been looking forward to retiring since the day he started working. He had planned for it, saved for it, and then when it happened, he said he hated it! So he opened this place."

"Is he married?" Dane asked, smiling at the story.

"No, typical cop," she answered. "He was married for a

couple years but, according to him, she couldn't handle the stress of not knowing if he was coming home or not. It's a dangerous job! I can't imagine being married to a cop. I think we all take for granted the lives some of our public servants lead, and the stress on their relationships. It takes a special kind of person to do that."

Dane nodded in agreement.

"Hey Dane," she quipped suddenly, "let's get these coffees to go and take a drive up the coast. What do you think?"

Dane thought for a minute. A drive on the curvy highway looking out over the ocean sounded like a blast, *and* it would be a way to prolong their date!

Diana frowned as Dane paused. "You're not the impulsive type, Dane?"

"No, no, that actually sounds fun, let's do it!"

They pushed themselves up and out of the soft cushions and walked hand in hand to the counter. Diana called for Mitch, who was back in his familiar spot ,whipping up a latte. "Can we get these to go?"

Mitch grinned and yelled over the whirring of the machine whipping a cup of milk. "Sure, anything for the two lovebirds! Be right with you!"

Mitch leaned over, grabbed a couple of cardboard cups, poured the remaining coffee from the ceramic mugs and handed them back to Dane. "You guys have fun now!"

"Thanks, Mitch. See you soon," Dane smiled as he reached for the half-filled cups. Dianna had already walked to the front door and stood holding it open for Dane. "Let's go", she said excitedly as Dane scurried by.

They climbed into Dane's car and spent the next two hours exploring the California coastline, getting to know each other better. Dane already relished the time spent getting to know

Dianna. It didn't take long for Dane to realize he was falling in love on their first date.

Michael and Dane walked into the softball park, gear in hand. Diana and Ruth were right behind them, laughing at their banter.

"You know that I haven't hit a baseball in years, right? And I can't even remember how long it's been since I hit a *softball*!" Dane confessed.

Dane had been an all-star baseball player in high school. As one of the nation's top pitching prospects, he had earned a full ride scholarship to Old Dominion University in Virginia. Dane was named Collegiate Baseball Freshman Pitcher of the Year and also won the Golden Spikes award the same season. He only played for one year, though, because he suffered a nasty broken arm in a snowmobiling accident. His bones were shattered, and his doctors had to screw the fragmented pieces back together. He hadn't been able to bend his arm for almost a year, and went through three more surgeries before he could finally start physical therapy. His doctor warned him not to try and pitch anymore, because the pitching motion put too much strain on his elbow.

That ended Dane's baseball career. To this day, he still had a screw in his elbow. It limited his mobility somewhat, but he had gotten used to it.

Michael laughed. "You'll fit right in! We're not that good, Dane. Most of these guys play because it's the only exercise they get! Did I tell you the name of the team?"

Dane shook his head.

The two men stopped walking, and Michael put his hand on Dane's shoulder. "We're the Yankees! But it's not what you think! It's spelled like this." Michael proceeded to spell the name, one letter at a time. "Y-a-n-k-e-a-s-e. Yank-ease! The team was started by a group of dentists. Get it, yank-ease? There's only one dentist left on the team now, though. They're a great bunch of guys!"

Dane started laughing. "I heard you were pretty good. Tyler told me you're the home run hitter on the team."

"Well, not so much anymore! My homes runs used to come easy. I hit seventeen one year in a fifteen-game season, which included a three-home-run game! But it's not that easy anymore. I get too anxious up there. I used to just wait for my pitch, but now I just don't have the discipline anymore. I think I'm nearing the end; time to retire."

Ruth grabbed the back of Michael's shirt and spun him around. "I thought I'd never hear you say that! You're really thinking of quitting?"

"I said retire. That's different than quitting! Besides, I'm not quitting yet; we got a game to get ready for, let's play some catch!" Michael and Dane walked to the other side of the field where a few of the teammates had gathered.

When they got there, Michael introduced Dane to the guys. "Dane used to be a baseball star, but it's been a while," he told them. "Before we start, though, I thought it might be appropriate to say a prayer in memory of Justin."

Dane looked at Michael as if to ask who he was talking about.

"Justin was our teammate. He was killed about six months ago while riding his motorcycle. It was right after the last game of our season. We're going to dedicate tonight's game to him," Michael told him. He looked up at his teammates and gestured for them to gather around him. "Let's all gather around and pray."

Dane was uneasy about all this touchy-feely stuff, but joined in anyway. He didn't want to be the one who threw cold water on their little ceremony.

Michael closed his eyes as his teammates all held hands. "Father, we ask You to be with us as we play. Keep us safe and help us represent You well tonight. We ask You to be with Justin's family as we play tonight's game in his memory. In Jesus's name, amen."

A few of Michael's teammates said amen after Michael, and walked toward the bat rack.

Dane yanked on Michael's shirt, pulling him away from the others. "I'm taking the place of your dead teammate? Michael, I wish you would have warned me!" he said.

Michael gently put his arm around Dane and walked with him to the end of the dugout. "Dane, don't worry about it. Everyone here is cool with it now. It was tough for a while – a few guys even blamed themselves, since he was killed on the way home from the game. But it's just one of those things, you know? When your time is up, you go! We all still miss him, but we have to move on. I think tonight will be a positive thing for everybody here. We suck as softball players, but we do a great job of representing Jesus to a lot of people. And believe it or not, we bring joy to our families!"

Michael turned and took a few steps toward the other end of the dugout, then turned quickly back to face Dane. "Oh and there's one more thing you should know. Justin was going to be my new assistant too, so you're not only taking his spot on the team, you're also taking his job, I mean in a roundabout kind of way. And the story is even weirder." Dane looked surprised and opened his mouth, but Michael put his hand on his chest as if to stop him before he could speak. "If Justin hadn't left early from the game to go see his sick Grandmother, he would have never gotten in the accident. And she wouldn't have gotten sick if she hadn't eaten out the night before the accident. She got food poisoning. It's crazy how things work ... how we're all so connected. It still blows me away. So many things changed because she ate some tainted food. So many lives were completely changed, forever!"

Danes mouth gaped open. "No way!"

"Yeah, way!" He turned Dane around and gently nudged him toward the field, patting him on the back. "Now enough of that, let's go. Grab your bat; you're our new leadoff hitter!"

When Dane turned to walk to the plate, Michael saw the long scar on Dane's arm. He was suddenly reminded of the story Dane told so eloquently over Thanksgiving dinner. The story of how Dane had left baseball, lost his scholarship and how that one pivotal moment changed his life forever. It brought back painful memories from a few years ago, when Hunter was forced to give up the game he loved.

# Chapter 13

*Three years earlier*

Michael, Ruth, and Hunter waited in the lobby of UC San Francisco. They were there to see Dr. Marconi, who was a specialist in movement disorders. Michael hadn't been to San Francisco in over ten years, and didn't like coming back to the city under these circumstances. But they were all determined to make the best of it.

Hunter had been having cramps for two years now. He'd said that he first noticed them when he was playing baseball. At first there were nothing more than slight cramps in his hand or foot. Michael fed Hunter extra bananas before practice and every game, hoping it was a simple mineral deficiency. Unfortunately that hadn't helped.

Then as his sophomore season progressed, things got more intense. The cramps lasted longer and became more debilitating. They hadn't stopped him from playing the game he loved; Hunter played half the season with his sophomore teammates, then found himself moved up to the varsity squad. He dealt with the pain and managed to get through the season with few people noticing he was suffering. After the season ended, so did the cramps.

But as the next season began, the cramping came back. This time when Hunter ran, he felt tingling in his feet, usually on the left side. The tingling continued up his arm and into his hand. Then his hand would cramp up into a fist, causing enough pain to make Hunter stop whatever he was doing and grab his hand to try and pry it open. Just like the previous year, the cramps only lasted about thirty seconds – just long and severe enough to hinder his game.

More importantly though, it worried Michael to the point that he was afraid something more sinister was going on in Hunter's body. They hadn't been able to cure the cramping with bananas or water, so it was far beyond Michael's personal knowledge.

Michael and Ruth took their son to the family physician. She prescribed medication, mostly to calm his nerves. Hunter tried that for a couple weeks, but found that it didn't help with the cramping. They went back to the doctor and she increased the dose, which ultimately had the same outcome; no help at all.

She decided to send Hunter to a chiropractor, thinking he may have a pinched nerve somewhere. After a few more weeks with the new doctor, the cramps returned. Now they were affecting his playing time, which was devastating to both Hunter and the team.

One doctor led to another doctor, with little help and no progress. This went on for two years while Michael combed the Internet at night, seeking a magical cure. One night before a game, Michael had Hunter drink vinegar. He'd read somewhere that it would cure cramps, and figured it was worth a try. Hunter never let his dad live that one down; drinking vinegar was disgusting, and more importantly, it didn't work.

In fact, nothing did. No doctor had an answer. Each doctor sent Hunter on his way to a more specialized doctor, telling him that they were baffled. So here they were, in Dr. Marconi's office. It would be the last stop. She was one of the top doctors in the country, specializing in movement disorders, and represented one of their last choices. They'd put her off because her practice was out of their network, and because of the distance they had to travel. Still, they weren't willing to give up without a fight. Michael had spent all night praying that she'd be able to give them an answer, even if it was one they didn't want to hear.

Dr. Marconi came into the waiting area then and introduced herself. She asked Hunter, Michael, and Ruth to come back to her office and sit down. First she explained about movement disorders. She talked about dystonia, a condition brought on by many different triggers. It was a nerve disorder. Michael remembered seeing a few videos on dystonia, and recalled that all of them had been very scary. Most showed a patient sitting in a padded room and repeatedly jerking into a shriveled-up ball. He hoped that Hunter didn't have that; he didn't think he'd be able to watch his son turn from a star athlete to a sick young man. The doctor did a quick examination of Hunter, then had him try to bring on a cramping episode. She had Hunter run up and down the hall, but he was never able to duplicate the symptoms.

In the end, the doctor asked him to come back into the office and sit down with his parents. After a little more explaining and investigation of the charts and records, she finally said, "Hunter, there's an old joke that goes like this. A man goes to his doctor and says, 'Doc, it hurts when I do this.' The doctor looks at him and says, 'Well, don't do that!'"

She threw his chart on her desk and sighed. "So unfortunately that is my advice to you. I can't give you a certain diagnosis here, other than the fact that you are in excellent physical condition, but if something is hurting you or causing these cramps of yours, I would recommend that you stop doing it."

Hunter was not amused. He sensed what the doctor was

about to say, and hung his head in despair.

"Don't play baseball anymore, and the cramps will probably go away. I know that's not what you wanted to hear, especially after chasing this thing for over two years, but that's all I've got for you."

The family thanked the doctor for trying to help. Michael shook her hand and walked out. They were all extremely frustrated, though they were beginning to see that this was out of their hands.

Hunter came to Michael later that week, while Michael sat at the computer in his office, again looking for a magic solution. The boy sat down on the sofa with tears in his eyes.

"Dad," Hunter said, trying his best to hide his tears from his dad.

Michael got up and sat down next to his son, putting his arm around him. "What's going on, why the tears?"

Between sudden gasps, Hunter said, "I think God wants me to leave baseball!" He hung his head as the tears finally appeared, flowing down his face. There was no holding them back now; Hunter knew the sport he had known and loved was slipping out of his reach, and there was nothing he could do about it.

"Why would you say that, buddy?" Michael was shocked. He knew how much baseball meant to his son, and he couldn't believe that he would give it up. It had brought him so much joy through the years.

Hunter inhaled and held his breath for a moment, collecting his thoughts. When he spoke, his words were slow. "Baseball has become my god. And I don't think God likes that. Doesn't it say something about that in the Bible?"

"Yes, of course Hunter. It's the very first of the Ten Commandments. I'd say it's pretty important to Him!"

Hunter leaned over in his father's lap and cried. "I have to give it up," he sobbed. Michael gently stroked his head, thinking back over his son's baseball career. There were so many little league games, tournaments, and high school games. Each one made Michael so proud of his son. He thought back to when Hunter first started to play baseball as a five year old. His initial joy in the game had never waned, even after all these years.

As Michael sat doing his best to calm his son, he remembered a prayer he'd always prayed about each of his children. He always asked God to open the doors his kids were supposed to go through, and to close the doors they were not supposed to go through. God had done it again. He had answered Michael's prayer, even though Michael didn't agree with it. The door of baseball in Hunter's life had been slowly closed. Michael knew that Hunter was making the right decision in seeing that, but that didn't make it easy.

"I think you're doing the right thing," he whispered. "And I think you're doing it for the right reasons. I love you, buddy."

"I love you too Dad," Hunter said. "Thanks for all you've done; even the vinegar! I know it's been frustrating to you too. Anyway, I'm going up to bed. Good night."

Hunter got up and slowly walked away, hanging his head in disappointment.

"Good night," Michael said.

Michael sat in his dimly lit office thinking about the decision Hunter had made and what impact this would have on his life. It was time for another talk with God. Michael lowered his head and folded his hands. He sat in silence for a few minutes then spoke softly. "I know I've prayed for direction in Hunter's life and I know he's doing what you want; following your will. But this one hurts."

Michael sat in silence again, longing to hear from God. After a few more minutes, Michael said, "Well, I'm just going to have to trust you on this one, Lord. I just ask that someday you'll show us that Hunter has made the right choice."

# Chapter 14

***Present Day***

"Dane, your security clearance finally came across my desk, so I can let you in on a few of my secrets. Let's head to the lab."

Michael continued to talk as they walked down the long hall with shiny metallic walls. "The first project I'm going to show you is a new type of delivery system. I've been working on it for a long time. I still can't fully explain why I'm getting the results I'm getting, but it's fascinating and it's going to blow you away!"

They stopped at a metal door with an armed guard.

"This isn't the lab!" Dane said as he looked around.

Michael explained to Dane that he actually had three different labs, and that this one was highly classified. Dane hadn't even known that this one existed, let alone been inside.

Michael chatted with the guard and introduced Dane as they slid their identification cards through a key slot on the wall next to the door, which slid open on well-oiled hinges. They entered a short hall, which was lined with more shiny metallic walls. Dane slid his fingers along the walls as he walked.

"What is this stuff, Michael?"

"This is a metallic magnetic epoxy. The formula is highly classified, but I can tell you this – the Navy sure is interested in this stuff! I helped develop it over ten years ago. It's pretty cool!" Michael stopped and the two men ran their hands over the walls. "You put it on just like paint, but when it dries it stays magnetic. We're able to bounce millions of light- and heat-sensitive rays off it, in a really small grid pattern, to make a passageway lined with it impervious to intruders of any size. The security guys love it because it makes their job easy! Another amazing detail ..." Michael stopped speaking and pressed his finger against the wall as he spoke, "is that when it dries, you can touch it without leaving a finger print impression of any kind!"

Dane leaned over and studied the wall, looking for any sign of Michael's fingerprint.

"Awesome!" he muttered, moving back and forth to get different angles on the wall.

They started walking again, moving down a long hall and around a few corners, until they approached another armed guard in front of another door. Dane walked a few steps behind Michael, waiting for his supervisor to clear him. This guard patted them down while making small talk. Once again, Michael introduced Dane to the guard. And again, they slid their identification cards through the card reader. Then they each had to place their finger tip on a scanner. As the light scanned their fingerprints, Dane looked at Michael, impressed. This was the tightest security he'd ever been through.

The door opened, and the two men entered what appeared to Dane to be an elevator. There were no buttons like in an ordinary elevator, though, and as the door closed they began moving automatically. It was a ride that lasted almost a minute. On the way down, Michael started briefing Dane about the experiment he was about to witness.

When they reached the end of the descent, Michael opened the door to the elevator and walked into a lab. Dane took a few steps inside and stopped to look around in disbelief.

"Whoa!"

"Pretty impressive isn't it?" Michael had walked to a closet behind a Plexiglas wall, and was now putting on a safety suit. When he was fully suited, he walked over to a massive piece of equipment in the center of the room. He watched Dane's face as the younger man gazed around with awe and smiled. Michael loved the chance to show off the lab he designed and helped build.

"Dane, you've heard of a Stirred Laboratory Autoclave, right?" he finally asked.

Dane nodded, and patted his hand on the side of a huge blue steel tube. "This thing?"

The autoclave was enormous. It looked like a giant steel cylinder lying on its side. It was about 8 feet tall and at least 30 feet long. On one end was a large door, resembling a bank vault, complete with a three-pronged twisting handle and lighted control panel with a digital timer.

"That's it alright," Michael said as he positioned himself in front of a workbench. "I'll get to that in a minute. For now, though, the experiment. First, I start with fluorine." Michael stepped a few feet to his right and opened the lid of a small freezer. As he did, thick white smoke billowed out and spilled onto the floor. It coated the concrete floor and formed a thin cloud which hovered about an inch from the ground before quickly dissipating. "We store our fluorine at cryogenic temperature, Dane. That makes it easier to handle." Michael plunged his glove-laden hand into the smoky freezer and pulled out a small test tube filled with yellow ice, then quickly slammed the lid. Immediately, the ice in the test tube began to thaw. Within seconds it had turned to a yellow, slushy liquid. He poured the half melted ice into a beaker and threw the empty glass tube in a trash container on the floor beside his workbench.

"Now I add liquid chlorine," he continued. As he spoke, Michael poured a small measured amount of chlorine into the glass beaker that contained the fluorine. When the two chemicals met, they began to form a heavy green gas that clung to the bottom of the beaker. The chemicals sizzled as they continued to meld together to form the gas.

"Then I take iodine – plain old salt – and add it to the fluorine and chlorine. We'll let that sit a minute before we cook it in the autoclave." Michael poured a tiny amount of salt into the beaker. When the salt hit the green gas, it seemed to solidify, forming a dark green jelled substance in the bottom of the beaker. Michael picked up the beaker and swirled the ingredients around before setting it back down on top of the stainless steel workbench. Dane hung over his shoulder, watching breathlessly. Michael turned and noticed that his assistant was still in street clothes, and gasped.

"Oh, I think I'm getting a little ahead of myself, Dane. I'm going to be using astatine next. I'm sure you know that it's highly radioactive, so we must take precautions. I'll wait until you get that suit on."

Michael pointed to the closet, where a line of safety gear was hanging neatly in a row. "Just find your size and get dressed. I'll wait."

Dane looked through the white rubber one-piece suits, and grabbed one that looked like it would fit. He slipped it on over his clothes, and then reached for a pair of safety goggles, strapping them over his face. When he was fully outfitted, he walked back toward Michael.

Michael smiled at his assistant. "Don't worry, these suits are just precautionary. That suit does look nice on you, though. You look like an official lab rat now. As I was saying, astatine is intensely radioactive." Michael opened a large metal door built into the wall directly behind his workbench. Inside were rows of drawers made of glass. He slowly pulled open a drawer containing several small flecks of astatine, a green substance resembling tiny rocks. He reached in with tweezers and picked up one small fleck.

"When we put that in the autoclave, along with our other ingredients, we get an interesting reaction." Michael dropped the green fleck into the beaker and carried it to the autoclave door.

"You want to open that for me Dane?" Michael asked, clutching the beaker with both hands. Dane opened the door and stood aside as Michael stepped into the tube. He placed the glass beaker down on a shelf inside the giant autoclave.

Dane stepped in after him, looking around the room. "Man, this thing is huge!" He cupped his hands up to his mouth and yelled, "Hello, hello, hello!" smiling at the ensuing echo.

Michael smiled at Dane's antics, then got back to business. "OK, Dane, let's get out of here and bake this thing,"

The two men walked out and Michael gently closed the door. He spun the handle around several times and turned his attention to the timer, where he punched a keypad.

"Fifteen minutes." he muttered. He pushed a green button and the giant autoclave began to buzz softly. He turned back to Dane to continue his lecture. "So let me explain something to you while we wait. Fluorine is the most electronegative element found in nature – it loves to attract an electron and fill its shell. And here's the interesting part: the chemical behavior of the halogens is the result of the seven electrons in their outer shell. There are two electrons in the S sub-shell and five in the P sub-shell." As Michael spoke, he smashed his hands together. "So the addition of only one extra electron by either ionic or covalent bonding will confer a noble gas configuration to the

ACCIDENTAL HEAVEN

halogen atom. But what I still can't figure out is why this liquid
we produce reacts the way it does to the oxygen!"

"Just don't cross the streams," Dane chuckled.

Michael looking at Dane in total surprise. "What?"

"Never mind. It was my failed attempt at humor. You know,
*Ghostbusters?*" Dane paused and looked surprised. "You're
the movie speak guy, I'm shocked you didn't get that one,
Michael!"

Michael shook his head and laughed. "Oh, so you're doing
me, doing *Ghostbusters*. I get it."

Dane looked around the lab and asked Michael questions,
pointing to a few pieces of equipment in the room that he did
not recognize. One by one, Michael explained what the equipment was and what it was used for. Just then the timer on the
autoclave dinged and the buzzing stopped. Michael spun the
lock on the door, stepped inside, and grabbed the beaker from
the shelf. As he walked back to the workbench, the jelled liquid in the beaker began to smoke. Slowly at first, but gaining
intensity with each step. Then it began to emit an orange gas.
He brought it back to the work bench and set it down.

Dane stood there, his eyes wide in amazement. "Wow,
that's amazing!"

Michael nodded. "If I capture this gas and compress it,
the magic begins!" Dane glanced at him, and noticed that his
boss looked like a kid on Christmas morning. He was really excited to show the next phase of his discovery to Dane.
He wheeled over a large copper container, about the size of a
5-gallon bucket, and placed it over the opening to collect the
gas, which slowly rose to fill the metal. Then he sealed the cylindrical container as the gas slowly dissipated, and took it to
another machine nearby. When the canister was settled in the
new machine, he closed the lid.

"That looks like the paint shakers down at the home improvement store," Dane said with a laugh, looking at the new machine.

"Oh it's much more than that," Michael said. "Watch." He pressed a button on top of the machine, turned a few dials, and stood back.

"What now?" Dane asked

"I'll show you in about ten seconds," Michael said as he stared at the control panel. After ten seconds, a buzzer went off and he unlatched the lid, reached in, and lifted out the container with the gas.

What happened next was incredible. The gas in the container had formed into a small ball, about the size of a ping pong ball, and had turned a bright green color. Michael reached in and grabbed it with a set of stainless steel tongs.

"What the…" Dane was speechless.

Michael took the green ball and set it into a large glass container about the size of a 1-gallon can. The ball hung in midair.

"Unbelievable, Michael. What is it?" Dane's curiosity had gotten the best of him. He was trying to do the calculations in his head that would somehow lead to this glowing, weightless green ball, but he just couldn't figure it out. He stared at the ball, totally mesmerized.

Michael glanced at his assistant and nodded. "Well, here it is in a nutshell Dane. Fluorine is a small atom, so its nine electrons are firmly bound and extremely difficult to remove. Therefore fluorine has the highest ionization energy in the group. The ionization energy of iodine is lowest. Similarly, the electro–negativity of fluorine is the highest, and for iodine it is the lowest. The fluorine replaces other halogens from the halide compounds either in solution phase or even in dry state.

Chlorine is the second best oxidizing agent of the group, and oxidizes bromide and iodide ions, but not the fluoride ion. What we have, in general is a halogen of low atomic number oxidizing the halide ions of the higher atomic number, so the reaction is at equilibrium. The temperature is constant. I just can't figure out why the vapor ball is able to stay suspended in the air like that. It must be a reaction to the oxygen, or maybe the copper, but I haven't quite figured that out yet."

He lowered his voice and spoke softly, as if he were speaking to himself. "Le Chatelier's Principle says that the equilibrium will adjust so as to reduce the concentration of the nitrogen. But that can only be achieved if the nitrogen reacts."

He looked up at Dane again, his forehead creased in a frown. "So you see, I'm baffled! A new equilibrium position is somehow established." He reached for a small ball-peen hammer on the workbench. "Now watch this!"

He tapped the glass container sharply with the hammer, and it shattered. As the glass fell to the bench top, though, the small glowing green ball didn't move. It stayed suspended in the air as the glass shattered and fell around it.

"I'm still not done Dane, there's more!" Michael muttered, hearing Dane's exclamation. "This little vapor cloud has enough density to physically hold weight over a million times its own weight, another baffling characteristic!"

Michael turned and walked into his office at the far end of the lab. As he did, Dane leaned over and gazed at the miraculous little vapor ball in front of him. He moved his hands over the ball, being careful not to touch it. He swiped his hand under the ball a few times, and then over the ball, almost expecting to knock the ball off an invisible thread. He couldn't believe his eyes, and didn't know if the ball was really floating on its own, or if it was a trick of some sort.

Michael came back from his office, holding a baseball. "Watch this!" He held the baseball over the vapor ball and let go. As he did, the baseball fell into the middle of the gas, but didn't fall all the way through; it remained suspended inside the vapor ball, and now they both hovered in midair.

Once again, Dane slid his hand under the ball, now a baseball enveloped in the gaseous cloud. "Unbelievable!"

"So," Michael explained, "this is very exciting, but there's more. Much, much more!"

Dane could see the excitement welling up in his boss.

"When we give this little green ball a charge while it's encapsulating a physical specimen like this baseball, this is what happens…"

Michael grabbed a small meter on a stainless steel stand and wheeled it over to the vapor ball. He lined it up so that the two metal probes sticking out of the meter were touching the edge of the ball, then reached for a switch on the side of the cart. When he flipped the switch, the ball disappeared.

Danes mouth dropped wide open. "What the hell?"

"Don't worry Dane, it didn't disappear!" Michael pointed to the far end of the lab, about 30 feet away, and motioned at Dane to follow him. "It's right there!"

Dane couldn't believe his eyes. There against the wall, still suspended in midair, was the vapor ball, still snugly enveloping the baseball. They both hovered in the air about an inch away from the wall.

Michael began to explain. "I'm not exactly sure why this happens, but it happens every time. This cloud holds the baseball and moves away so quickly that we can't even record the movement with our cameras. It doesn't crash into the wall, though; the cloud pads the baseball, so that it doesn't make an impact. Every time I do this, I get the same result. It travels faster than the speed of light; actually quite a bit faster. The problem is that we can't measure how fast it goes; we just know that it does! And the cloud provides so much protection that whatever I place in the cloud is padded against impact. I've even done this with an egg, and it doesn't break! So our next phase of this experiment is going to be dropping a camera into our little vapor cloud to see if we can record the outcome. We also need to send it somewhere beyond the wall, and see where it stops! More importantly, I suppose, we need to see *if* it stops. Then there's the matter of steering our little ball here so we can be assured it will hit its target. I've been working on that too, but still need to perfect it."

Dane sat down, trying desperately to wrap his mind around what he'd just seen.

"Can you bring it back?"

"Yeah," Michael said. "Funny you would ask, because I'm not sure why it comes back, but it does." He explained the process as the two walked back to the starting point. "All I do is reverse the iconic ionization, reverse the polarity, and hit the switch." When they arrived back at the work bench, Michael turned a few knobs and flipped the switch down, and the gassy ball reappeared, right back where it started from, clinging to the probes.

"It's hard to tell what we could use this for," Dane murmured, deep in thought. He was still baffled and having trouble connecting the dots. "If it works with a camera, what next? How much weight will it hold? Could we use it to deliver bombs? What about other weapons, or spy satellites ... or rescue apparatus or even food? I mean, the possibilities are endless!" He stood rubbing his chin. "What would happen if you dropped something like a mouse into this thing, would it survive? Have you even thought about that, Mike?"

"No I'm not that far along, Dane, but I doubt any living creature could survive. There's no evidence of oxygen in there; but I wouldn't rule anything out just yet. There is one slight problem though; it only lasts for 48 hours, then dissipates into light green dust. Then about 24 hours later, the dust disappears. I'm completely baffled as to why! I'm only certain of one thing; the possibilities are definitely endless! But before we get there, we have a lot more work to do."

# Chapter 15

**Dane met Diana** at the beach at 6 in the morning. He thought it was a little too early to surf, but according to Diana, dawn was the best time to catch the 'most awesome waves!' She said the winds were offshore or calm and the beach was less crowded. She'd lived here longer than he had, so he took her word for it.

When he saw her unloading her board in the parking lot, he couldn't believe his eyes.

She was even beautiful in a full wet suit! Dane had fallen hard for Diana, and astounded at how quickly it had happened. He knew she was special from the moment he first met her. The feeling he had when he was with Diana was like no other, though he still had trouble understanding it sometimes.

Mostly because it was so different from anything he'd ever felt for anyone before.

He'd always had a hard time getting close to anyone. He had lots of friends and a few girlfriends through the years, but has always ended things when a relationship got too serious. But with Diana, everything was different. He opened up to her like no other, and she did the same. For the first time in a long time, Dane felt he was truly happy.

"Good morning sunshine," Dane said as Diana leaned her board against the side of the Jeep.

"Hey sexy." Diana leaned over and kissed Dane's cheek. "Ready to catch some waves?"

Although surfing was something he'd always wanted to do, Dane was still a little hesitant. "I guess," he said, looking at the ever-increasing size of the waves. "But now that I'm here and I see the waves and picture myself out there, I've got to admit that I'm a little scared!"

His mind wandered back to when he got on a snowmobile for the first time. His friends had told him how easy it was and how much fun it would be, and of course that it was safe. That was the day Dane managed to slam into a tree and break his arm so badly that it ended his baseball career.

*Surfing will be different though*, Dane thought. He knew he had the ability to surf; he'd always been athletic enough to do anything he put his mind too. The thought of standing on top of the water with huge waves crashing all around him made him a little nervous, though. In the end, he took a deep breath and tucked away his fear; after all, he'd already decided to do this, and he wasn't going to let Diana down. And she was an expert surfer, ready to show him the ropes. He'd been on his own that fateful day on that snowmobile, with no one to tell him how to steer.

Diana snapped him out of his memory when she patted him on the back and said, "There's nothing to be scared of, Dane, I'll show you everything you need to know."

Dane smiled warmly at her. "If only my parents could see me now. I told my mother when I was a teenager that some-day I would move to California and learn to surf. Back then it was just talk; I can't believe it's actually happening!" Deep down, he was also thrilled to have such a gorgeous teacher.

Diana laughed, then pointed to the surf board in the Jeep. "Grab that board there, it's an oldie but still a goodie. Let's take it to the beach and I'll give you a rundown of what to do before we go into the water."

Dane's heart began to flutter. He wasn't sure of it was because he was spending time with Diana or because he was picturing himself in the ocean! He grabbed the board, hoisted it over his head, and followed Diana to the sand, vowing to get out there on the water no matter what it took.

As he walked, he peppered Diana with questions. "So why is my board so much bigger than yours?"

Diana giggled at Dane's lack of knowledge of surfing. "It's easier to get up on a bigger board Dane, you'll see!"

"And why so early?"

"I told you Dane, the best waves are happening right now! Relax will you? We're going to have a blast. You'll love it, I promise!"

Dane loved the fact that Diana was actually going to teach him to surf. "I can't believe you've been surfing since you were ten!" he said as he walked behind her through the parking lot. "That's amazing!"

After a quick lesson on the sand about paddling, shifting weight to actually let the wave push you along and how to keep your balance, it was time to give it a try.

As they stood on the beach, Diana added, "Oh, one other thing Dane. If you fall off your board, remember to come to the surface covering your head. You don't want to pop to the surface and get run over by another surf board! Believe it or not, that's how most surfing accidents happen!"

"OK," Dane said, covering his head and ducking slightly. He looked back at his teacher and smiled. "Like this?"

"Perfect!" she snickered. "Dane, you're going to be great out there."

She pointed to a secluded area in a cove. "Let's paddle out there and get used to the feel of the board for a bit."

They strolled out into the water, boards under their arms.

Dane followed Diana, trying to remember all the instructions she had just given him and carry the board as easily as she did. Diana ran into the surf, threw her board on the water, and leapt into the air, landing directly on top of her board. Within minutes she had managed to paddle out to the exact spot where she had just pointed. Dane struggled to get on the board, but once on, quickly learned how to paddle. A few minutes later he met up with Diana.

As the two bobbed in the waves Diana said, "Good job, Dane, you learn quickly!"

"Thanks," he said with a grin. He looked below his board only to see his arms and feet lost in a patch of thick gooey slime! "But what's with all this seaweed?"

"It comes and goes," she said with a laugh. "Don't worry about it; it won't keep you from surfing. Besides, when we actually get to some waves, it will be gone!" She paused for a moment, watching the waves come toward them and measuring the distance. Then she turned back toward Dane.

"OK," she told him, "time to see if you were listening. Follow me!"

Diana lay back down on her board and started paddling straight out toward the bigger waves, a couple hundred feet out to sea. Dane reluctantly followed, still thinking of the peculiar feeling of seaweed on his legs. Within minutes, Diana had turned her board and was perched on it, ready to catch a big wave rolling in. As it approached, she yelled for Dane to follow, but he suddenly froze. He watched motionless as Diana caught the wave and jumped to her feet, cutting through the wave as she rode it a few hundred yards.

Dane just watched, disappointed in himself. He'd never been afraid of anything before. Maybe the seaweed had creeped him out and caused his sudden reluctance, he thought.

Whatever it was, he needed to put it behind him, as another big wave was approaching. He was determined to do this!

He paddled into the break and jumped to his feet, barely managing to land on them and stand. He held his arms out to steady himself, weaving back and forth on the board as the wave pushed it forward.

He stood for almost five seconds before crashing through the water.

When he fell, he tumbled below the surface and into the ocean foam. He turned in the water, searching for the surface and kicking hard with his feet. Just before breaking through to the sky above, he put his hand up over his head, remembering what Diana had told him about breaking to the surface. He popped up, shook the water from his hair, and wiped his eyes, laughing.

Just then he saw Diana, sitting straight up, clapping her hands and shouting. He was thrilled to see Diana so happy, sharing in his triumph. He'd done it, he'd actually surfed, if only for a few seconds! And his girlfriend was right there, watching it all happen. He'd never been so happy. And he couldn't wait to try again.

Ruth held her phone in front of her and read the text from Michael. It said that he and Dane would be working late on their newest project. She poured a glass of Chardonnay and walked slowly upstairs, pausing when she reached the top of the landing. She stared at a picture of the boys in their baseball uniforms, which had hung on the wall for years. She had walked by that picture a thousand times, but this time stopped and remembered all the fun times that seemed to revolve around baseball.

Michael had coached each of the kids at some point in their baseball playing days. He had coached twenty-five different baseball teams over the past nineteen years. He'd always been the type of father who was really involved with his kids, and even went so far as to start up a brand new youth football program in San Diego because he didn't think the current league was teaching the kids the right life lessons. The new league he started taught Christian fundamentals and strict discipline to the kids. He had just recently announced his "retirement" from coaching. Ruth wasn't sure he would really retire, but when Michael made his mind up to do something it usually got done! He had loved coaching, and Ruth had loved watching him. They each cherished their time with the kids.

Through the years, they had used baseball as a way to bond as a family. A typical vacation for the Owens family had centered around baseball tournaments. They had been to tournaments all over California and Nevada.

As Ruth sipped her glass of wine, she remembered one particular tournament Hunter had played several years earlier. It had been in Fresno in the middle of August. Fresno was suffering through one of the worst heat waves they'd ever had. The first day of the tournament was on the twenty-second consecutive day over 100 degrees. The temperature at game time had been 112! The last game of the tournament lasted fifteen innings. The boys on the team were exhausted by the time the game ended, and the parents in the stands weren't in much better shape.

Michael, Ruth, and the rest of the family had been right there. Whenever any of the boys had a game to play, the entire family had sat in the bleachers and watched. They always supported each other in everything they did. Ruth smiled at the memory and shook her head at the thought of sitting on those hot aluminum bleachers. She loved her family, and nothing brought her more joy than watching her sons in any athletic endeavor, but baseball had always been her favorite.

But now Ruth was alone in the house, while Michael was away working, and she was in a melancholy mood. Ruth thought back to those vacations and remembered them fondly, but felt now as though she'd been missing out on something more in life. She had felt uneasy playing the role of mother at times, though she couldn't put her finger on the reason. Brandon's birth had been the happiest day of her life. But things had changed for Ruth, slowly at first but with growing intensity over the past few years.

Her discomfort had grown; she wanted more, but she wasn't sure what exactly that meant. It bubbled up to the surface in her life from time to time, and now was one of those times. It made her very uncomfortable; her family meant the world to her, but there was so much more to life. Most of the time, she was able to bury those feelings of discontent.

Was there more to life than just being a mother of four kids? As her children grew, she became more and more dissatisfied with her life. She could never talk to Michael about it; he would surely take it the wrong way. She had to rely on her faith to lead her through these times.

She poured another glass of wine and thought *maybe I'll just ask God for forgiveness*. She tried to pray about it, but when she folded her hands and closed her eyes, she felt as if a huge wall had gone up, blocking her conversation with God. It bothered her that Michael had such a great relationship with Jesus. Why couldn't she have that? Michael had said he heard God speak to him. *I never heard anything like that* Ruth thought. *Maybe God doesn't like me as much,* she mused. Or maybe she just wasn't being honest with herself. She tried to be a good Christian, but had to admit to herself that she didn't always do the right thing. Most of the time she could justify her actions, but that was getting tougher and tougher. Lately, she felt like she was growing apart from Michael. She knew that this was partially her fault, given her choices, but worked hard to keep up appearances.

She closed her eyes and lay back on the sofa. This restlessness must be something she needed to bury, but how? She had to find a renewed sense of purpose in her life, whether it be as a great mom, great wife, or something else. It was the something else that frightened her.

Dane picked up Diana at 6 o'clock. She was excited to take him to her favorite dinner joint. The Steakhouse at Azul was a very nice, upscale restaurant, and had a wonderful view of the Pacific Ocean. As Dane pulled out of the driveway, Diana started telling him about what she had planned.

"So this place is in La Jolla right on the water, and has spectacular views. I reserved a great table right by the window, so we should have a front row seat to a spectacular sunset! Tonight is my treat! It's my way of saying thank you for the happiest month of my life!"

Dane hadn't even realized it had been a month since they first met in the dog park. Time was really going quickly, Dane thought to himself. *It's true — time really does fly when you're having fun!* He laughed at the thought; he'd heard Michael say just that the other day. Maybe Michael was starting to rub off on Dane; he had been spending quite a bit of time with him and his family, and felt like Michael's family was becoming his second family! *That's a good thing,* he thought. Michael seemed to have it all figured out, and Dane was happy the two of them were becoming closer friends.

ACCIDENTAL HEAVEN

As the valet opened the car doors at the restaurant, Dane was jolted out of his daydream. Diana jumped out, excited to share this experience with Dane. They got out and stood at the edge of the parking lot overlooking the ocean for a few minutes. The sun was beginning to set in the distance.

As they embraced, Dane asked, "Is it always this beautiful here? I mean, we're coming up on Christmas pretty soon and it's still warm!"

Diana sighed, "I don't know Dane, sunny every day, 80 degrees, it gets so old."

The two shared a laugh, then Dane turned and looked into Diana's eyes and whispered, "I love it here." He paused for a minute, taking in the beauty of the surroundings and his company. "And I love you Diana. You really make me happy!" He drew her close, closed his eyes, and gently stroked her back. It was the first time he had shared his feelings with her.

Diana nestled her head into Dane's chest and whispered back, "I love you too, Dane. I feel the same way."

Dane smiled to himself, blissfully happy. Once again, she'd given him the response he had hoped for. *She loves me,* he thought. Nothing could have made him happier.

Suddenly Diana exclaimed, "We should get inside. I'm so anxious to show you this place and that sun isn't slowing down any!" The two turned and walked arm in arm to the door, where they waited in line behind an elderly couple. They overheard the maître'd ask, "Reservations?"

The gentleman in front of them replied, "Yes, reservations for two. The name is Houston; Steve Houston."

"Table for two, Houston, right this way." The young man, dressed in a black tuxedo, held out his arm and the woman took hold. They were escorted to their table.

When he returned he asked ,"Name please?"

Diana said, "Table for two, Diana." Here we are, he said as he pointed to the reservation list on the podium in front of him. Right this way. Once again, he held out his arm and this time Diana grabbed hold. As she did, she turned around to Dane and smiled. Dane walked closely behind winding his way through the fifties style restaurant until they came to their table. It was a booth secluded from all the others and looking over a rocky cliff below to the water.

All the booths in the steakhouse were covered in black tufted leather with tall leather backs. It was the type of joint you would expect to see Frank Sinatra and the rat pack sitting enjoying a meal before excusing themselves and lighting cigars on the patio! It was a very elegant place, with white linen table cloths, fresh flower centerpieces and a huge wine rack along the entire back wall. Dane smiled at Dianna as he took his seat, sliding over snugly brushing up against her leg.

"Very stylish", he said as he continued to look around. The ambience was perfect and the aroma of sizzling steak filled the air. Dane was really impressed. The waiter immediately brought over the menus as a busboy poured each of them a glass of water. The waiter introduced himself and told them about the specials of the evening, all of them involving fresh fish.

As they looked over the menu, Dane raised his water glass and proposed a toast. "To the fastest month of my life, and perhaps the happiest! Thank you for bringing that happiness to me. I never knew life could be this much fun. I look forward to waking up each day, just to see you smile! Here's to many more years of happiness." The couple clinked their glasses and smiled.

"Cheers," Diana said. She was beaming.

Dane couldn't help but think about his life. It seemed to

be coming together as if he were living a fantasy. Once again, his thoughts turned briefly to Michael. *He said everything is connected. I sure am happy I broke my arm in that accident. If it weren't for that, I would still be on the east coast. I may have never met Diana. Man, Michael was right again. Everything does happen for a reason!*

"Sorry I'm late, Michael, traffic was horrendous," Dane said as he hustled into Michael's office. "I've been out here for over ten months, and I'm still not used to it! I still don't think about leaving early to account for it, either."

Michael looked up from behind a stack of papers on his desk. "I don't think anyone ever gets used to it. You just learn to live with it."

"You wouldn't believe it, though – there was a mattress in the middle of the freeway, on fire! And then I heard on the traffic report that there was another mattress on fire on another freeway!" Dane shrugged his shoulders in disbelief. "How is that even possible?"

Michael laughed. "I've been here almost my entire life, and it never ceases to amaze me the stuff you hear! I don't think I'm used to it either ... it seems like there's always something new! But let's not let the interesting commute distract us; this is going to be a break-through day. Let's head down to the lab."

Michael walked swiftly down the stainless steel hall, with Dane following closely behind him.

"Dane, why don't you come over tomorrow night?" Michael said as they walked. "I think there's a Padres game on."

"Sounds great Mike, what time?

"Game starts at 7, but you can come over anytime, the mountains are always blue!"

"Huh?" Dane asked, puzzled.

"I'm a Coors Light guy; it's my way of saying the beer is always cold!"

"Oh, alright then, sounds great! I'll see you at 7! So big day, huh? What are we working on?" Dane asked.

Michael stopped abruptly, turned, and spoke softly to Dane. "We can't talk about classified stuff out here. It's very important that nothing that we do or say leaves the lab. I cannot stress that enough; nothing leaves the lab."

"Got it, chief!" Dane felt like a kid getting scolded by his teacher for chewing gum in class. He knew better – he shouldn't have asked anything until they got into the secured lab. But he didn't like to let Michael down with his carelessness. He wasn't going to be making *that* mistake again.

Michael nodded and smiled, and the two men started their trek again down the hall again. They made their way past both security check points and boarded the elevator down to the lab.

Once inside they walked into Michael's office. Michael said, "Dane, I hope you understand how serious it is that nothing we say or do ever leaves the lab. I'm sorry to give it to you like that, but you could have your security clearance revoked if any leak is ever traced back to you."

"No problem sir, I get it!"

Dane walked over to the closet and pulled down his safety suit. Michael stopped him abruptly and said, "Dane, We don't need those! I ran a few tests early this morning and I have concluded that the danger to us is very limited; to the point where we won't need to be completely covered. But I would still use caution. Our little ball of gas appears to be user-friendly, but that's just preliminary. That's what I was studying this morning when you arrived."

Dane smiled and added, "That's awesome, Mike!" He hung

the suit back up behind the Plexiglas wall.

"So do you remember when I told you I wanted to try putting a tiny camera in the ball of gas?"

"Yea, great idea Mike, but do we have to call it the 'ball of gas?' Can't we give a better name, maybe make it fun, or something … I don't know, sexy? How about Marilyn?! Let's call the little gassy ball Marilyn!"

Michael smiled. "Marilyn it is! Going back to the point, though, I had our IT guys build me a very small HD camcorder, about the size of a ping pong ball. It's almost all screen, so it can capture images from 340 degrees, almost a complete circle. I hope to slow the images to frame by frame, so I can calculate how fast our little ball travels."

"Wow Michael, you got this thing figured out, don't you?" Dane was almost as excited as Michael.

"I don't think I have it figured out, but I'm gaining on it. My mind can't work fast enough to answer all the questions, but that's what makes my job so interesting! So check this out."

Michael picked up a small cardboard box from his desk, reached inside and pulled out a shiny metallic ball, which glistened in the light of the brightly lit lab.

"Sweet!" Dane took the ball and rolled it around in his hand. "This is the camera?"

"Sure is, Dane. And all we have to do is slip this thing into Marilyn and record the results!"

Dane laughed. He loved the fact that Michael had let him name the new creation Marilyn. Michael started laughing along with Dane, and Dane laughed harder. Michael had a better sense of humor than he'd originally thought; he'd just had to dig deeper to reveal a little more of the man's "comical" side!

"Come on over here Dane and bring the camera."

Michael walked over to his computer keyboard and began typing feverishly, then looked up at Dane and said, "Check this out."

Dane leaned over and gazed at the monitor, which showed an extreme close up of his hand. He held the little round camera up in the air in front of his face, and looked back down to the screen. There was his face, along with a panoramic view of his surroundings.

"That's awesome!"

"It sure is! Looks like it's working perfectly," Michael said. "Now let's introduce this thing to Marilyn!" Michael started the sequence that would create the gassy ball they now called Marilyn. A few minutes later, they had their ping pong ball-sized creation, floating in midair in the lab. Dane was still clutching the small camera.

"Michael, where are we going to send Marilyn?"

Michael scratched the top of his head. Dane already knew that when Michael did that he was deep in thought. He also knew something genius was about to happen. Before Michael could speak, Dane blurted out, "Let's send her to the moon!"

Michael started laughing, and then stopped suddenly as Dane's logic sunk in. "That's actually a good idea Dane, but I think we should start with the Naval base across the highway. Let's make sure she hits her target first and we can keep control of this baby; then, I don't see why the moon wouldn't be the next logical step. Let me make a few calls and see what's available. I'll be right back."

Michael turned and walked back into his office, where he picked up the phone. Dane pulled up a chair and stared at Marilyn. *How is this even possible?* he wondered. His impulsive nature and curiosity suddenly got the best of him. He looked around the lab and noticed a small box, about 12 inches square, sitting on a pile of papers in the corner of the lab. He wanted to move things along faster than Michael, so he tip-toed over and grabbed it, all the time wondering what would happen if he dropped the box into Marilyn instead of the camera. He came back to Marilyn, still hovering about 3 feet off the lab floor, raised the box up over Marilyn, and let it go. Miraculously, Marilyn absorbed the box. The gas completely covered the box and mimicked its shape perfectly. Now, instead of a gassy green ball, there was a gassy green box hovering above the floor! Dane was amazed.

"Fascinating," he whispered.

He looked back to see Michael still sitting at his desk talking on the phone. He scanned the lab for anything else to drop into Marilyn. His mind was racing; how big would this gas grow? Would it cover anything, regardless of its starting size?

Dane walked over to the safety closet and grabbed a rubber boot. He raised it up over Marilyn and dropped it in, on top of the box. The boot merged into the floating body, now completely covered by the gas. The package now resembled a green box with a green boot on top.

"What the hell?" Dane couldn't believe his eyes. He heard Michael's chair squeak, and realized that Michael was finished and on his way back.

Dane unconsciously reached into Marilyn and removed the boot and the box, setting them behind a control panel and out of immediate view. As he set the objects down, he looked at his hand. He had just put it into Marilyn without any thought to his personal safety, but the gas hadn't harmed his skin at all. He rubbed his hands together and looked at them again. He hadn't thought at the time about the possible danger of sinking them into Marilyn; he'd just reacted to the fact that Michael was about to catch him playing with his creation. He raised his hand up to his nose and sniffed. Nothing. *Michael said, 'user-friendly'*, he thought.

He glanced back at Marilyn and noticed it had returned to the exact same size. "Unbelievable!" he sighed.

"What's unbelievable, Dane?" Michael had obviously heard Dane muttering to himself.

"Oh, just this whole thing, Mike, it's unbelievable!" Dane was afraid to tell his boss what he'd just done. He didn't think he'd done any harm, but he didn't want to deal with another lecture today.

Michael nodded, smiling. "Sure is. OK, I just spoke to the base and we can have the test fire range all day tomorrow if we want. Let's get over there at about 9 and see what Marilyn can do. We should get back up topside and to the office. I've got meetings all afternoon and I need to get ready."

Michael and Dane drove to the naval base together in one of Sem-Con's SUV's the next day. Marilyn made the short trip secured in a vault in the rear. Michael also packed his laptop, recording equipment, tables, the new camera, and the all-important probe used to ignite Marilyn and send her on her way. They pulled onto the base and made their way past a roundabout, which had the American flag flying proudly in the center. The base was beautiful; articulately groomed lawns, flower gardens, and large trees dotted the landscape, all designed to enhance the Navy's image. It was a relatively small naval base; only 5 square miles of land, but the layout offered plenty of seclusion, which was just what Michael wanted.

They drove quickly through the check point at the main entrance; Michael knew the security guards at the gate, so all it took was a quick flash of his ID. Then they continued past the housing area to the far end of the base.

The test range they would be using had an area Michael was very familiar with, as he'd used it hundreds of times before. It was a secure area and he would be able to send Marilyn almost a quarter of a mile straight forward, which would give him a good idea of just how fast she was capable of traveling. Michael had used the range to test fire weapons many times before, so today was not unusual.

One thing was different though; he had never taken Marilyn into an uncontrolled environment. He had many questions that needed answers. Would external conditions such as barometric pressure, temperature, or even sunlight change the outcome of the tests? What about wind or the moisture from the ocean a few hundred feet away? He had all the calculations to make Marilyn do what he wanted, but needed these questions answered before moving on. Today promised to be an exciting day.

They turned off the paved road onto a gravel path and parked. Dane started to unload and set up for their test as Michael walked to the end of the range. He approached a tall cinder block wall peppered with small bullet holes. This would work, he thought as he ran his hand across the chipped brick. He took out a tape measure and found the center of the wall, both horizontally and vertically. Then he took out a marker from his pocket and drew a small circle where his two measurements intersected.

"Dead center," he said.

He walked back and found that Dane had set everything up perfectly. "Let's introduce Marilyn to the great outdoors, Dane!" he said as the two walked back to the SUV.

"This is exciting stuff, huh Mike?" Dane asked with great anticipation.

They opened the vault and there was Marilyn, resting comfortably in the exact position they had left her, hovering in the center of the space in the vault. Michael grabbed her with the tongs he'd brought from the lab and placed her in a glass container. Dane carried the container across the gravel. As he was walking, though, he tripped on a small rock and fell forward. Dane put his hands out to break his fall. As he did, the container Marilyn was riding in went flying. It exploded into hundreds of small shards of glass as it hit the rock. Marilyn fell with the container, but stopped just above the rocky ground motionless, hovering about a foot from the ground.

Michael heard the crash and turned quickly, just in time to see Dane tumble. "Holy crap, you okay Dane?"

"I'm okay Mike, I'm so sorry!" Dane looked at the crushed container guiltily, an angry flush creeping over his cheeks.

Michael waved him off. "Don't worry about it. Look at that! She's just sitting there! I guess exposure to atmosphere isn't going to change her."

"That's excellent. And now we know she's pretty tough too, Mike!"

Michael was happy with Marilyn's progress so far, though he was also a little disappointed in Dane's haphazard manner of handling her. He warned the younger man to be more careful, then lifted Marilyn with the tongs and set her on top of the table. Slowly, he let go. She didn't move! He took the tongs again and moved her up to eye level and let go. Once again, she stayed right where she was placed.

"That's interesting." Michael said. "She stays right where you leave her. After all the tests I've run on this thing, you'd think I would have known that! I think it's time we see how fast she is, now that we know she can survive a fall."

Michael picked up a handheld laser scope and pointed it

toward the wall he'd visited a few minutes earlier. "One thousand, three hundred twenty-two feet, that's one quarter mile plus a few feet. Perfect! Let's see if my calculations are correct. If they are, I'll hit my mark."

Michael set up the laptop and programmed a target destination. Then he set up the electric probe and positioned it precisely, according to his calculations. He brought Marilyn over and set her just in front of the two prongs. Dane watched anxiously as Michael prepared to flip the switch.

"Michael," Dane said suddenly.

"Yes, Dane?" he replied as his finger fell from the switch.

"How much juice does she need to fire? In the lab I thought you had this thing hardwired to electricity, but out here it's a battery. Is that enough?"

"It certainly should be Dane, but that's what we're going to find out."

Dane continued, "Shouldn't we put the camera in?"

Michael said, "I'd like to see what she does out here on her own first. Then we'll use the camera. You ready?"

"Absolutely," Dane said with obvious excitement in his voice. He could hardly contain himself, though he thought Michael was still being too cautious.

Michael put his finger on the switch and said, "Here goes!"

He flipped the switch and Marilyn disappeared. Michael grabbed a pair of binoculars off the table and stared at the wall in the distance.

"There she is," he exclaimed enthusiastically. "Right in front of my mark." Michael turned around and held his hand up.

Dane met his high five and yelled, "Yeah, baby!"

"Dane, run down and get her. It's time to try the camera!"

Dane took another glass container from the table and started jogging away.

Michael yelled, "Walk Dane, please walk carefully this time!"

"Ok, boss,." Dane smiled back at Michael as he slowed his pace.

Michael shook his head and quietly said, "What am I going to do with him?"

At the wall, Dane grabbed Marilyn with the tongs and stuck her into the glass container, then walked slowly back toward Michael. He was clutching it with both hands as he gently set it down on the tabletop. When the container was settled, Michael handed him the camera, which he had retrieved from the car.

"Here Dane, drop it in when I give the word."

Dane rolled the camera around in his hands as he watched Michael at his laptop, getting the camera ready. When it was set up, he looked up at Dane. "Go ahead, drop it in."

Dane leaned in and looked closely at the gassy green ball, holding the video camera over her. Then he let it go. Just as every other time, Marilyn caught the object and suspended it in midair.

"That never ceases to amaze me, Mike," Dane said. "Unbelievable! Is the camera on?"

Michael looked at his computer screen. "Sure is."

Dane came over and leaned on Michael's shoulder, mesmerized by what he was witnessing. The screen looked slightly green in color, and seemed to be recording a moving atmosphere around it.

"It almost looks alive, like some type of green lava flow. Pretty crazy stuff!"

Michael nodded. "It's not exactly what I expected, but I'm not going to let that slow us down. Let's get Marilyn on her way." Michael duplicated the previous calculations and coordinates as Dane slid the prong in place behind Marilyn.

Once again, Dane's enthusiasm got the best of him. "Can I hit the switch this time Mike?"

"Sure, Dane, in just a minute." Michael continued working, hunched over his keyboard, every few seconds looking up at the screen. He picked up the binoculars again and focused on the wall.

Finally he was ready. He kept the binoculars in front of his face and snapped, "Hit it Dane!"

Dane flipped the switch, and once again Marilyn was gone in the blink of an eye.

"Wow!" Michael gasped. "In a split second she just shows up. Perfect shot again! We need to pack up and get this camera back to the lab. Let's get out of here. You get Marilyn, I'll pack the stuff."

Michael was really anxious to study the recording, so he rushed through the packing and then the drive. Within twenty minutes they were all packed up and back in Sem-Con's parking lot.

As they pulled into the parking space, Michael's cell phone rang. He answered using the blue tooth on his car stereo.

"Michael?" a voice asked.

"Yeah?" Michael answered, looking at his dash board.

"Hey, Mike, we have a little problem that's going to require your immediate attention. Can we borrow you this afternoon? We need a little training. I thought we could cover it ourselves, but we're in over our head. You got any plans today?"

"Nothing that can't wait, sir." Michael glanced over at Dane and rolled his eyes. "We can be there in about half an hour."

Michael knew the voice on the other end of the line. It was Bill, a senior advisor to the Pentagon. Bill was training a few officers on the use of a delivery system Michael had turned over to the Pentagon about a year ago – an air buster grenade launcher with a laser rangefinder. It could be a little tricky since it was so different, but once the troops on the ground got used to it, it had the capability to do some serious damage while limiting their exposure. Of course they needed to be trained on it first. Evidently that was where the problem came in.

Michael hung up and turned to Dane. "Looks like Marilyn's going to have to wait until tomorrow!"

Michael walked out his back door, stopped, and took a deep breath of cool, salty air. He made his way over to the outdoor kitchen, grabbed a beer from the fridge, and popped it open.

Just then, the doorbell rang. Duke, who was by Michael's side, ran barking toward the door. Michael followed quickly, opening the door for Duke. The dog raced out the door and started sniffing Dane, who was standing there holding a 6-pack of Corona.

Michael grinned at his visitor. "Come on in Dane, game's about to start. I've got it on out back, follow me!"

Dane had been to Michael's house a few times since Thanksgiving Day. He had noticed the large deck in the back but had not gone outside.

He looked around when they got there, impressed. "This is really something, Michael. This deck is huge!"

"It's my favorite part of the house," Michael said with pride. "I built it myself!" He pointed to the outdoor kitchen at the far end of the deck. "And check this out, all brand new. I just finished the kitchen last month. I even built the pizza oven!" Michael ran his hands over the brick oven, which resembled a giant bee hive.

"You built this?" Dane asked.

"Yep! Well, I ordered the parts online, and then had to put it all together. Turned out pretty nice, though. We have yet to fire it up, but I bet the pizza is going to be phenomenal!"

"Wow, Mike, this whole thing is really sweet!" Dane walked around the kitchen slowly, taking in every detail. He pulled up a stool from below the granite counter top and sat down.

"Can I get you a beer, Dane?" Michael asked, gesturing toward the beer in his hand.

Dane held up his Coronas, shaking his head. "I brought these. Corona has become my favorite since moving out here!" He grabbed a bottle from the 6-pack and handed Michael the remaining five. Then he opened his beer and held it up to Michael. "To Marilyn!"

Michael grinned, holding up his Coors Light, and gently clinked the bottle necks together. "To Marilyn!"

He turned to put the beers in the refrigerator, but paused when his phone rang.

"It's Ruth, excuse me for a second," he said, glancing at the phone and then Dane. "Hi honey." He listened quietly. "Sure no problem, Dane's here. We're just going to watch the game, so take your time."

Michael hung up and looked at Dane, who had turned his attention to the game that was about to start. "I was wondering where she was. Turns out she's working late, so she'll be awhile."

"Does she have to work late a lot?" Dane asked.

"Not much, but every once in a while. She has a meeting tonight. She's had a lot of night meetings lately; must be budget season! Her job can be a little stressful."

"Does she like it?"

"She says she loves it," Michael said quietly.

"I guess we're all lucky to be doing something we enjoy." Dane answered.

Michael jumped at the chance to change the subject. Ruth had been making him distinctly … uncomfortable lately, and he wasn't in the mood to talk about that to anyone else. "You like working at Sem-Con so far Dane?"

Dane laughed. "You kidding? I love it!" He beamed at his boss, then grew serious. "Can you believe it about Marilyn? I mean, she hit that wall in the blink of an eye! Pretty amazing! Have you figured it out yet? Were you able to look at the video?"

"No, I locked it away in the safe and it's been there since we got back yesterday. To tell you the truth, I'm not any closer to understanding now than I was the first time she shot across the room. I'm hoping the video helps. But, it's pretty crazy, and I'm not the kind of person who's just going to guess. I mean, I *have* to know how it works. I have – I mean *we* have – lots of work left to do. But for now, I'm extremely happy with the results."

Dane sipped on his beer and gazed at the label, slowly rubbing the frost from the bottle with his thumb. "Mike, I've been meaning to ask you … you really believe in all this God stuff, I mean Heaven and all?"

"Wow Dane, you sound like me the first day I met you. Jumping right into the heavy stuff right away! We just sent a little green gassy ball across an open field to a wall a quarter mile away, defying all the laws of physics and gravity, and every other law of nature, and you want to talk about Heaven?" Michael snickered. "Man, you've been hanging around me too much!" He sat down and sighed, trying to decide where to start. "Well, here's the thing. I certainly believe that Heaven's out there somewhere, but my belief in God is all faith! Well mostly, anyway."

"Mostly?"

"Yeah, I say mostly because I had a near-death experience a few years ago. I had a dream, but I think it was more than just a dream. I actually think it might have been a journey; a peek into eternity! I actually think I heard God speak to me before too! But with that said, I have to admit that there's still a really tiny part of me that finds it difficult to believe. It's the scientist in me! I want proof that God exists, but I think that's perfectly natural. I'm human, Dane, we all are. None of us has the capacity to grasp the big picture like God does."

Michael took a swig of beer and wiped his lips with the back of his hand. "I mean, we can't wrap our mind around a being that was never created; our minds just don't work that way. So the tiny part that doesn't believe just doesn't have the capacity to comprehend! I picture myself on my death bed someday and it kind of scares me. Sometimes I think ... what if I'm wrong?"

Michael got up, walked over to the railing of the deck, and bent over, resting his forearms on the rail. He turned and looked back toward Dane, who was still leaning on the bar behind him. "But not believing always leads me back to wondering where all this came from." Michael's voice got quiet. The waves of the Pacific Ocean crashed on the rocks below. "And that non-belief is just a sin, for which I always ask forgiveness. It's harder for me to believe that my life is just a circumstance of chance, where a bunch of atoms banged into each other and happened to land perfectly, in total order, to create this world ... this universe. And it's not just me, or all humans for that matter. It's everything! It boggles the mind if you think about how everything had to go *right* to make all of this. And those questions always lead me back to the one; where did it all come from?"

Dane sipped his beer, watching his boss intently. He got up and walked over to Michael.

"Maybe you're right, Mike. Maybe there is a God."

"Now you're coming around, Dane!" Michael smiled.

Dane nodded slowly. "Would you be more comfortable talking about the Heaven stuff later, when the game's over? I hope you don't mind me asking you this stuff. I feel like we're becoming friends and talking about God with anyone else kind of makes me uncomfortable. But you seem like you have all the answers."

"I have a few answers, Dane, but I certainly don't have them all."

Dane shrugged and continued. "I'm just really curious where all this faith comes from. Diana is the same as you – it all seems to make sense to her, without as much as a question. It's really phenomenal to me, how you guys can have that much faith in something that has no scientific proof!"

Michael straightened up and said, "What are you talking about, no scientific proof? There's never been scientific proof of the existence of God, but every scientific discovery ever made only further proves biblical stories. There have been countless discoveries that prove the existence of tribes and people once thought by the scientific community to be nothing more than myth. The Hittites were once thought to be a Biblical legend, until their capital and records were discovered in Turkey. Then there was Sargon, the king of Assyria. In Isaiah Chapter 20, the Bible mentions King Sargon. Most people thought that was just a myth until they discovered his palace in Iraq. There are lots of stories like that. But there has never been a discovery that disproved the existence of any Biblical record. Most people don't realize that. The only ones that do are Biblical scholars or priests or something! You're not going to hear anything like that in today's media!"

"Wow, I never realized that; all those discoveries." Dane was surprised. "That's amazing. I have to know more, Michael. Inquiring minds need to know. I'm a scientist too, you know, but you guys seem to have such peace. I noticed that the first time I met you. Diana has it too. I can't put my finger on it, but a small part of me wants what you guys have!!"

"You should start going to church with me, Dane, or with Diana. It would do you good. I always tell people what it says in the Bible; seek the truth! You won't be let down!" Michael was surprised at how open Dane seemed to be, suddenly wanting to learn more about his faith. Nothing could have made him happier. He wanted to just jump in and try to convert Dane to Christianity right there on the back deck. But Ruth's words echoed in his head; *be an effective witness.* Michael was pretty sure Dane would be scared off if he pushed things now. Dane was certainly curious, but the timing didn't seem quite right. *Soon*, Michael thought; *all in God's time, not mine.*

Suddenly an excited voice on the television interrupted the conversation. "There's a long fly ball deep into right, and out of here! And the Giants take the lead on the first pitch of the ball game."

"That's not how you want to start a baseball game," Michael said in disgust.

He was a Padres fan, and they were playing the Giants, his favorite childhood team. Michael had a long standing grudge against the Giants because a few years ago they had taken Bruce Botchy, who had been the Padres manager for twelve years, and had led the team to a national league pennant in '98. Michael had always felt that the Giants stole Botchy from the Padres. Botchy was a good, honest man with a knack for managing. Michael had been a fan of his since the Padres hired him as manager in '95, but seeing him manage the Giants – a team just a few hundred miles up the coast – still hurt. It made this game very personal, and Michael was hoping against hope that the Padres would pull it out.

Dane walked into Michael's office just before 8, carrying two lattes.

Michael smiled when he saw his assistant, "Coffee? You're earning some serious brownie points!"

Dane laughed. "Well after that beer last night I figured you could use some!" It hadn't taken Dane long to figure out that Michael was a fan of coffee, especially lattes.

Dane handed Michael one of the paper cups and asked, "So, what are you working on this morning? Check out the video yet?"

"No," Michael said as he got up from behind his desk. "I figured you'd like to see that too. Let's go check it out."

They walked out of the office and down to the lab. As the lab door closed, Dane asked, "We going to send her to the moon today, Mike?"

Michael grinned. "If everything checks out, that would be the next logical step. We're fast tracking this one already, so why not?"

That seemed to make Dane's day. He grinned, ecstatic.

Michael opened the safe and removed the video camera. Marilyn was still in the safe, hovering right in the center of the space. They left her in her place for the moment, taking the camera to the computer to download the stream. Within minutes, they were ready to start unraveling the mystery of just how fast Marilyn was capable of traveling.

"OK, here we go Dane," Michael said. "This camera

captures half a million frames per second, so we should be able to calculate her speed relatively easy." Michael looked at the first few minutes of video, and then stopped it. It showed Marilyn in front of the probe and the next second showed the wall.

"Let's slow this down," Michael said as he adjusted the playback on his computer. "Now, let's try again."

Once again Michael advanced the video, this time frame by frame. He didn't see any difference. One frame showed Marilyn in front of the probe, and the very next showed the wall.

"Wow, she's fast alright. Time to freeze it frame by frame one more time." This time, Michael froze the first frame and studied carefully. This frame showed Marilyn, clearly waiting for takeoff. The next frame showed a flash, which Michael assumed to be the charge, and the very next frame showed the wall! Michael studied the screen again, watching as Marilyn hovered in front of the wall, motionless.

He turned and stared at Dane, his mouth open. "Dane, do you realize what this means?"

Dane stared at the screen. "Yeah, she's wicked fast!"

"That's an understatement, Dane, she reached the wall in less than one millionth of a second! That wall is exactly one quarter of a mile away. I can't even comprehend it. We still have no movement on video, until she stops at the wall. We have to send her to the moon now if we want to get a real measure of her speed. We really have no other choice!"

Michael and Dane spent the rest of the morning and most of the afternoon preparing for the next step; sending Marilyn to the moon.

Michael sat at his desk, pouring over his calculations. Dane walked in and pulled up a chair next to his boss. Michael was leaning his chin on the palm of his hand as he pointed toward his computer screen.

"Here's what I've got so far." Michael said quietly. "We already know that the moon is 388,400 kilometers from Earth, so setting the right course shouldn't be that tough. And we know that the moon is 3,476 kilometers wide, so it gives us a pretty large target. The only problem I can foresee is gravity. We don't know what effect the lack of gravity will have on Marilyn. I don't think it's going to be a problem with her movement, but it may hinder her stopping! She may end up smashing right into the surface of the moon. By my calculations, we'll be in a direct line to intersect with the moon at precisely 4:02 pm. And there's only one way to see if I'm correct!"

"You're right Michael, but personally I don't think she will. Smash into the moon, I mean. She just keeps surprising us. I have a feeling that she's capable of much more than we realize. My money says she's just beginning to show us what she can do!" Dane had all the confidence in the world that Marilyn's trip to the moon would be a success.

Michael walked to a computer in the back of the lab to retrieve the coordinates necessary to make sure Marilyn hit her mark. Dane looked in fascination at the ball in front of him; what an incredible creation. How was this even possible? She still fascinated Dane every time he saw her, and neither of them were any closer to understanding what she was or how she worked.

"Got it," Michael said. "Are you ready to make history?" Michael paused and thought about making history. "I mean make history again!"

ACCIDENTAL HEAVEN

Dane was way ahead of Michael, and smiled. "Um, yeah boss. Every step is history isn't it?"

Michael laughed. "That's true, I guess. Let's get Marilyn back to the lab."

Michael pointed to a large control panel at the back of the lab. It sat beneath a large circular metal disk on the ceiling. As Dane walked back, carrying Marilyn, the disk on the ceiling began to move.

"What's that?" Dane asked.

"That used to house a very old telescope, but I had it removed a few years ago. I just never completely filled in the tunnel. For once, my procrastination paid off, because we need an airway to get Marilyn out of here."

Dane walked under the metal disk, which had stopped moving, and looked up. He saw an opening about 6 feet wide and several hundred feet long. At the end of the tube, he saw blue sky.

"That's bad, Mike! So this is the launching pad to the moon?"

Michael loved the fact that Dane was so excited about the new discovery. He could tell that he was enjoying his new job, and this pleased him; it was always nice to work with someone who was as enthusiastic as he was himself. "Yep, this is it. To the moon, Alice!"

Michael wheeled the stand that held the electric probe over toward the globe, and carefully placed it under Marilyn. He sat back down at the control panel and started entering the coordinates that would send Marilyn on a trajectory to intersect with the moon.

When he told Dane earlier that hitting a target as large as the moon would be easy, he knew that wasn't exactly the case. He could carefully calculate *how* to get there, but he really didn't know how fast Marilyn would cut through the atmosphere. Would the lack of gravity speed things up? The truth is, he just didn't know. He would have to set his coordinates and try again if he failed.

It wouldn't be the first failure he had encountered during his time at Sem-Con. Two years earlier, he'd watched as a $4 million prototype shoulder launch rocket crashed and burned in one of his experiments. Although it had failed, the lessons learned from that disaster had proved invaluable. That's what research and development was all about, though; test and test again so that when it counted, the product would work flawlessly.

The next launch of that weapon had been a complete success, and the army was now using that particular rocket in Iraq, in certain limited situations. The feedback from the field was very positive. It made Michael proud to be an American, even though he rarely got any credit for the results he enjoyed.

He hoped that this particular experiment would someday yield the same kinds of results. But first, the experiment had to happen. Michael looked at the clock on the control panel. It read 4:01pm. He stood up and put his finger on the switch that would launch Marilyn.

"Well, here we go," he murmured.

Michael and Dane watched anxiously as the clock ticked to 4:02. The moment it did, Michael flipped the switch to give Marilyn a charge and just like that, she was gone. Michael looked at his computer screen. It had turned from the slightly green color to a dark grey.

Doubt started to creep into Michael's mind. Something must have gone wrong, he thought.

The screen had never turned grey before. Then again, maybe it was just the effect of space, the lack of atmosphere. "I almost expected to see streaks of light or something", he said. "You know, stars zipping by!" He shrugged it off and decided the only thing to do now was be patient.

"Well, she's on her way. Let's check it again in the morning. I'm going to get this place cleaned up – I've got a meeting tonight at church, so I'm out of here in a few minutes. You can take off as well if you want. I'll see you in the morning."

"Alright, cool Mike," Dane said. He'd already taken off his lab coat and hung it in the closet. Now he walked out the door to the elevator. As he did, he yelled back at Michael.

"Thanks Mike, see you in the morning. I can't wait to check on Marilyn!"

# Chapter 16

**Michael and Ruth** walked into the church social hall and stood at the door, looking for a seat. There would be a dinner before the meeting started, so the room was set up with round tables, each seating eight people. Michael pointed to a few open seats next to their friends, Phil and Sherry. Phil had become one of Michael's closest friends and he was thrilled to find seats at their table. He was the first person who had approached Michael and welcomed him to Redwood Heights on their first visit to the church. They'd hit it off immediately and had remained good friends ever since.

"What's up, Michael?" Phil asked, always excited to see Michael. Within minutes the conversation turned to the Dallas Cowboys, as it always did between those two.

An air of excitement filled the hall during dinner, as word began to spread that the church was going to launch a brand new program tonight. It was the brainchild of Donny Lambert, a retired pharmacist, who had attended the church for over forty years. Donny had spent the last ten years going on mission trips around the world. He had a great sense of humor, and loved talking to strangers about Jesus. Donny's campaigns for the church were always very exciting and everyone anticipated hearing from him.

Within minutes of Michael finishing his meal, Donny made his way to the stage to address the crowd. As he did, the doors in the back of the room burst open with a bang. Everyone turned to see what the noise was all about.

Through the doors came a small school bus, about 6 feet long, made of large sheets of cardboard and painted yellow. There were eight crudely cut windows on each side and a large hole in the front representing the windshield. The bus followed Donnie's footsteps toward the stage. A young man was inside the contraption, holding it on his shoulders as he walked.

Michael quickly recognized the young man inside as his youngest son Tyler. He turned to Ruth and asked, "Did you know Tyler was doing this?"

Ruth seemed as shocked as Michael was. "No!"

As Tyler made his way toward the stage, he began yelling. "Here comes the bus, here comes the bus, all kids get aboard!"

Just before he arrived at the stage, Tyler stumbled and the front of the bus gripped the carpet, causing the bus to stop abruptly. Tyler giggled as he picked up the bus and moved a few more feet, before setting the bus down. As he lowered his body to the ground inside the bus he started laughing as he thought about his misstep. This led the audience to laugh along with him.

Donny asked for everyone's attention, and began to explain his plan. "I want to introduce you to the latest program for summer camp." He told them that he envisioned the church sponsoring children who lived near the church to go to summer camp. His idea was for members of the church to pay for kids from the surrounding neighborhoods to go to camp at a cost of $50 per child. The camp was held for two weeks each year in mid-July, and accepted kids aged eight to twelve. The sponsored kids would spend two weeks in camp, and when they came back, the hope was that the parents would start attending the church. By reaching kids for Jesus, Donny hoped to eventually bring their entire families to know Christ as well.

It sounded like an excellent idea to Michael. As Donny was

on stage explaining his program, Michael heard a voice next to him say, "I want you to give $1000."

Michael turned to reply. As he turned he said, "I don't have $1000 to give!" He was shocked when he found that no one was standing next to him. There was certainly no one close enough to have whispered in his ear.

Ruth heard Michael's reply and asked, "What?"

Michael, feeling a little shaken, looked at Ruth and said, "What?"

Ruth was confused. "You said something. I didn't hear you, and asked you what you said."

The voice said again, "I want you to give $1000!"

Michael suddenly recognized this voice. It was the voice of God! It was the same voice that had told Michael to give money to Pastor Chase. Michael had prayed for a long time to hear from this voice again, but until now God had remained silent. Michael had just figured that He was busy with other, more important things, and didn't have time to talk to him. *This must be important to God, if He's talking to me again*, thought Michael.

He got up, excused himself from the table, and walked out to his car. He sat in the driver's seat and closed his eyes, trying to gather his thoughts.

Finally he rested his head on the steering wheel and said, "Lord, I don't have an extra $1000 laying around right now. I don't know how I can do this. I've been paying for Hunter's college tuition, and things are just a little tight right now!"

God said, "You'll get it back!"

Michael opened his eyes and looked straight ahead, out the windshield. He almost expected to see someone standing in front of him, holding out a handful of money.

But he'd been through this before. For some reason, he was able to actually hear the voice of God. He was, however, very surprised. He knew he couldn't say no to God; this had to be very important for God to finally break his silence with Michael. But how could he say yes, when he knew that it was beyond his means?

Still, it had been months since Michael had first heard that voice. It had told him to do the right thing before, and now it seemed that he had a new mission! There was no other choice; he had to find a way to give $1000. He knew that would pay for twenty kids to go to camp and spend two weeks getting to know Jesus. The eternal implications were profound. When Michael thought about it, he realized that it was a very worthwhile cause.

"OK, God, I'm going to trust you. I'll write the check," he said quietly. He got out of the car and started walking back to the meeting. On his way in, he saw his friend Phil.

"Phil!" Michael yelled across the parking lot.

Phil turned and waved when he saw him. "Hey Mike! I wondered where you went. I came out looking for you!" He changed direction, and the two men met near the edge of the parking lot.

"It happened again!"

"What happened, Mike?"

"God spoke to me again. I heard Him again!" Michael was really excited and anxious to share this revelation with his friend. Phil looked at him, confused, and Michael continued. "Remember, I told you how I heard God that one time, and He asked me to give money to Chase? Well, He just asked me to give $1000 to this summer camp thing."

"No shit!" Phil didn't normally use that kind of language, and quickly offered an apology. Then he asked, "What did He say, exactly?"

"He said I want you to give $1000. And that I'd get it back!"

"Really! So are you going to do it?"

"Yes, of course! I have nothing to lose! He said I'd get it back!"

Phil looked a little puzzled. "I don't want to rain on your parade here Mike, but are you sure it was God?"

Michael thought for a moment. It had to be – it was the same voice he'd heard before, he was certain. "I'm positive. I just got my checkbook, and I'm going in there to write a check right now. Hey, here's a wild idea; why don't you do the same? Donny said they wanted to raise $25,000 so they could send five hundred kids to camp. That would make them closer to their goal, all in the first night! I bet Donny would be pretty surprised!"

Phil smiled. "You think God wanted you to tell me so I'd write a check too?"

"Ok, I don't know, but maybe! I mean, why not?" Michael thought for a moment.

Phil continued his in-depth analysis of the situation. "Of course, God knows how this is all going to play out, right? I mean, He knows that you're giving the money, and now because of you giving, I'm going to give some too. Sounds to me like God is an efficiency expert! He knows how to get a real bang for the buck! Alright my friend, I'll write a check too, for $1000. Furthermore, I'm going to go into the meeting and tell everyone what you heard and what I'm doing about it. Then I'm going to issue a challenge to the entire congregation! Let's send some kids to camp!"

Michael got to work early the next morning, anxious to check on Marilyn's progress. She should have reached her destination by now, he thought. This could be a really exciting day. He made his way past security and headed straight for the computer, but his excitement soon turned to disappointment. The screen looked exactly as it had the night before – a slight grey tone.

"Nothing happened?" he asked aloud. He was pretty sure Marilyn that would have hit her mark, but it didn't look like she had ever left the atmosphere. He checked the electrical probe, thinking that maybe Marilyn had malfunctioned and somehow returned, but she wasn't there. He opened the telescopic tube and looked up at the sky, as though that would give him some answer. The sun was just beginning to turn the dark sky into a light blue. His cell phone rang, interrupting his star gazing. It was Dane.

"Good morning, Dane."

"Morning Mike, I'm on my way, but I figured you would probably get there a little early. Are you at work yet?"

"Yeah," Michael said as he looked back at the computer screen.

"Did she make it yet?"

"It doesn't look like it." Michael paused, still wondering what could have possibly gone wrong. "When you get here, come down to the lab. I'll be here."

Michael hung up, but continued talking as if still having a conversation with Dane. "I'll be here alright, trying to put this puzzle together." What could possibly have gone wrong? Michael went to the screen that had been scheduled to record Marilyn's journey. He went to the beginning of the recording and began playing it frame by frame, finally reaching the exact point where Marilyn was launched. In one frame, the screen showed the green haziness they had observed, which looked like green lava. In the very next frame, the screen went grey, and stayed exactly that way. Michael couldn't figure it out; if

Marilyn hadn't gone to the moon, where was she? Would she be back? And why didn't the recording work?

Back to square one, he thought. He was very tired, and this didn't make him feel any better. The night before was just a blur now; he was still having a hard time believing God had spoken to him again. He needed coffee, which always gave him the spark he needed. He decided to head to the cafeteria; by the time he got back, maybe Dane would be in the lab.

# Chapter 17

**Ruth stepped out** of her car, cell phone in hand. She looked around the parking lot as she dialed.

"Administration, Elaine speaking."

"Hi Elaine, it's Ruth. How are you?"

"I'm good, how are you? Or should I say, where are you? It's 8 o'clock!"

Ruth and Elaine had worked together in the administrative office of Tri City Medical for almost ten years. Elaine was the oldest of the three secretaries who worked in the office, and was nearing retirement. The administrative office was the heart of the large 550-bed hospital, and an extremely busy hub; except on days like today, when all the bosses were out.

"I don't think I'll be coming in today, not feeling too good. Do we have anything urgent going on? Do you think it's safe to take a personal day?" Ruth already knew the answer to this question; she had checked the day before, and knew that all of the administrators were out today. They weren't scheduled to return.

Elaine confirmed what Ruth had already decided for herself. "Ruth, it looks like you picked a perfect day to call in sick. Everyone is away today, should be pretty quiet here," she said.

"Thanks Elaine, I'll see you tomorrow."

Ruth pressed end on her phone and continued walking. She pushed open the door to the coffee shop and walked in; this wasn't her usual coffee shop, but she'd chosen it for a reason. It was a few miles from her home. As she looked around her eyes met the eyes of a familiar face.

"Have you been waiting long?"

The man sitting in the farthest corner of the coffee shop spoke. "No, but I would wait forever!"

As Dane was walking down the hall leading to the lab, he came across Michael, who was coming from the cafeteria, carrying his coffee.

"Hey Dane, I'm glad you're here," Michael said, relieved.

"Figure it out yet?"

"No, nothing. Let's get down there so we can talk." The two men walked quickly through security and got on the elevator.

"So," Dane said, "what's going on?" He was careful not to speak until the elevator doors closed.

"The screen's still grey. It doesn't look like she went anywhere."

"That's impossible, Mike, we saw her leave! If she's not here, then where is she?"

"I don't know, that's what I can't figure it out!"

The elevator doors slid open and the two men walked briskly to the computer screen and sat down.

As Dane sat down, he gave Michael a sheepish grin. "Well, I have a confession to make."

"Oh no, what?" Michael asked, afraid of the answer. He had seen Dane touching things he shouldn't be touching in the lab at times, and had scolded him repeatedly. The younger man was too keen on touching things without thinking about it, which went against the careful processes usually required in a lab. He knew Dane would become a very good assistant, but at times he wondered how long it would take. He felt like he was training a new puppy, and hoping that the effort would be worth it in the long run. For now, he tried to remain calm, though he was suddenly wondering what Dane had done to Marilyn, and whether that had led to this malfunction.

Dane spoke nervously. "Well, you remember when we were about to put the camera in Marilyn for the first time?"

"Yes Dane, of course."

"Well, when you went to your desk to call the naval base, I kind of put something else in first, just for a minute." Dane was hesitant to go on, nervous about the consequences of what he had done. But he had to get it off his chest. "I put a box in her ... in Marilyn!"

"You did *what?*" Michael yelled, emphasizing his last word. "Dane, this is a controlled environment, with strictly enforced rules and very exact, precise, controlled scientific results! You can't just throw things in willy nilly! What the hell were you thinking?"

There was no hiding Michael's dissatisfaction now. This was worse than he'd realized and he was mad to the point of boiling over.

"Mike, I know all that. I honestly don't know what came over me; I've always been the type of person who wants to skip ahead! I had so much confidence in Marilyn that I just did it. I'm really sorry, Michael."

Michael didn't answer. He just stood there, looking furious, and Dane gulped.

Then he continued with his explanation. "But don't panic. I took it out, and everything was fine!"

"*WHAT?*" Now Michael was *really* angry. "You took it out? With what?"

Dane backed up a few steps. "Michael, you're scaring me!"

Michael turned around and walked a few paces away, taking a deep breath, and looked back at Dane. "OK, you're right,

I'm sorry." He took another deep breath, trying to control his sense of betrayal and frustration. "You need to tell me everything. I *hate* when people do things behind my back, Dane, especially when it has to do with one of my experiments. We have to be completely open, honest people here. This is an extremely sensitive experiment we're working on, and you can't do something – unauthorized, I might add – and then just hide results. Everything must be plotted so that we know what to do next. We need to record all the results, as I have said, in detail."

"Mike, I reached in and grabbed it with my bare hands, and, well, nothing happened. I took it out, set it down, and then you came back after you got off the phone."

Michael sat down slowly, shaking his head. He thought about this new revelation and wondered what effect, if any, this would have on Dane.

But then Michael also started thinking about the bigger picture. Dane had touched what started out as a highly radioactive gas, and nothing had happened. Michael had no doubt that he'd done it in a panic, afraid that Michael would catch him fooling around with the gas. He certainly hadn't been thinking at the time, or he wouldn't have done it. But in his panic, he may have just accidently saved them months of research. It certainly confirmed his preliminary test results; Marilyn *was* user-friendly!

"Let me see your arm," Michael said, reaching out to Dane.

Dane held his right arm out in front of Michael, who grabbed it and looked at it, running his hand over the skin. "It appears normal. Does it feel any different, warmer than normal, itchy at all?" Dane shrugged. "No, it feels fine."

While Michael was still holding Dane's arm he said, "Dane, don't ever, ever do something like this again, do you understand? This stuff could seriously harm you, or worse!" He paused, but his curiosity overwhelmed his anger and disappointment. He gave Dane a wry grin. "So what happened to Marilyn when you dropped the box in?"

"Marilyn completely covered the box and mimicked its shape exactly!"

"Fascinating," Michael said, deep in thought.

"Michael, I swear I won't do anything like that again. I don't know what I was thinking."

"Alright Dane, but I need to document your behavior. You keep doing things like this, and it's dangerous and unacceptable. I'm going to write you up and keep you on a very short leash for a while; at least until I feel you can be trusted again."

Dane hung his head, but knew he deserved these consequences.

Michael shook his head and looked back at the computer screen. "Let's get back to business. You know, I'm really not sure what we *should* be seeing right now, but I think it's something different."

"Did you try panning out?" Dane asked.

A light bulb went on in Michael's head at Dane's words. How could he have missed that simple answer? he wondered. Aloud, he said, "Of course, that's brilliant!"

He grabbed a small toggle switch on the control board and pulled. As the camera angle pulled away the image began to clear.

Dane pointed to the lower left of the screen. "Michael is that a rock?" He pointed to small, dark object. It looked like it had a shadow below it. "What is that?"

"Holy shit Dane, it *is* a rock. She's there. Marilyn is at the moon." Michael leaned closer to the screen and squinted. "We're looking at a close up of the surface of the moon."

"Are you sure?" Dane asked.

Michael's mind was racing now. "She's there alright; the picture hasn't changed since the moment we sent her up yesterday. But do you realize what this means? Not only is she there, but she got there in one single frame of the most super slow-mo camera we've ever designed. She was there in the blink of an eye ... uh, a snap of the finger."

Danes mouth dropped open, then he smiled at Michael. "Holy shit," he exclaimed exuberantly. "I think congratulations are in order. If she got her there that fast, how quick can you bring her back? Why don't you bring her back now and find out, Mike?"

"Of course." Michael moved to the chair in front of the electrical probe and began the sequence that would bring her back.

In a matter of minutes, he said, "Hang on, here she comes!" He flipped the final switch and there was Marilyn, right back where she started from, hovering above the floor. Michael and Dane looked at the computer screen, which had turned from grey to the familiar light green.

Dane looked at Michael and shook his head. "Un-freaking-believable!"

The two men gave each other high fives and embraced in a joyful hug. Michael let out a loud whoop, his mind racing about the possibilities of this new discovery.

Michael sat down at the computer in his home office and logged on. It was early morning, and he'd only had a few sips of his first cup of coffee. He was on the computer this morning to check on his stocks and perhaps make a few trades; he'd an account with an online brokerage for over ten years now, and enjoyed taking care of his own investments. He would mostly buy stocks and hold them for a week or two, then sell when they hit his target price. Sometimes he had to hold for quite a while, while other times he would buy and sell all in the same day. He usually stuck with stocks in sectors he was familiar with, but occasionally he bought some he didn't know that much about.

He had gotten pretty good at recognizing the right economic indicators, and used that to his advantage when trading. He had bought some housing stocks before the bubble burst, and was lucky to come away with a profit. Now housing stocks were one of his favorite stocks for day-trading, since they had become so affordable and volatile. It wasn't unusual to see a one-day swing of 10 percent! This was also a fun and challenging way for him to make a few extra bucks, and gave him a good break from scientific thought and research.

Every once in a while, he would hear about a stock or see it mentioned in a business magazine, and would buy shares on a whim. He'd been watching one particular stock for the last couple of weeks, and had decided that today was the day to buy. The stocks were only $1 apiece, so he pulled the trigger and placed an order to buy 4,000 shares; the market wouldn't open for another hour. This particular company was mentioned in an obscure article in the back of the *New York Times* business section, and he loved to speculate!

He checked a few other stocks in his account and found one that had hit his target price, so he placed a sell order. He glanced through the rest of his portfolio; everything else looked good, so he logged off.

"That ought to do it for today," he said to himself. He pushed his chair back from the desk and looked down at his feet. Duke had crawled under the desk and laid his head on Michael's shoes.

Michael slowly stroked Duke's head, "What a good boy, Duke; you want to go for a run?"

Duke knew that question and Michael already knew the answer. The dog jumped up, ran to the front door, and sat down to wait for his master.

Michael got up and put his running shoes on, grabbed Duke's leash from a table in the entry, and walked quietly out the front door. Duke waited patiently on the porch as Michael snapped the leash on Duke's collar. With so many things happening in his life, he felt the need to get away, and had decided to go back to basics and start running again. He hadn't gone for a run in over a month, and he really missed it.

He stepped out his front door and smelled the ocean, which was only a few hundred feet away. There was a bike trail that followed the coastline just on the other side of Michael's house, and he had run on that trail hundreds of times, praying as he went. Jogging was his designated time to spend with God.

Michael was already running when he leapt onto the path. Duke, as always, was right by his side. His run always started with thanking God for blessing him with such a wonderful life. It typically ended with Michael asking how he was worthy of that life. He was very grateful, but like many other Christians in America, he wondered what he had done to deserve all this.

Michael had jogged almost a mile when he came across an old man, sleeping on a bench overlooking the ocean. The man was wearing a ratty old shirt, full of holes. He had plastic garbage bags duct taped around his feet and legs. He looked as if he hadn't shaved in a week. A newspaper was pulled up loosely over his chest to protect him from the morning dew.

*How ironic*, thought Michael. This guy was homeless, probably penniless as well, and yet was resting on prime real estate with one of the prettiest views of the Pacific Ocean in all of California.

Michael stopped running, reached into his pocket, and pulled out a $10 bill. He slipped it into the old man's shirt pocket without disturbing him.

As Michael started running again, he began to talk to God. "Lord," he whispered, "how can you shower me with such a beautiful life and let guys like that fall between the cracks? It doesn't make sense to me. He must have made a few bad choices in his life, but now what?" Michael couldn't understand how God could just turn his back on a guy like that. He was obviously suffering. Somehow it just didn't make sense. *I guess some people don't use their free will the right way,* Michael thought. *But still, how does God allow such suffering, such sadness and hurt in the world, without stepping in and ending it?* That was always difficult to explain to non-believers, and was almost always the first question people asked when the conversation turned to religion.

As Michael ran on, he thought of a story his mother had told him as a child. It had stuck with him all these years. It was the story of a little boy watching his mother sewing. She was making a quilt from pieces of his worn-out clothing. From the child's point of view, the quilt looked like a bunch of ratty old pieces of random cloth. He asked his mother what she was making, and his mom told him that it was going to be a very beautiful blanket. The boy doubted her, because from his point of view, the quilt looked shabby. But when she was done, she held it up for the little boy and he could finally see the beauty of the quilt.

Michael had used that story many times to explain to

non-believers that faith was all a matter of perspective. From our point of view, he told them, our lives may look like tattered cloth, but from God's perspective, they were beautiful, and everything would be completed in His time. That was always another tough topic for Michael to explain to non-believers – the issue of God's timing. Maybe some-day that old man would find Jesus and turn his life around. Maybe Michael should stop and talk to the old guy. Was God whispering thoughts into Michael's ear, he wondered? He re-membered what happened in the hospital when the old man died before Michael had to chance to talk to him about God. Here it was five years later; had Michael done anything to help his cause? Was this just a reminder from God, somehow telling Michael that he hadn't done enough? He decided that he would talk to the old man soon, maybe even on his way home from the run.

Michael and Duke came to the 5-mile marker on the trail. and Michael stopped to rest for a moment. The sun was begin-ning to rise over the city in the east, and Michael gazed over the ocean as the light reflected off the waves. *What a view,* he thought. He leaned over and rubbed Duke's back, enjoying the light and the water before him. The dog licked his sweaty hands in return, and Michael laughed.

He decided that it was time to head home, and turned back to follow his footsteps back along the trail. As he ran he saw the old man in the distance. He knew he should stop, but the old man was still asleep. Michael stopped and knelt down next to the man, wondering. He was definitely asleep, but Michael was afraid he would never have the chance again. He had never seen this guy before and was afraid if he missed this chance he may never have the opportunity again. Michael was sure he would please God by taking a minute to witness to the old man. Besides, he told himself, he didn't want to repeat the experience with Ed in the hospital.

Michael reached out and gently shook the old man. "Hey buddy," Michael said, "you alright?"

The old man opened his eyes and seemed startled to see someone so close. "What?" he said gruffly, with a raspy voice.

Michael smiled his most friendly smile, hoping the man was a morning person. "I stopped a few minutes ago to give you some money. You look like you could use a good meal. Are you alright out here?"

The old man wrinkled his face and yelled, "Get the hell out of here! Leave me alone!".

Michael stood up and took a few steps back, trying to show the old man that he meant no harm. "I just wanted to talk to you about a way out of this life. I want to share Jesus with you," he said quietly.

The old man threw his newspaper off and sat up abruptly. He screamed again, "I don't need Jesus, get the hell out of here, I said! LEAVE ME ALONE!"

Michael held out his hands, confused. "Sure buddy, no problem." He turned back onto the path. Duke was still busy sniffing the old man, and Michael gave him a tug, not wanting him to get too close. "Come on boy!"

*Wow*, Michael thought as he jogged away. *Talk about a grump.* As Michael ran on, he wondered what the old man's problem was. He obviously knew who Jesus was, and had turned him away. *Free choice*, Michael thought. *Well, I guess I still have to find a happy medium; to become an effective witness.* Michael silently promised God he would eventually figure it out.

Michael made it to his front porch a few minutes later. He opened the front door and released Duke, who ran straight for his water bowl. Michael went to the kitchen, poured a glass of water, and walked back to his office, thinking that the market would be open by now.

He sat down and logged in to his online trading account, curious whether the trade had been made yet on his newest speculative stock. He scanned the stocks in his account line by line, looking for it. When he came to his latest purchase, he almost choked on the water he was drinking. It showed he had bought the stock, 4000 shares at $1.00 per share. But the current price was $1.25! It was too good to be true! He decided he needed to dig a little deeper to find out what was going on. He clicked on the stock symbol to quickly answer his question. That one click brought him to news about the stock. There were trade rumors flying and that particular company was right in the middle of those rumors. The news sent the stock soaring, up 25 percent in minutes!

"Wow, big move," Michael stood up at his desk and clapped his hands, then sat back down quickly, realizing he could wake up Ruth who was still upstairs asleep. What timing, though! He had bought the stock at exactly the right time, and was already reaping the benefits. It was hard to contain his excitement. Just like that, he'd made $1000! He began to log off, but before he could get up from his desk a voice echoed in his head.

"You'll get it back!"

He paused, swallowing heavily. He had just made his $1000 back, just like God had told him he would! Once again, God had proven to Michael that He was completely in charge, and since Michael was obedient, God had kept His word.

But now, Michael had a problem, one he started wrestling with right away. *God told me I would get it back, which I have; only it's on paper. It's not real money until I sell,* he thought. *Should I sell now and get the $1000 back, or should I hold out for more? If it went* *up 25 percent in minutes, how far could it go? What if it goes up 50 percent, I could make $2000!*

Michael decided to pray about it. As he sat at his desk, he closed his eyes and rested his head on the desk top. "God," he whispered, "thank you for this great news. You did it again! Thank you!" Michael paused and looked at Duke sniffing his folded hands under the desk. "Help me answer the question of what to do now? Should I sell? Or should I hold it a little longer?"

Michael sat in silence, waiting to hear the voice. He sat for several minutes, and heard nothing. Suddenly Ruth's alarm buzzed from upstairs. Michael had waited for God's voice and took the alarm as a sign that he would have to make this decision on his own. Before lifting his head he asked God once more, but this time asked for discernment and wisdom to make the right choice. He whispered amen and opened his eyes. The computer screen still showed the stock price at 1.25 per share. Michael thought about the conversation with God the night he heard the voice. *God said, you'll get it back*, he thought. And with the stock price at $1.25, he had gotten it back, to the penny! Michael put in an order to sell all shares immediately. He refreshed his screen and in a matter of seconds it was done. He had made sure his profit was $1000 dollars, just as God said. Now it was time to say thank you again.

Michael bowed his head and closed his eyes, this time more overwhelmed than just moments ago. He felt so humbled by this dramatic series of events and witnessing God's power, but felt that it wasn't enough to just bow his head and close his eyes. He felt a need to show God just how much he revered Him. He slid out of his chair and to his knees on the floor, then started praying. The power of the Lord showered down on Michael like a ton of bricks, and he began to cry.

"Thank you, Lord, you are so true to your word. You are truly in charge of everything!" Michael lay on the floor, quietly weeping and in awe of what had just happened. He lay there for several minutes, until the silence was broken again by the same alarm clock upstairs. Michael opened his eyes and slowly picked himself up off the floor. "Snooze button," he said to himself quietly, laughing and wiping away his tears. He sat back down in his chair, this time staring at the computer.

"I'm sorry I ever doubt you, Lord," he said aloud. Michael reached up and logged off, then picked up his phone and ran upstairs to make sure Ruth was responding to the alarm. As he did, he flipped through his contacts. When he found Phil's name, he pressed dial.

Phil's phone went straight to voicemail. "Darn it," Michael whispered in frustration.

He left a quick message for his friend. "Hey man, it's Mike. I just made a stock trade and God gave me $1000 back. He did it again! God just proved He can do anything, and I don't quite understand it all, but He definitely did it! I don't really comprehend the big picture here Phil, but I'm obedient and He keeps rewarding me!" Michael started to end the call, then held the phone back up and said, "Praise the Lord. Talk to you later, buddy!"

Dane drove this highway all the time. He had seen it in the dark, in the fog, and the rain. But this night was different, somehow. It was darker than he'd ever seen, and there was something odd about the road in front of him. The light from the sliver of moon above was blocked by the low clouds and intermittent fog.

The best of David Gray played softly in the background,

comforting him a bit. Diana slept peacefully in the seat next to him. They'd attended a fundraiser at a comedy club, and had such a fun night. Diana had heard about the event a few weeks earlier, and had surprised Dane with two tickets. All the money raised was going to the local SPCA in San Diego. She started attending the annual event years ago and usually went with her parents, who had always supported the cause. Diana had a soft spot in her heart for animals of all kinds, and loved helping organizations she felt had the best interests of animals at heart. It was another of the traits that Dane found so endearing.

As they drove home, Dane thought about his future. He could only see Diana in that future now. He wondered what would their kids look like, and how many they would have. He didn't even know if she wanted a family, but what woman wouldn't? When you're in love, that's the next logical step, he thought. Dane had always wanted a big family. He was an only child and always longed for brothers and sisters. He looked out his window and saw a small house on a hill in the distance. His mind wandered as he envisioned Diana and him raising a large family in a house just like that. *Something close to the beach*, he thought, *so we can walk there. Diana can teach our kids to surf and we'll get a little dog, just like she had when she was a kid!*

He shook his head, trying to stop his imagination from running ahead. He needed to focus on the road ahead, literally rather than figuratively. It was black, and quite slick with the recent rain. A light fog hovered a few feet off the pavement, causing him to strain his eyes to see. Suddenly Dane saw an image right in front of the car.

"What the heck?!" he mumbled, leaning forward.

At first it appeared to be a black shadow, resembling a large head with one eye. Then it was more than just a shadow;

it was a huge black cow, right there in the middle of the road. It came out of nowhere, appearing out of thin air and then charging toward the car.

Dane took his foot off the gas pedal and almost got it to the brake, but the animal came at the car too quickly. The front of the car smashed into the cow's shoulder, hurling it into the air. Dane heard the crash and saw the cow's head smash through the windshield right in front of him. Airbags went off and the car started spinning from the impact, turning completely around and whirling into the mud on the side of the road. The front tire caught the soft ground and dug in. It was just enough to start the car rolling. Dane was pinned behind the wheel by the airbag as the car began to flip end-over-end. He heard more crashing, and the sound of glass and metal being smashed against the ground. He peered out the window, trying to get an idea of where they were heading, and saw the ground coming up toward him. Then his world went completely black.

# Chapter 18

**Diana had been** asleep and resting peacefully in the seat next to Dane. She'd felt a slight bump on her head, and rolled over. Then she began to feel dizzy and slightly nauseous. *I need to wake up; I'm going to be sick,* she thought. Fright set in. She had struggled to open her eyes, but had found herself in a deep sleep, unable to pull herself from its grip. The sick feeling was soon replaced by a comfortable, warm feeling ... a feeling of serenity. Diana kept her eyes closed and thought, *that's more like it*. She willed herself to fall back to sleep.

Suddenly she was jolted awake and opened her eyes, gulping in a deep breath of air. She was floating, she thought, as if she were completely weightless. As she floated ever higher, she threw her hands out to her sides to gain the balance she felt slipping away. She looked around but everything was so dark that she was unable to see. She strained her eyes to look through the blackness, looking desperately for anything familiar. She reached for Dane in the seat next to her, but she felt nothing. This made her sit up and panic even more.

"Dane!" she cried out. Her call was met with silence. Again she cried out, yelling loudly this time, "Dane, Dane where are you?" She looked all around in the emptiness and saw what appeared to be very faint car headlights, shining up a grassy hill below. They revealed several dimly lit trees in the distance. *This must be some kind of crazy dream*, she thought.

She felt as though everything had gone wrong, but she couldn't remember why. As she looked down on the scene below her, though, she realized that she wasn't just imagining things. She was actually floating and getting farther and farther away from the lights. They were car lights alright, but they began to fade. She was stricken with a sick sense of fear and anguish. *What is happening?* she wondered.

She looked back down at the scene below; it was a car — Dane's car, lying upside down on a road. But now it was tiny and fading from view. She was scared now, and struggling to make sense of it all. She remembered driving with Dane, but that seemed like ages ago.

As she floated upward, her sense of balance returned and she began to feel more warm and secure, as if she were being held in her mother's arms as a baby. The sensation of warmth and comfort grew, and she felt more at peace than she ever had before. She knew she had to be dreaming, but the sensation was unlike anything she had ever experienced. All of her senses seemed to be working perfectly … in fact more than perfectly. She could smell a very pleasant aroma, which reminded her of her mother cooking in the kitchen when she was a child. She closed her eyes and smiled at that thought; it was one of her favorite childhood memories. She had always loved spending time with her mother.

Her warm thoughts quickly vanished as she heard wind whistling by her, but strangely, didn't feel any breeze. The comfortable, warm, soothing feeling was overwhelming. Music began to play quietly in the distance, a very soothing melody. She felt like she was being cradled in someone's arms, but that couldn't be! Then she felt movement under her body and realized she *was* being held! She looked up and to her surprise found that she was in the arms of a rather large being that had a friendly, almost familiar face.

*This dream just gets weirder and weirder*, she thought.

The creature looked at her, smiled, and said, "You're not dreaming. I'm carrying you home."

"Is this Michael Owens?"

"Yes."

"This is Officer Art Gardner, with the California Highway Patrol."

Michael sat up in bed. "Yes?"

"You are listed in the phone of Dane Robinson as his 'ICE contact.'"

"Ice?"

Ruth rolled over. "What's going on, Michael?"

Michael was frowning and rubbing his face. He'd been in a deep sleep, and was struggling to make sense of this phone call.

"Yes sir; in case of emergency," the voice on the other end of the phone said. "Mr. Robinson has been in an accident."

The cobwebs in Michael's head disappeared in an instant, and Michael sat up. "Oh my goodness, is he alright?"

"He is being transported to County General Hospital as we speak, sir. Are you family?"

"No, I'm his boss. He doesn't have a family. Was he alone?"

"No sir. Sir, you should get to the hospital as soon as possible."

"Was there a young woman with him? Can you tell me what happened?"

"That's all the information I have at this time sir, you should get to the hospital as soon as you can. County General Hospital, sir."

The line went dead, and Michael hung up the phone. He put it on the bedside table and stared at it, shocked.

"Michael what's wrong?" Ruth had only heard one side of the conversation, but had pieced together the scenario without the details.

"Dane's been in an accident. I need to get to the hospital."

"I'll go with you," Ruth insisted.

"No Ruth, I need to go right now." Michael threw on the jeans he had laid on the laundry basket near his bed the night before. He grabbed a shirt and a baseball cap and threw them on. Then he unplugged his cell phone and stuck it in his pocket, hastily grabbing his wallet and keys. When he had everything he needed, he raced out the door and down the stairs.

Ruth was still sitting in bed.

As Michael bolted down the stairs, she yelled after him, "Call me!"

Michael rushed into the emergency room at County General Hospital, praying as he walked. "Lord, keep them safe," he murmured under his breath. He kept telling himself to stay hopeful, that it probably wasn't as bad as he was imagining. He pictured walking into a room and finding Dane and Diana there, talking and laughing as usual, maybe getting some bandages. He was sure that they would be upset because Michael had been called in at such a late hour.

He walked quickly up to the reception desk, looking for the nurse in charge. "Can you tell me where I can find Dane Robinson?" he asked.

"Who are you?" The woman behind the glass was not what Michael would call the friendly type; surely they should put a nicer person in this kind of situation! He took a deep breath, though; fighting wouldn't get him to Dane any quicker.

"I need to find Dane Robinson. The CHP called me and

told me he was here, that he had been in an accident."

"Are you family?"

"No, I'm his boss. He doesn't have any family."

"I'm sorry sir, but I can only release information to family."

Michael growled deep in his throat; he was desperate to find out about Dane, and this woman didn't seem like she was going to be easy. "He *has* no family. I'm his only family left in this world. I'm his boss, and his friend." Michael paused, trying to get his point across. "I'm his ICE!"

The woman behind the glass did not look impressed. "Just a moment, sir." She got up and left her desk, walking through a large swinging door.

Ten minutes later she came back through the door. "Follow me, sir." She gestured for Michael to follow her, and led him down a hallway to a room enclosed in glass. There were a row of seats against the wall, and she motioned to them. "Have a seat, I'll let the doctor know you're here."

Michael sat down on one of the cloth-covered chairs to wait, wondering what the next few minutes would bring.

Suddenly a doctor walked briskly through the large swinging doors on the other side of the room. "Are you looking for Dane Robinson?" he asked.

Michael jumped to his feet. "Yes, is he alright?"

"Please sit down, sir."

*Oh God,* Michael thought. *I've seen this in movies. It's never good when they tell you to sit down.* He dropped into his seat, swallowing heavily.

The doctor walked over to sit next to Michael, and took out his clipboard. "Dane's going to be fine. He rolled his car and got a few bumps and bruises, but he should be able to go home tomorrow. I have him pretty heavily sedated though, so he'll be asleep until the morning."

MICHAEL MCKINSEY

Michael allowed himself a large sigh of relief; *one down, one to go*, he thought. "That's great, thank you. Was he alone?"

The doctor looked down. "No, I'm afraid not. Did you know the young woman who was with him?" he asked.

"Did I?" Michael probed with a sense of urgency in his voice. "Did you say 'did I,' as in past tense? Don't you mean *do* I?"

"I'm sorry, but she didn't make it. Her head trauma was too much. I'm so sorry."

"Oh my God." Michael started to cry as the emotion hit like a ton of bricks. He covered his face as tears suddenly burst forth and he fell forward out of his chair onto the floor. His mind was a blaze of questions without answers – how could this have happened? How could the Lord have seen fit to take Diana away? Where was the justice in the world? The doctor knelt by his side, laying his hand on his back.

"It's going to be alright sir," he said as he patted his back. He turned and shouted down the corridor for a chaplain.

Michael just lay on the floor sobbing. All he could think of was Dane. This would be devastating to his friend. His whole life had changed when he met Diana, and now she was gone. Her dying – in this way – was going to change the way he looked at everything, and Michael's heart broke for his young friend. Finally he sat up, realizing that he was going to need to be a lot stronger than this for Dane. The younger man would need a shoulder to lean on for a while, and Michael was the only one he had. *God give me the strength to be there for him,* he prayed.

# Chapter 19

**Michael came down** the stairs and noticed a glare coming from the office. It had been nearly a week since Dane's accident, and neither Michael nor Ruth had been able to sleep much. Still, Michael thought, it was strange for Ruth to be awake and on the computer this early in the morning.

He opened the door and found Ruth sitting in the chair with her back to the door. "Hi baby," Michael whispered.

Ruth jumped. "Oh my, you scared me!" Michael crept in and leaned down to kiss his wife on the cheek. As he did, he could see the computer screen and read a few lines. Ruth was typing an email. At the top it read, 'to my sweetheart.' Michael looked at the bottom and read 'from your lover girl.'

Ruth frantically closed the email on the screen, but it was too late; Michael had seen enough. He couldn't believe what he'd just read and his face grew still.

As he stood up and backed out the door, he quietly asked, "Ruth, who are you writing to?"

"Oh no one," she answered quickly. "Just a work email." She closed the window on the screen, got up hastily, and dashed upstairs. Michael followed more slowly, his heart heavy.

Ruth had taken a seat at the vanity table and started putting on her make-up, as she always did. She didn't look at him when he entered the room, and he could see that her chest was heaving.

Michael again asked, this time not as quietly, or as patiently, "Ruth, who were you writing to?"

"No one, it's just work stuff."

"Ok, then who is your sweetheart, and who is lover girl?"

"What?!"

"Your email said to my sweetheart, from your lover girl!"

"No it didn't. You must have read it wrong!"

Michael turned and went back downstairs without answering. He knew what he saw, but had he read it correctly? *Is she cheating on me?* he wondered. *What have I stumbled into?* It brought back some uncomfortable feelings; suspicions from long ago. As he slowly walked down the stairs, he remembered back to an unpleasant time in their marriage when Michael had suspected Ruth of cheating on him with her boss.

One afternoon, twenty-five years ago, Ruth had paged Michael. From time to time, Michael would take to the road to visit some of his suppliers. He enjoyed getting out of the lab and into the 'real world,' getting caught up on the latest advances in the research field. Back in those days, pagers were how the couple communicated; Ruth would call Michael on his pager, and Michael would find a pay phone nearby and pull over to return the call. On that particular afternoon, she paged Michael when he happened to be driving past her workplace on his way home. He had pulled into her parking lot and called her office from the lobby downstairs. She had calmly asked him to pick up the kids; that she had to work late again. Brandon and Haley were still very young, and attended daycare while Michael and Ruth worked. When he told her that he was calling from the lobby downstairs, she had screamed. It wasn't quite the reaction he'd been expecting, and it didn't sit well with him. He remembered feeling very strange, and suspicious that something wasn't quite right. She had, after all, been spending many late hours at the office. She had always told him it wasn't good to just drop in to the office anyway;

she said she was just too busy. He left to get the kids that day, but always wished that he had gone upstairs to see what was happening in her office. He'd always wondered what he would have found. Was Ruth alone with her boss? If so, what exactly were they doing? And why had she screamed about his presence in her building?

There had been other signs of infidelity at the time, but Michael hadn't paid attention to them. Back then, hiring a private detective was the only way to find out for sure if your spouse was cheating on you. Michael didn't want to do that, and deep down he hadn't felt that it was necessary. He had believed that Ruth was a good person, who loved the Lord and her family. Besides, how could someone with the Holy Spirit living in them ever cheat on her husband and children? He had convinced himself that it was his imagination playing tricks on him. Some part of him had realized that he was refusing to see what he didn't want to see, but he had ignored that voice and gone on with his life.

As they say, though, when you don't have all the answers your mind goes to the darkest place. It had taken a long time for Michael to bury the images his mind had conjured up after that episode.

They had talked about the incident and Michael's suspicions late into the night once when he couldn't stand it any longer. Ruth had successfully convinced Michael that nothing was happening; it was all his imagination. Michael believed her and thought they had put it all behind them, but that didn't last long.

Just a few days later, Ruth came home crying from work. When Michael saw her, he gave her a hug and asked her what was wrong.

A secretary that worked in another department had

stepped in front of an oncoming truck in front of the hospital, she told him, and had been killed. Worse, it didn't look like an accidental death. Apparently, she had been having an affair with Ruth's boss. He had broken it off, and the woman felt so bad that she decided to end her life. They found a suicide note in her locker that afternoon.

Ruth spent that evening on the phone with her boss. She had told Michael she needed to know the truth. The secretary had admitted to an affair with Ruth's boss in her suicide note, but he denied any involvement. After a few glasses of wine, the conversation got very personal between the two. When Ruth finally wrapped up her conversation, Michael confronted Ruth about *her* relationship with her boss and opened up that freshly sealed can of worms again. After another long talk until the early hours of the morning, Ruth had once again convinced Michael that nothing was going on and that he had nothing to worry about. Although on the surface Michael believed her, deep down he still had doubts.

A few days later, Ruth swallowed half a bottle of pills and told Michael that she wanted the pain to end. Michael rushed her to the emergency room, where she had her stomach pumped, then filled with charcoal. The next day, she was very upset and extremely embarrassed by the ordeal. She swore to Michael that she had made a huge mistake in trying to end her life. They talked and agreed to go to marriage counseling. Michael hoped that a few sessions with a counselor would convince Ruth to tell the truth once and for all about her involvement with her boss. After five sessions, Michael was convinced that their marriage was going to survive and that Ruth truly regretted her suicide attempt. He was also convinced once again that she had not had an affair, and he took the counselor's advice never to bring it up again. It was a very tumultuous time in their relationship, but Michael believed they were a stronger couple for their effort. He also decided that the best thing for his young family was to go along with the self-imposed gag order. He never talked about that night again.

But now, with this new discovery, Michael wondered if things had ever completely stopped between Ruth and her boss.

This time would be different, he knew. They lived in a different age – the age of technology – and Michael would pour everything he had into an exhaustive search. She passed things off a little too quickly to convince him to take her at her word this time. He knew what he'd read in that e-mail, and it was anything but innocent. And if something was going on, he now had all the tools to find out. He walked into the office and sat back down at the computer. First he started by looking up the history on the computer; he had watched Ruth close the email, but he also knew that she hadn't erased any history. He clicked on the history tab, which showed a sign-in page for Gmail. They didn't use Gmail in their home, so this page he opened was totally unfamiliar to him. It should respond only to her information, though, which would help him. In the user name slot, he typed the letter Q, but got no response. He deleted the Q and typed in W. Still nothing. Eventually he typed in every letter across the top of the keyboard. E, followed by R, then T, but still nothing. Until he came to the letter U. The computer auto-filled the rest. The email sign in came up as USTCheerleader@googlemail.com. The password was auto filled in as well. Michael was puzzled, but felt sick at the same time; UST was Ruth's college in Texas – University of South Texas. Michael paused before hitting "Enter," hesitant about what he might find.

When he pushed the "Enter" key, Michael's whole world changed. It was a moment he would never forget; that moment in his life when all song lyrics took on a whole new meaning.

Ruth had always been very outgoing, and Michael had on occasion wondered just how outgoing she actually was. Through the years, he had grown to trust her again, although it took a long time. Now he was having second thoughts. Had he trusted her too much?

The first page to pop up was a Gmail inbox full of e-mails to Ruth. He began opening each email, one by one, and reading every word. As he read, his world slipped away, piece by piece. He stopped reading after about ten emails. He'd had enough, and he couldn't stand what he was seeing. He decided to go upstairs and confront Ruth with what little information he had.

It was pretty clear that she was having an affair, though the extent of it was still unknown. Michael knew he would need to find out more, but the first place he would start was with his wife. If she confessed, it might just save the marriage and prove to Michael that the affair had ended. Or that she was willing to end it. If not … well, Michael didn't want to think of the consequences, at least not yet.

He went back upstairs and found Ruth in the bathroom, still putting on her makeup. "What's going on, Ruth? I need answers," he said quietly. Shouting wasn't going to do any good right now.

She sniffed. "Nothing, Michael, stop being so jealous!"

Michael raised his voice and said, "Stop lying to me! I've read enough to know you're seeing some guy named Mark. I need answers! Who is he?" Michael yelled.

"Michael, I have a very important meeting that's going to take most of the day. We have people coming from the state to begin a review of the hospital. It's critical that I don't miss this. Can we talk tonight?" Ruth's voice was shaking.

"Without answers right now, I won't be here tonight."

"Where will you be?"

"Hotel!" Michael yelled again. "Don't protect this guy. If you do, it will be obvious that you value your relationship with him more than you value me!"

"Michael stop, there is no relationship!"

Michael sighed, turned, and started dressing hastily for work. He didn't believe a word she was saying, but he had only the emails to react to. It was obvious she was buying time, but Michael chose to finish this confrontation at a later time.

As Michael threw on his clothes, he thought angrily that this was the worst possible timing. Dane had just been in a car accident, his girlfriend was dead, and now this. He slammed the dresser drawer closed and marched into the bathroom. If nothing else, he had to get ready for work.

As he walked, he looked up at the ceiling, trying to contact God again. "Really God? Me? *My* family? I can't believe this! Is this because I complain to you about the suffering in the world? Are you laughing at me right now, saying, 'I'll show you suffering'? Or is this 'free choice' rearing its ugly head?"

He hurriedly brushed his teeth, packed an overnight bag, stuffed an extra outfit in it, and turned to walk out.

Ruth saw him and the bag and asked, "You're really spending the night in a hotel?"

Michael quipped back, "Yep!" He took a few steps toward the door, then turned back around, walked into the closet, and grabbed a black suit. He walked past Ruth, still sitting at the vanity and said, "I'll see you at Diana's funeral this afternoon. Nice timing, Ruth."

Michael was disgusted. Was there ever a good time to find

out your wife is having an affair? Michael knew the answer, but right now – when one of his friends was in trouble and suffering a loss of his own – had to be the worst.

Michael pulled on the black slacks he'd brought from home. He hated funerals, and this one in particular. He smiled, though, as he remembered Diana and how sweet she had been. She'd always been so happy, and she and Dane had been so in love. The smile faded from his face at that; everything had changed in the blink of an eye. One event, and so many more lives changed forever. It was eerie.

He thought back to the conversation he'd had with Dane not too long ago at the softball game. His friend Justin's grandmother had gotten sick, Justin had gone to see her, and had been killed on the trip. That tragedy opened up the position to replace Justin as Michael's assistant, which Dane filled. Now this. What consequences would Diana's death cause? Sweet Diana, what a shame. Such a waste of a precious life.

Michael thought back to his early morning runs and his conversations with God. All the pain and suffering in the world had suddenly become very personal. It really bothered him to see his young colleague in such pain. He knew that Dane would be okay eventually, and he also knew that he himself would play a big part in bringing Dane back from this devastating blow. And he knew that it would be a long road back.

The funeral would be a celebration of Diana's life, and should be a celebration of her entering Heaven to begin a new journey with her Savior. It should be a time to acknowledge that Diana was reuniting with loved ones who had passed away, since Diana was a believer. But Dane wasn't. That would make that road even longer for him.

Michael also knew the funeral would be very awkward. Ruth would be there. His mind began to wander at that thought; he hadn't spoken to her all day and he wasn't anxious to see her. There were just too many questions, too many hurts. How could she do this to their family? How could she do this to him, the man she had promised before God and their friends and families to love? He knew he couldn't rest until she told him the truth about everything. If there had been an affair, and it certainly seemed possible, Michael was determined to get all the facts, regardless of how bad they were. He needed to know so that he could put his mind to rest and decide what he was going to do about it.

But that would have to wait. Right now, he needed to minister to his friend. Michael got in the car and drove to Dane's to pick him up.

He pulled up to the parking lot outside Dane's apartment to find him waiting at the curb. He looked defeated, beaten down by the tragedy, and stood with his shoulders hanging low. His normally confident swagger seemed to have disappeared. He hadn't shaved, and Michael noticed black circles under his swollen eyes. He looked like he'd been awake for days. Dane opened the door and sat down in the passenger seat next to his boss. He closed the door, folded his hands, and slumped over in the seat, to stare at the floor with his head hung low. He didn't say a word, but let out an audible sigh as he looked around the car and into the empty back seat.

Michael looked at his friend and asked, "You okay?"

Dane's only response was, "Where's Ruth?"

"She's going to meet us there." Michael figured he'd wait a while before telling Dane about Ruth. There was only so much pain and heartache this guy could face. He'd find out soon enough.

"I don't know if I can do this, Mike."

Michael smiled at Dane, and spoke softly, trying to reassure his friend. "Dane, you always hear people say that those we lose are in a better place, right? I believe that Diana *is* in that place. The hard part is not knowing for sure. But Dane, if you had my belief, there would be no doubt. Right now, Diana is probably having dinner with Jesus himself. She's getting reacquainted with loved ones who she hasn't seen in years, some she's never even met!"

Michael felt himself slowly crawling up on his soapbox, but thought that Dane needed to hear this, if only to feel a bit better. "I have the peace that passes all understanding, to quote one of my favorite bible passages. Jesus said, 'Do not let your hearts be troubled. You believe in God; believe also in me. In My Father's house are many mansions; if that were not so, would I have told you that I am going there to prepare a place for you? And if I go and prepare a place for you, I will come back and take you to be with me that you also may be where I am.'"

Michael paused. That was Michael's favorite Bible passage, and he wanted Dane to think about it; let those words soak in a bit.

After a moment, he continued. "Dane, that's assurance from Jesus himself that Diana is in Heaven right now. And trust me, Dane, she's loving it! Let's get you through this celebration of Diana's life. And please realize that it *is* a celebration. We're sad because we miss her, but she's not sad, Dane. She is more happy and more alive that we can possibly imagine! You've got to believe that, or else life is just hopeless. You've got to let it get into your heart, to give you hope and comfort. You're going to hear a lot of those things at the funeral. Just try to keep an open mind. I'm going to pray that God allows you to hear things differently today. Let God speak to your heart today, Dane, and let Him comfort you."

Dane managed to smile slightly. "Man, Mike, I wish I had your faith. I promise I'll try. But this is still the hardest thing that's ever happened to me." He hung his head once again and fixed his eyes on the floor. "Let's just get there and get it over with."

Diana's pastor delivered a beautiful and comforting message. He had a way of sympathizing with the family of the deceased, while giving a strong message of hope. After all, hope was all a Christian had when a loved one died the way Diana did. She was so young and so full of life, and hope was the only thing that made it acceptable that she was gone.

Dane had asked Michael to speak on his behalf. He knew that he would never be able to face Diana's family and friends while stumbling through a eulogy, and didn't even want to try. He missed her badly himself, and still blamed himself for her death.

Michael stepped to the podium after the pastor was done, stopping to touch Dane's arm in comfort on the way by.

"As believers," he started, "we all know where Diana is. The Bible says that to be away from the body is to be with the Lord."

Michael looked at Dane, who was slumped over in the front pew, Diana's casket a few feet in front of him. The scene didn't seem real. He looked out at the people attending the funeral. Most of Diana's family were sobbing, wondering how someone so young and full of life could be gone. It didn't make sense to anyone there. His eyes came across Ruth, and his heart dropped. There she was, sniffling in the second row, sitting right behind Diana's family. Michael couldn't help but wonder if the tears were real, considering the secret life he had just stumbled upon.

His attention was drawn back to Dane as he suddenly sat up and lifted his eyes slightly, catching Michael's gaze. He wondered what it was that got his attention. Was God finally reaching out to Dane, Michael wondered; or was God letting Michael know he needed to concentrate on his friend rather than his situation at home? If only God could convince Dane that Diana was in Heaven; maybe that's what God was silently telling Michael – it's in your hands right now. That was it, he realized. He needed to focus and get through the speech he had prepared for his friend, who was really hurting, rather than worrying about himself and his own life. Since Dane didn't believe in God, Michael's words could be meaningless, but he had to try.

"We cannot even begin to understand how that all works, and more importantly how it's possible for Diana to have no desire to come back here. Diana was a believer in Jesus Christ, though, and that says it all. To believe in Jesus is what we should all strive for; to love the Lord like Diana did. Her entire life was spent trying to please her God. And now she's reaping those rewards. Rewards Jesus promised to every one of us while He hung on the cross. Jesus told the thief hanging on the cross next to him, 'Today you will be with me in para-dise.' Have you ever wondered what Jesus was talking about? Paradise! The modern day definition of paradise is a place, situation, or condition in which someone finds perfect hap-piness. Think about that; Diana is perfectly happy right now! Have you ever been perfectly happy? I think the answer is no. In our human condition, there is no such thing! Oh, we can be happy, but *perfectly* happy? Impossible! In this world we live in, where there is sin, we can't have that."

Michael paused and looked at Ruth. "Sin kills any chance of true happiness." Ruth looked down as if she knew Michael was talking directly to her.

"Sin affects all our lives, whether it be through hate, racism, theft, or infidelity," he continued. "Sin affects us all. And because we live in a sinful world, we can never be truly happy. But friends and family ... Diana is truly happy." Michael forced a smile to Diana's family sitting in the front row. He looked at Dane, who finally gave Michael a half-hearted smile.

He said again, "Diana is *truly* happy!" He was glad to see Dane finally getting engaged and showing interest in what he had to say. Heaven was a wonderful place, Michael was sure. He told the story of his own near-death experience after Brandon's wedding, and it seemed to resonate with the crowd. He saw a few people still sobbing while he spoke, but others were smiling. It was the message of hope he wanted to give to Dane and Diana's family.

# Chapter 20

**Michael had a** sick, uneasy feeling in his stomach as he sat down at his desk in the home office. He wondered if it was from the lack of sleep, the emotional wretchedness lingering from the funeral yesterday, or anticipation of what he might find. He had called in sick to work already; since Dane would be out for a few more days, any further progress with Marilyn would have to wait.

The funeral went as well as a funeral could, and Diana's family had let Michael know that they would look after Dane for a few days. The young man had even moved into their guest room for the time being, so that he wouldn't be alone. Ruth had already left for work. He would have the entire day, and more importantly, the computer all to himself. He'd spent the previous night in a hotel not far from home. Michael had managed to get one hour of sleep again last night, bringing his total since the accident to just over ten. He was exhausted.

There was nothing for it, though. He had to do what he had to do. Sighing, he logged on to Ruth's email accounts and checked them all for any recent correspondence with Mark. He thought again that if he had some answers, it might make things easier to understand. He didn't see any new emails, since the ones he had discovered that early morning yesterday. He was about to log off when he noticed a tab at the top of the page. It simply said, 'Account.' Curious, he clicked it open. Up popped all of Ruth's information: her work phone number, address, and strangely enough, another email address that didn't look familiar.

All he could say was, "What now?"

When he clicked on that email address, another sign in page came up. The user name and password were auto-filled, just like the last email account. Michael clicked on this new email account and started feeling sick again.

Up came an entirely new set of emails. Only these were from different names – all men.

"Oh my God," Michael murmured; he couldn't believe what he had stumbled upon. He read a few of these emails, each from a different man. He didn't recognize any of the names. *Who were these guys? What the hell is going on here?*

He was stunned by the language in these emails. It was becoming pretty clear to Michael that he was married to someone he didn't really know. Most of the emails complained about Michael, and how Ruth felt alone. Did she really feel this way, or was she just saying that to get sympathy? It didn't make sense to him at all – Ruth seemed so happy. Was this why she was conducting these relationships? He had to get to the bottom of this, and figure out exactly what was going on. Suddenly his thoughts turned to Brandon's wedding. Ruth had been on her laptop constantly in the hotel room there. Could this have been going on way back then? The thought of that really scared Michael, but then again, if something was going on he needed to know.

"Come to think of it," he said aloud, "she slammed the laptop closed more than once. She must not have wanted me to see anything on that screen."

Then there was the fact that she'd left him alone in the hospital so much of the time. She'd always had an excuse, but he'd wondered then why she wasn't around more, when his life was in danger. Now that thought came back to him tenfold. He had to know everything, every little detail, no matter how hard it was to hear. From what he was able to piece together, she had been seeing one man pretty regularly. His name was Mark Anderson, from Virginia Beach.

The other guys seemed to only be occasional emails. Although the language was sometimes very graphic, he didn't see any evidence that she had actually spent any time with these men ... at least not yet. They just seemed like play things, just dirty chats!

But Mark was a real problem. Ruth had told him that she loved him, pretty consistently. That was disturbing, to say the least. But Michael wanted to know all the details. And he had come up with a plan to put all the pieces of the puzzle together. First he thought, he'd start with the calendars. He walked upstairs to see if by chance Ruth had left her calendar home. She always kept a binder copy on a table in the master bedroom. That was a tradition that started when the kids were all little. Michael and Ruth had to have a way to coordinate all the practices, games, dance lessons, etc. for all the kids, and the calendar worked perfectly for years. When he got to the bedroom his heart sank. The calendar was gone, but he had a revelation. What if she was meeting these guys during the day, instead of going to work? She had worked for the same place for so long; she had hours and hours of personal time she could take, along with weeks and weeks of vacation time. Michael opened the drawer where Ruth kept her check stubs. He thumbed through them and found two or three days off every pay period. That must be it, he thought. *I don't remember her taking any personal time off, for anything!* He took all the stubs back downstairs to his office.

He sat down at his desk, opened the top drawer, and grabbed the phonebook. He checked to see if his cell phone was in its holster on his belt, and walked out onto the deck, where he sat down at the bar. If this guy was coming from Virginia Beach, he would need a place to stay. He opened the phone book and started looking for hotels nearby.

"Let's try the Holiday Inn," he said to himself, reaching for his phone.

He dialed, and got an immediate answer. "Holiday Inn, may I help you?"

"This is Officer Thomas with the San Diego Police Department."

"Yes, sir?"

"I'm investigating a series of crimes that occurred a while back, and I need your help."

"Yes sir, glad to help any way I can." The voice on the other end of the line seemed very eager to cooperate.

Michael continued, "We're looking into a gentleman from the East Coast, and trying to piece together a timeline that puts him in our area when a couple of crimes were committed here. Is it possible for you to access records and cross reference the name?

"Yes sir, that's certainly possible. I just need his name."

"Thank you," Michael said. He knew he would be in trouble if anyone discovered that he was impersonating a police officer, but this was the best plan he had. So far it was working perfectly. "We appreciate your cooperation very much. The suspect's name is Mark Anderson. Can you tell me if he stayed at your facility anytime this year? He's from Virginia Beach." Michael was unsure how the hotel personnel would respond to such a question, but he figured it was worth a try.

"I show a Mark Anderson from Virginia Beach staying with us three nights in April of this year, sir," the voice answered after a few moments.

Michael was floored. It worked! "Wonderful, could you give me the dates?"

"Yes sir, he stayed here the nights of April 8th, 9th, and 10th, and checked out on the 11th. Three nights total."

"Thank you." Michael hung up and whispered to himself, "Wow that was too easy!"

He picked up the check stubs and quickly found the pay period that matched the dates he had just gotten from the clerk. Sure enough, the stub showed Ruth had taken three personal days off on April 8th, 9th, and 10th. Now he knew that Mark had stayed in town for three nights and four days, and Ruth had taken the same three days off. This worried him, and increased his suspicions; what else would he find if he kept digging? He knew he needed more than just one visit. He had to have more. He picked up his phone again and called Brandon in Irvine. Michael knew one day at his computer wouldn't be enough time to piece all the information together. He needed a plan to give him more time.

"Hi Brandon, its Dad. You mind if I drive up and stay with you for a couple days?"

Brandon paused for a moment. "Sure, of course. What's going on?"

"I'll tell you when I get there in the morning."

"Tomorrow?" Brandon was shocked.

"Yeah, that ok?"

"Sure, Dad. Is everything alright?" Brandon sounded a little worried; Michael was not exactly the spontaneous type, and he'd never come to stay with them before.

"Yep, I'll talk to you when I get there. See you in the morning."

Michael ended the call with Brandon, then dialed another hotel nearby.

This desk clerk, though happy to help, had no record of Mark Anderson checking in during the past year. Michael figured he would try another. He pulled out the phone book and began to mark hotels to call, working from the nearest ones to those in the neighboring cities. He talked to four more desk clerks, but none had any record of Mark during the past year either.

Michael was frustrated. Maybe he had been all wrong. *What if it was just a coincidence?* he thought. Was Ruth really capable of doing this? She was after all, the mother of his children. She certainly *seemed* like a good, decent person, and he had always thought that she was. Well, for the most part. Did she deserve the benefit of the doubt here? Was he jumping to the worst possible conclusion, for no reason?

But when he called the Fairfield Inn, they had bad news for him. Mark Anderson had checked in for three nights and four days back in February. Michael slammed his fist against the wall. That was what he'd been afraid of, though he still had to prove that Ruth had spent that time with this guy, or it would be a moot point. Right now all he had was the fact that this guy had been in town and Ruth had taken three days off, which happened to coincide with the dates he was here. It seemed to be enough, but Michael wasn't satisfied. He looked through the pay stubs again and once again, Ruth had taken two more days off in February that matched up with the dates Mark was in town. *It's not looking good*, he thought.

Michael called another hotel nearby. This time the news was devastating. Mark Anderson had stayed there three times in the last year, each time for three nights. Michael hung his head as he once again thumbed through the pay stubs. Just like every other time, the dates matched. Michael was deflated. It was as bad as he thought. His mind jumped from there to the next conclusion: if she was still lying to him, that probably meant that this affair wasn't over.

"So that's how she does it," Michael said. "She kisses me goodbye in the morning, goes to work, and makes a beeline for a motel, where she meets this bastard."

Suddenly his blood was boiling. Ruth had been living a secret life right under his nose, and that of his family, and no one suspected a thing. And why would they? Ruth had been a very sweet, very innocent person, who loved Jesus! But now he was uncovering her other side, and it was getting ugly.

"What a hypocrite," Michael thought. "I hate hypocrites!"

As he said that, he realized that he may not have all the answers, even now. The time coming up at Brandon's would be invaluable. Not only would it provide him some much needed time away from his wife, but it would allow him a chance to finish his investigation. His mind flew through the possibilities, working like a prosecuting attorney's. He needed to have all the facts, all the dates, all the receipts, all his ducks in a row before he confronted Ruth again. The thought of talking to her about this made him sick, but he knew he needed to; just not right now. This was do-or-die time, and Michael was afraid of what was about to happen, but there was no going back now.

He decided to pray. Prayer always brought clarity. *If God wants me to end my marriage over this, He'll let me know*, he thought slowly. He walked back into the house and sat down at his desk. The adrenaline rush he'd experienced when talking to the hotel clerks was wearing off quickly, and exhaustion once again came over his body. He folded his hands and laid his head on the desk. He began his prayer but only uttered the words, "Dear God" before he fell into a deep sleep.

"Michael," Ruth whispered as she gently shook Michael's shoulders. "Michael, wake up," she pleaded. Michael slowly lifted his head off the desk top and looked around the office.

"Are you alright?" she asked.

As Michael shook off the cobwebs, he managed to mumble, "Yeah, fine."

Ruth sat down in the sofa across from Michael's desk. "Would you like to talk now?" she asked eagerly.

Michael thought about that for a minute. He knew there were still questions, and he wasn't looking forward to hearing about his wife's intimacy with another man, but he knew this time would have to come. Reluctantly he answered, "Sure. But I'm still going to Brandon's tomorrow. I'm going to stay there this weekend. I need time."

"Okay," she answered. "I understand."

She seemed calm and willing to share. He wondered if she would tell him everything now, but then realized that it wouldn't be that easy. Still, he figured he would start with a few easy questions and see what type of response he got.

Michael sat back in his chair, looked Ruth in the eyes, and asked, "Who is this guy, Mark? When is the last time you saw him, and what's going on between you two?"

Ruth swallowed hard and said, "He's just a friend from high school. He was my boyfriend."

Michael couldn't help but chuckle. "High school?" he asked.

Ruth sneered. That look alone told Michael volumes. Her tone had suddenly changed from willing to stubborn. "Yes, Michael, high school."

Again Michael laughed. "That was what, thirty, forty years ago, Ruth? Are you kidding me?"

Ruth said sternly, "Not quite forty years, Mike. You know

that." She paused, taking a moment to breathe deeply and look at the ceiling, as if she was searching for the right words. "My dad was an alcoholic, something else you already know. Because of that, we moved around a lot. Mark and I were high school sweethearts right up until my dad uprooted us my senior year. When Mark first contacted me, he wanted to get together and talk about old times. It grew into a little more than that."

Michael stopped her. "Ruth, I don't think I want all the details right now. I need more time to think this through." What he was really thinking was that he didn't know enough yet to know whether she was telling the truth or not. He needed more information so that he could catch her in any lies. "I just want to know when the last time you saw him was, and if you plan on seeing him again," he said finally.

Ruth hung her head and answered slowly. She began to cry, struggling to get the words out. "I haven't seen him in over six months. And no, I don't plan on seeing him again. The last time I saw him we agreed to just email every once in a while."

Michael suspected that this was a lie, but he had no proof; the dates he had confirmed from the hotel clerks were still jumbled in his sleepy head. He knew he had to get the facts completely straight before going any further. And he needed sleep.

Michael stood up. "Okay Ruth." He walked out of the office and up the stairs, thinking vaguely that it was time for him to pack for his trip to his son's. Ruth followed and stood at the bottom of the staircase.

"Where are you going?" she called up.

"Packing for Brandon's. I'm done talking for now." *Another self-imposed gag order*, he thought. And again, it was for his own protection.

Michael drove north on I-5 early Saturday morning. All he could think about was the real possibility of divorce. He'd never imagined he would ever consider leaving Ruth, but how could he stay? Michael was a man of principles, and she had violated a sacred trust. It was the one reason that God allows for divorce in the Bible. How could he forgive her and stay with her? Every time he saw her he would have a reminder. Did he want to live the rest of his life like that? And how could he ever trust her again? All these thoughts echoed in his mind as he drove.

He wondered now how the kids would react. He spent the next hour mentally walking through scenarios in his head. He thought of each of their children, and wondered what their reactions would be. Should he tell them? How should he do it? *How tragic*, he thought. Their opinion of their mother – and their relationships with her – would forever be tainted.

And how would it affect the lives of all their friends and the relationships with people at church? *How she could do this to us?* he wondered for the millionth time. He still didn't have an answer.

He remembered when Ruth's brother, Allen, went through a divorce several years earlier. His ex-sister-in-law had edu-cated Michael about living with the child of an alcoholic. She told Michael that Allen had intimacy issues, which was a new idea for Michael. Allen couldn't open up and trust like any person raised in a 'normal' home, she told him. It was one of many scars left on all Ruth's siblings. *Was Ruth scarred?* Michael wondered. All her siblings struggled with a number of issues – addictions, infidelity, alcoholism, and problems with intimacy. Intimacy had cost Allen his marriage, and now it looked like it would do the same to Ruth. Adult children of alcoholics, especially alcoholic fathers, tended to defend their parent's behavior, and might idolize them and completely understand their behavior. Most alcoholic fathers were very controlling, emotionally and physically. This created "longing" in their daughters, or a plea to be accepted and loved. It was a hunger, an emotional need that was never met. Michael had seen these traits in his wife, but never realized their origin. And now it seemed that Ruth had succumbed to these traits, and by doing so had changed their lives forever.

He arrived at Brandon's early in the morning, with one mission. He had to find out the rest of the details of the affair, or affairs, and he had to find out fast. Michael wanted desperately to save his marriage, but wasn't sure it would be possible with all the things he'd learned over the last couple of days. He had to make a decision about that as well.

Michael's mission now was to find out the last of the details and go home to compare notes with Ruth. He still didn't know what she had to say for herself. Up until now, she hadn't expressed any remorse for what she'd done.

Michael had a quick breakfast with Brandon and Heather, and sat down to break the news. They were mortified when Michael told them what he'd discovered. He told them that he couldn't stand to see her and hoped a few days away would help calm him. He also told Brandon he needed time to uncover the rest of the sordid details of the affair. He had found out quite a bit in the few days he had played detective, but needed more time to nail things down. Michael felt he needed to be thorough; develop a timeline to correspond with the details of Mark's visits to San Diego. He was never one to allow for loose ends.

Michael sat down at Brandon's kitchen table, fired up his

laptop, and started what he hoped would be the last of his detective work. He logged on to Ruth's email and found that she'd had no contact with Mark since he looked yesterday. He started looking into credit card statements, which led him to accounts with liquor stores, flower shops, and even Victoria's Secret. He scoured over purchases and compared them to dates Ruth and Mark had spent together. The facts were lining up and becoming more and more disturbing.

Then he stumbled on a purchase that he had overlooked before. It was for a hotel stay in La Jolla last month, which Ruth had charged to her American Express. He jotted down the name and address of the hotel, and grabbed his cell phone to do as he'd done before, pretending to be a detective. He asked about Mark Anderson from Virginia Beach, but the hotel had no record of him staying there. He looked at the statement again.

Suddenly he realized that they *wouldn't* have a record of Mark staying there; the hotel was booked in Ruth's name, not Mark's. This was a new revelation. Up until now, she hadn't paid for any of the hotel stays, at least not that he'd seen. Could this be a new man? This was a completely different set of circumstances. Michael couldn't imagine his sweet wife driving all the way to La Jolla, checking into a hotel room, and spending the day with another man. Then again, this wouldn't be the first time she'd done it; there were numerous examples of her spending days with Mark.

He took a deep breath and tried to force his heart to beat steadily. He'd known that it would be this way. A disturbing question was starting to grow in his mind, though, and it was getting harder to ignore. Who was Ruth, really? He was beginning to wonder if he'd ever really known her.

He slammed his laptop shut and walked outside, to sit in

Brandon's patio chair and relax for a moment. He closed his eyes, laid his head back, and prayed. "God, this is killing me. My wife is not who I thought she was. This can't really be happening. I need help. I need guidance."

Michael stopped praying and just thought for a few minutes. Suddenly it all became very clear. Michael would go back home and ask Ruth to tell the truth. If she told him about La Jolla, he would stay with her. If she didn't mention this latest detail, Michael would know his marriage was over, that she was still lying and would never be able to tell the truth. More importantly, he would never be able to trust her again. He walked back inside and began to pack, calling to Brandon that he had to leave. Brandon asked him to stay one more night and return on Sunday, and Michael gave in. It would give him a chance to go play golf with his son, something the two of them cherished. It would also give Michael the chance to solidify his ultimatum to Ruth.

It was the worst round of golf Michael could ever remember playing. It may have been because he was using rental clubs and not his usual Pings, but deep down Michael knew that this was just an excuse. The truth was that he just couldn't concentrate. He had a feeling his marriage was about to end. He couldn't imagine life without Ruth, but he didn't want to be one of 'those' guys that looked the other way while she slept with a slew of other men.

"Sure," he thought, "I can forgive her. But I don't want a daily reminder of what she did." This was going to kill his family. The implications of his impending decision were weighing very heavy on his mind. It would affect generations to come. Grandchildren would eventually hear the truth about why

Grandma and Grandpa weren't married, and it would color how they viewed their grandparents.

Brandon promised to remain supportive whatever his decision would be. He also promised to call his close friends along with his brothers and sister and ask them to pray for the family.

In the afternoon, Michael hugged his son and left. He was anxious to get this over with, no matter what was going to happen. He knew he couldn't keep waiting; he'd only been sleeping for one to two hours a night, and it was starting to take a toll. It would be a long drive home, and he hoped that he'd be able to keep his eyes open for the entire thing. When he started the car, he asked the Lord to see him home safely, and for guidance on what to do when he got there. He prayed all the way home.

# Chapter 21

**Michael pulled into** the driveway and Ruth pulled in right behind him. As they got out of their cars, the tension was thick.

Michael looked at Ruth and asked, "Where were you?"

Ruth answered sternly, "Grocery store."

"Oh. How was church? Did you go?" Michael asked.

"Yes, I went. I needed to go Michael. It's what we do. It's what *I* do."

"Ruth, remember you told me once that I needed to be a good witness, but I also needed to be an *effective* witness? Do you honestly think you can be an effective witness for Jesus right now? I mean, based on what I know you've been doing for the past few years, I'd say that's going to be a challenge! Most Christians, especially me, hate hypocrites."

"Michael," Ruth answered, not amused at Michael's tone, "God has forgiven me. Now you need to!"

"That's funny, Ruth, because you haven't even *asked* for forgiveness! Until now, all you've done is lie to me and try to blame everyone but yourself. You have coddled your relationship with this guy. That's not something a cheating spouse does if they want forgiveness and are truly sorry for what they've done! "

Ruth glared at Michael, but didn't answer him.

Finally he said, "Let's go upstairs, we need to talk." He stopped in the kitchen, opened a bottle of pinot noir, and grabbed a couple glasses before following Ruth upstairs. They sat down on the sofa in the master suite. The sofa faced a wall, which was covered with pictures of the kids. Michael got up and walked slowly to the pictures, stopping and looking at one they had taken at Easter about twenty years earlier. He thought of how innocent their lives had been back then, how simple. Things had become so complicated lately. He couldn't help but think of how their lives would change from here on out, whatever the final outcome of their talk would be. Even at this point, Brandon must have talked to each of his siblings and asked for that much-needed prayer. Their opinion of their mother had to have changed dramatically. And it had happened so fast, almost overnight. That had to be tough for them, he thought. He knew how tough it was for him, and he had the benefit of age and experience. He'd also had an image of his wife as a great Christian woman, a wonderful mother of his children, and the woman who had held his future, his dreams, in her hands. Now it looked as if she had thrown it all away. And for what? Sex? How sick!

He turned and sat down again, and started to pour the wine. He thought that it may put him at ease and help him accept his wife's answers a little more readily. It may even help put Ruth at ease, and make it easier for her to open up.

He handed her the glass. Michael, for his part, knew that this was game seven of the World Series. The bases were loaded, with two outs in the bottom of the ninth, and the count was full. It was her last chance.

He knew that this was going to be tough for Ruth, but he also hoped that she realized the consequences of continuing the lies.

"So," Michael started in a hushed voice, "I hope you've had time to think about the dire consequences we are each facing here. I'm hoping you can once and for all tell me everything.

I want to know the truth about your relationship with these men. Please don't hold back."

"Fine," Ruth quipped, rolling her eyes.

Michael took a sip of wine and looked up once again at the pictures of the kids. *Not a good start,* he thought, but he continued in his quiet voice.

"Ruth when did this start, what happened, and when was the last time you saw this guy? And what do you want now?"

Ruth looked at Michael, and did not look happy. "First of all, I don't appreciate you looking at my email account. Michael, I work for a hospital, and I deal with confidential issues. There are HIPAA laws!"

"Okay, look let's not get sidetracked. Besides, it was a personal e-mail account I stumbled upon. It had nothing to do with work." Now Michael was wondering if there was more. He never thought about her work e-mail. He concluded quickly that using a work e-mail would be far too risky and decided to continue with the facts he had uncovered. "It's time you owned up to what you've done to our family, especially if you want this to work. If you want me to stay."

Michael hadn't expected this level of resistance. He'd hoped that she would ask forgiveness for what she had gotten herself into, but so far, it didn't look like that was going to happen.

Ruth growled in frustration. "Fine, Michael, I'll tell you everything." She took a deep breath. "I've been feeling like maybe I've made a few mistakes in my life. I thought if I met with Mark and realized I wasn't actually in love with him all this time, it would somehow ease my mind and help me accept who I am. I didn't want to move away back then, but I still felt I was missing out on something. Yes, I've seen him a couple times, but it was innocent. Nothing happened!"

Michael knew that was a lie, but he remained silent. He had uncovered numerous liaisons with this guy, but he wanted to see if she could tell the truth.

"My dad used to move us every seven years. I think it was because his company or boss found out he was drinking, so he would run away. But because of that, he uprooted his family. That was really tough for us, all the kids. We had friends and then suddenly we were yanked away from our lives and forced to start over somewhere else. It was really hard."

Ruth began to cry softly. Through her tears, she continued. "So we had to start over because our dad was a drunk!"

Michael was disgusted again, but knew he couldn't control his wife and certainly not her feelings; he didn't even want to. She was somehow blaming her current failings on her child-hood and her father. He knew that he should have expected this, but it still made him sick. He decided to get things back on track; he wasn't going to let her sidetrack him.

"When was the last time you saw him?" She was telling him some of the truth now, but the real test was yet to come. He remembered the promise he'd made to himself on the way home – if she mentioned La Jolla, he'd stay; if not, he would take it as a sign that she would never be able to tell him the truth, and he would leave. It would kill Michael to divorce the mother of his four beautiful children, but he would have no other choice. The trust would be destroyed. He still loved her, but without trust, what was left? He knew this would tear apart his family, and his own heart as well. He had never pic-tured his life without Ruth by his side, but now he felt like he had no choice.

"Michael, I told you..." Ruth was still crying, although Michael was skeptical about the tears; he'd seen that façade before. He'd begun looking at his wife as a stranger, unsure of who she really was. Everything seemed fake to him at this point.

"The last time I saw him was over six months ago!" she sobbed.

"In San Diego?"

"Yes."

Michael sighed and stood up, shaking his head. "Ruth, what about La Jolla, last month?"

Ruth was shocked. Her mouth dropped open, but the silence was deafening.

After a few minutes and a few more sobs, she whispered, "Mike, I didn't want to hurt you anymore."

Michael grabbed his wine glass, got up, and turned toward the door. "You lied again, Ruth. Every time I see you, you have your nose buried in your lap top! All those times at Brandon's wedding, five years ago? You've been involved with this guy that long?" Michael already knew the answer to that question, so he didn't wait for her to respond. "And if it wasn't him then, who was it? You've been cheating on me for that long, cheating on your *family*, and you're incapable of telling the truth or even asking for forgiveness. I found evidence of wine purchases, flower purchases and even lingerie the day before your 'boyfriend' arrived in town. I also found out he gave you a cell phone and you have been loading minutes on a phone card for years!. You have been living a secret life for a long, long time. I don't know you anymore, and quite frankly, I don't know that I ever did. But I do know one thing; you are a liar and a hypocrite, and you know how I feel about both!"

Michael turned and walked out the door, heading downstairs. In that instant, he expected to hear Ruth follow him, or at least cry and beg for the forgiveness she still hadn't asked for. But there was nothing – she didn't leave the room. The man she had been married to for thirty years was walking out, and she did nothing. Those actions spoke louder than any words possibly could have. She just sat there and let him go. That was more proof for Michael. He knew it was over.

# Chapter 22

**It was Dane's** first night alone since Diana's death, and the silence in his apartment was more than he could handle. He had spent every night since the funeral with Diana's parents. He knew he couldn't stay there forever, though, and had stayed much longer than he could have imagined. He'd headed home this morning, but now dreaded the fact that he was alone. He sat on the couch with the dogs, who were both asleep, and reached for the remote.

He'd been drinking, and dozed off while watching the evening news. He was jolted back from his state of semi-consciousness by the commercials, and decided that he would make a quick trip to the kitchen for another beer. He knew it wouldn't take away his pain, but it did bring temporary comfort. He wanted to escape into a state of mind that brought solace from the reality he was now facing.

He hated that he'd lost Diana, and felt that nothing could ever replace her. Worse was the fact that he was alone again. Dane didn't do 'alone' well. He never had. It brought back the unwelcome feelings from when his mother passed away. He missed Diana desperately, and ached to hold her again. He knew he needed to sleep, but also knew it wouldn't ease his pain, which was gripping him tightly. It would still be there when he woke up. *Just an escape,* he thought. *That's what I need. I don't want to face life without her.*

He thought about Diana and how her life had seemed so perfect until she met Dane. He thought about what Michael had said when he explained how all people were connected. What would have happened if Dane had never met Diana; would she still be alive? Or was her fate to die on that day at that very moment when Dane hit the cow? Dane had to come to grips with the fact that he caused the death of someone he loved very much. But how could he live with that for the rest of his life?

He thought back to the last conversation he'd with Diana, before she fell asleep. They'd been talking about Heaven. Dane smiled at that. What if Michael was right? What if Diana was right? What if Heaven was real? Was Diana there? Would believing that help him through the days? When he thought about his life in the world, and his future, all he could see was darkness, despair, and loneliness. He didn't think he'd ever meet anyone who had made him as happy as Diana had, and that made everything worse. Even thinking about Diana being happy didn't ease the ache of having to go forward alone.

It didn't take him long to realize that life wasn't worth living, at least not without Diana. Without her, what was the point of going on? Suddenly he realized that he could end his own life, so that he wouldn't have to think about living without her. He started thinking about how to do it, and an idea popped into his head. He could jump into Marilyn and blast himself into space. He sat up, impressed with the idea.

Bella opened her eyes and looked at Dane, and he finished the conversation he'd started in his head by speaking to the dogs. "I could jump into Marilyn and poof, it's done! I'd be like one of those monkeys they shot into space. Heck, maybe I'll end up famous; like a pioneer! I may even help Michael solve problems with the old girl! I end my life, and further Michael's research!" The beer was obviously fueling his thought process, though he felt as though this was the most brilliant idea he'd ever come up with.

But then reality hit. What if it didn't work? What if he put himself into Marilyn and it didn't go anywhere? He could burn up in the gas, or go blind, or something even more terrible! What if he got into space and just kept going? He could end up suffocating or burning to death.

*Anything is better than living without Diana*, he realized. Any of those deaths would be better than facing his life without her. He looked at his hand and thought back to when he'd stuck it in Marilyn. Nothing had happened. There were no lasting scars, and no pain! This could be the perfect way to end his life. But did he really want to do that? The alcohol had convinced him that ending his life was his best option.

"Actually," he said aloud, "it's my only option."

He looked down at Bella, who looked up at him sadly. "Don't worry guys," he said as Lucy woke up and gave him the same gloomy look. "Michael will adopt you. I guarantee it!"

He got up, grabbed his car keys, and started out the door. Just before he closed it, he thought to himself, *Michael has been such a great friend; it would be really rude to just kill myself without explaining why*. The last thing Dane wanted was for Michael to blame himself. He knew the effect blame had on him, and he wanted to save his friend from the same torture. He darted to his bedroom and grabbed a notepad off the dresser, then sat down and started writing a suicide note.

Michael had asked Ruth to move out, and planned to file for divorce. She had grabbed a few clothes and some makeup and moved in with her mother earlier in the day. Now Michael found himself all alone, and he didn't like it one bit. Both Tyler and Haley were out late with friends.

Michael knew that Dane was alone tonight as well – this was his first night alone, and he was probably feeling the pain of Diana's death. He decided that he should check on his assistant. He called Dane's cell phone, but it went straight to voicemail.

"Come on, Dane, that's not like you," he mumbled. He left Dane a message to call him as soon as he could, then called for Duke. "I know it's late, boy, but let's go for a run," he told his old friend. Duke started prancing around in circles in the entry way and wagging his tail.

Michael threw on his running shoes and locked the front door. He and Duke started running down the driveway that led to the bike path along the beach, and he started talking to God like he always did on his runs.

"God, how could You let this happen?" he asked. "I've asked You a thousand times and will probably ask a thousand more before I die. It makes no sense how You could let this happen to me; to my family, my precious family ... who really love You a lot!"

The emotion of the moment took over Michael's body, and suddenly he started hyperventilating. He sat down on a bench along the path, and hung his head. Duke sat down at his feet and watched the waves. "What a great life you have, boy!" Michael said as he struggled to catch his breath.

Then Michael heard a faint but familiar voice; the waves of the ocean made it barely discernible. He hadn't heard that voice in a while, but he knew who it was.

The voice said, "Michael," very softly. Michael raised his head and looked at the ocean.

"God?"

He looked out over the expanse of the ocean. The very thought of God's creation hit him. How incredible! Michael couldn't help but realize how small and insignificant his problems were in the big scheme of things. But this was such a personal hurt. It killed Michael to think of what was happening to his life. He had done everything he could to be a good father to his children and a good husband to Ruth. He was a good man and a good Christian. Couldn't God help him a little more; couldn't he protect his family? That free choice thing popped into his head again. Michael had no control over the circumstances he found himself in. It was all spinning out of control. But he had a choice about how he reacted. *Jesus knows each one of us,* Michael thought. *He knows the number of hairs on our head, that's what the Bible says. He cares deeply about each one of us. How could he let this happen?* He still couldn't help but be consumed with his hurt.

The voice said again, "Michael."

Michael said, "Yes Lord, I'm listening."

The voice sounded different this time. Michael knew it was the voice of God, but it was so quiet this time. The voice said again, "Michael, I gave up a lot too, but it was worth it."

Michael was confused. God was comparing His pain to Michael's? He knew when he became a Christian, he gave up what was best for himself and agreed to live for what was best for the kingdom of Christ. Is that what God meant?

Then he realized that God had sent His own son to die for the sins of the world. It never made much sense to Michael living in this modern era, but back in Jesus's day there was a price for sin. Now, because Jesus had paid for humanity's sins, everyone who believed was forgiven. God had suffered a great loss, and so had Michael. Was it the same, he wondered?

Michael closed his eyes and hung his head again. "You're

right, Lord, that had to hurt, watching Your son on the cross," he whispered. *But it all ended pretty well,* he thought. Was that what God wanted him to learn from all this? That it would be worth it? When? This was a pretty tough lesson, and a pretty tough way to learn it.

Michael was struggling to make sense of Diana's death, and Ruth's infidelity; two tragedies, so different yet so similar. They would both change the course of history for a lot of lives, and they were both causing a lot of pain in the moment. He wanted to believe that some good would somehow come from these things, but it was so hard to see right now.

He finally stood up, stretched, and resumed his run without an answer. Once again, his thoughts turned to Dane. He knew Dane wasn't a believer, and wondered if Diana's death was going to be the thing that pushed him into believing in Christ. Michael had prayed about it; was this God's way of answering his prayer? That would certainly be good for God's kingdom! Would one life be worth another? Well, Michael thought, in light of eternity, of course it would.

But from Michael's perspective it was hard to take. That would help explain Diana's death, but what about what he was going through? It was impossible for Michael to justify Ruth's infidelity. He believed that the greatest gift God had given humans was free will, and Ruth had certainly exercised her free will. But she had used it to do harm, and how could that be part of God's plan? There was no consolation there. It would definitely take time to understand how this was for the greater good.

He picked up the pace and pushed himself forward, seeking to clear his thoughts. Duke ran right by his side down the path that led back to his house. *So much to think about*, Michael mused. *This is going to be a long run!*

# Chapter 23

**Dane arrived at** Sem-Con after hours. He knew it wouldn't be easy to get into the lab this late, but he had a pretty good relationship with all the guards. He figured he could always tell them that he was expecting Michael later, but he would have to come up with a reason not to call and verify with Michael right at that very moment. He needed a way to get in without Michael being alerted. He wanted to get this over with as quietly as possible.

The note Dane left for Michael explained it all. He'd told Michael that he was sorry for the trouble this would cause, and appreciated the break he'd given him with the new assistant position. Dane explained his feeling of hopelessness, and wrote that he just couldn't see a reason for living anymore. His joy was gone. He hoped that it would ease Michael's guilt, and make him feel at least a little bit better.

He walked through the front doors without a problem, and passed down the steel hallway, still fascinated by the shiny glow of the walls. He walked slowly, running his finger along the wall, and remembering the first time Michael had taken him down that same hallway to the lab. He got to the first guard and slid his card. The guard surprisingly didn't even ask him why he was here so late. He continued on to the next guard and breezed right through, no questions asked!

Once on the elevator, Dane exhaled. That had been easier than he expected. When he got to the bottom floor, the doors opened slowly. The lab was dark, cold, and empty; nothing like it had been on the first morning. Dane turned on all the lights and started firing up the equipment to produce a brand new Marilyn. Within a matter of minutes, she was there, glowing green just like every other time.

Dane sat down at the control board and started looking for a wide open coordinate that would catapult him into space forever. *Forever*, Dane thought. *I wonder when it will kill me.* Probably within a matter of seconds. He hoped.

Michael came back to an empty house. The kids were still out, then, and that was probably best. He grabbed his cell phone and tried Dane again. For some reason, he thought the timing may be right to ask Dane to become a believer. He felt as though God was coaxing him forward, urging him to contact Dane. Michael suddenly felt compelled to contact his friend, and that would be a very good motivator. Whatever the reason, Michael knew he had to talk to Dane, and it concerned him that Dane wasn't answering. He felt as if God had given him a mission. He had to see Dane and at least start introducing him to the kingdom of God. If all went according to plan, Michael would talk to Dane and within a few minutes, his assistant would become a believer. *If it's really a plan from the Lord, that's how it will go. One life for another*, he thought.

Michael knew that belief would bring Dane some peace over Diana's death. He thought back about his words to Ruth – be an effective witness. That's just what he planned to do with Dane. But he had to get a hold of him first. His phone went straight to voicemail again. Where was he? Michael's mind went to the worst place, and he pictured Dane as Diana's death sunk in, needing a friend to talk to. He grew more concerned, and started making a list of places Dane might have gone.

Dane finished programming a brand new coordinate to an area that showed absolutely no interference, as far as the computer could calculate. He locked it in and began the new, crudely made timer. As he did, he also programmed the computer to completely erase his tracks; it would leave no record whatsoever of where he had gone. In five minutes, he hoped it would be over.

*Now for the tricky part*, Dane thought. Getting into Marilyn was going to difficult. He took a few steps back, took a deep breath, and jumped toward Marilyn, feet-first. When he was in the air, he curled up in a cannonball as if he were jumping into a swimming pool. Then he hoped with all his might that he wouldn't miss. He didn't; in a matter of moments he was engulfed in green haze, which meant that he'd hit his target. Now he found it difficult to move, but not impossible. He could see Marilyn covering every inch of his skin.

He'd been holding his breath when he left the ground and jumped. He was amazed to find that he could breathe in Marilyn, though. He took a cautious breath, and then another, and exhaled in relief. He could breathe! This was completely unexpected. He had thought that once he was inside Marilyn he might suffocate.

He took one last look around the lab. *So it comes to this*, he thought. *My life is over, just like that. I wonder what happens to people like me.* Dane thought about his dogs. He hoped he was right in thinking Michael would adopt them – he had asked Michael to take care of them in his note. Michael was fond of dogs, and Duke would love a few little sisters! And his parakeet, what would happen to him? *Oh well*, he thought. *Michael will make sure he finds a good home.*

Dane was stricken with a sudden wave of sadness, thinking about everything that had happened, and all that he was losing. He hung his head low between his knees. He'd had everything to live for, just a few short weeks before. Now it was all going to end. He glanced at the clock, which showed five seconds to launch, and closed his eyes. At least that didn't give him any time to change his mind.

Michael tried Dane's cell phone one more time and just like before, it went straight to voice mail. He frowned. Now he was really getting worried. He grabbed a jacket and his keys, anxious to go find Dane and see if he was alright. Michael yelled for Duke, thinking that he would take his friend with him for moral support.

The two of them ran out, slamming the front door behind them. Michael didn't know why, but he knew that he needed to find Dane. His thoughts were turning dark again, and that meant that Dane must be in trouble.

# Chapter 24

**The ride Dane** expected never happened. Instead of falling asleep, suffocating, or even smashing into a star, he found himself suddenly looking at a shiny, clear wall. He rubbed his eyes, trying to see, but the green atmosphere of Marilyn made it difficult to focus. He felt no motion whatsoever, though, and he didn't think he'd gone anywhere.

He held out his hands and touched the wall. It was very thick, and smooth. Glass, he thought. Beyond the wall the horizon reached before him – hills, brilliantly bright green hills. Dane couldn't believe what was happening. He was supposed to be dead, and instead he found that he'd never felt more alive.

He stretched his hand in front of his eyes, and looked at it as he opened and closed his fist. This was fascinating. It appeared that Marilyn had absolutely no effect on his body. He could breathe and move, and the fact that he could see was so surreal!

He looked around again in wonder; now he just had to figure out where she had taken him. He looked through the glass wall again, trying to decide if he was imagining things, but what he saw beyond the wall was hard to imagine. In the distance, above the hills, he saw sky, a beautiful, extremely colorful sky. The colors were all the colors of the rainbow, and some that he'd never seen before. The hills had trees that looked almost like pine trees, but were perfect in their shape and color. Not a single tree had any dead branches; in fact, the shape of every tree was exactly the same. The colors of the trees were so bright, so vivid. Everything he saw was so beautiful and so alive, there was no way to describe it.

His mouth dropped open when he saw what looked like people walking along a path at the bottom of the hill in front of him. Some of them were walking, but others were running, pulling each other along as if they were anxious to get wherever they were going. Some were even skipping, like school kids going to recess. They were all smiling and looking really happy.

He thought about climbing over the glass wall to try and get in, but couldn't even see the top; it seemed to go on forever. Marilyn was holding him right there, in front of the wall, and showed no sign of moving any farther.

He looked back through the glass and saw more people, now hundreds of them, all joining in the processional. They were all dressed in brightly colored clothing. Some were wearing robes, others pants, and some of the women were wearing brightly colored dresses. Who were they? he wondered. Where were they going? Had he somehow discovered a new planet? Maybe something had gone wrong, and Marilyn had just taken him to another area of Earth, but that had never happened before! Dane was sure of the coordinates, and hadn't seen even the slightest obstruction in his trajectory into space. Marilyn had worked perfectly every other time. But this time … well, the only explanation was that something had happened, and she'd taken him somewhere very, very cool.

How would he ever be able to describe this place to Michael? His thoughts turned from happy to sad again when he remembered why he'd ended up here in the first place. He had wanted to end his life, and instead he had made a fantastic discovery. But when he put in the coordinates for Marilyn, he made sure that they would be erased afterward. Even if he could somehow make it back alive, there would be no way to duplicate his journey.

Michael knocked on Dane's door and stood back. He waited a few seconds, then rang the doorbell. After a moment, he decided to look through the windows. He was getting nervous and very worried about his friend, but peered through a small opening in the drapes in the front window, hoping to find Dane sleeping on the couch or watching TV. The light was on, and so was the television, which worried Michael even more. Dane wasn't on the couch or in the room, and Michael didn't think he'd leave without turning off the TV.

Michael had to get in to see if Dane was alright. He looked around for where Dane may hide a key. He looked under the door mat and under a few flower pots, but didn't find anything.

He turned and walked toward the manager's office, growing more worried with each step.

Dane leaned against the glass and tried to focus on the material instead of looking through it. It seemed pearly, and almost luminescent, but Dane was able to see right through it. He made a fist and tried knocking on the glass, but it made no sound. Of course there would be no sound, he realized. There weren't any molecules to vibrate! The lack of sound virtually proved that he was in space, yet here he was, able to breathe and move with no restrictions at all. If this was space, he thought, he should have burned up a long time ago. But he was safe, and still alive. Marilyn had made the impossible

possible. What a miracle! Michael would never believe it.

All thought of killing himself had vanished, and suddenly Dane couldn't wait to get back to the lab to tell Michael about his discovery.

He watched as the crowd of people beyond the glass stopped and huddled around, forming a large circle. Suddenly a large winged creature appeared, cradling something in its arms and covering it with its wings. It seemed to appear out of thin air. The creature was mostly white and covered in feathers, but also had what appeared to be human skin on its face, arms, and legs. It wasn't wearing any clothing, so Dane figured that it must be some type of animal. It appeared to be at least a foot taller than any of the people.

He looked closely at the creature, trying to see what it carried. It had been cradling a young woman, and now set her down. As he set the woman down, she stood for herself and looked around, first up at the sky and then at the line of people eagerly waiting to greet her. The crowd surrounded her, and she started hugging them, one by one. They all made their way to her, to hug her and talk to her. Some hugged her longer than others, and each stayed near. Some people cried as they hugged her, and the woman began to cry with them. It was as if she had been lost, and was now coming home. Everyone seemed very happy to see her. Soon she was surrounded by a circle of people who evidently loved her very much.

Just then the crowd parted and a man wearing a white robe approached them from behind. He was the last person to reach the woman, but greeted her with open arms. She fell into his arms and began to cry uncontrollably. The robed man held her up briefly, and then helped her back to her feet. As he did, he turned his face toward Dane and Marilyn.

Dane saw this, took in the man's face, and then pushed back from the glass and gasped. "Oh my God!" he whispered. He glanced back at the man in the white robes to confirm his first impression, but he'd been right. The man was Jesus.

Dane rubbed his eyes. "The winged creature must be an angel," he mumbled aloud. "What else could it be?" He remembered back to when Michael had told him about his near-death experience at his son's wedding. They'd had many talks about religion and God, but that particular conversation had a real impact on Dane. Dane had never believed in God, but he'd never forgotten Michael's account of his near-death experience. Michael always cried when he told that story, he'd said. He'd even talked about it at Diana's funeral. Dane remembered now how Michael had described the colors of the sky. It had been particularly amazing, Michael had said, and unlike anything he'd ever seen before. Dane looked at the sky above the crowd and the green hills.

"That's it," he said to himself. "That's definitely what Michael saw – those colors *are* indescribable! And the trees are exactly as he said, they're all perfect!"

Dane looked back at the crowd and noticed something else. "The people … every one of them is in great shape. None of them are overweight; in fact, none of them are old! They're all perfect! Oh my God, it's exactly like Michael said it would be!"

Steve, the apartment manager, turned the key and opened Dane's door. He leaned in and yelled, "Dane, it's Steve, are you here?"

Michael pushed Steve aside and walked quickly through the living room, looking around on his way down the hall. He walked into Dane's bedroom.

"Dane!" Bella and Lucy jumped off the bed and started sniffing Michael's feet. It didn't take long for Michael to realize that Dane was not there.

As Michael turned to leave, he saw the note that Dane had left for him. He picked it up and began to read the words, his heart sinking. By the second line, he was already crying.

Bella backed up and barked a few times, realizing that something was wrong. When Michael got to the end of the letter, where Dane had stated his intention, he dropped the note and stared at the dog in front of him.

"Oh no," he whispered, heartbroken.

"What?" Steve asked from the doorway.

"Dane's on his way to the lab to kill himself!"

# Chapter 25

**Dane watched as** Jesus and the young woman began to walk away. The crowd followed, some hand in hand, others clapping and cheering. They were all so happy.

When they disappeared, he wondered what he had just witnessed. Was it possible that this person had just died, and was indeed coming home? "This is completely nuts," he said to himself. "It just can't be! But what other explanation is there?"

Suddenly he noticed a light in the sky, not exactly like the sun, but very bright. "That's something else Michael talked about, that bright light," he said quietly. Just then he noticed the trees again, and how they shimmered in the light. "Michael said they shimmered like diamonds when the light hit them. He's right! Damn it, Michael was right." He looked around him in awe. "This is incredible!"

The minute Michael got in his car he was on the phone with the Frank Johnston. Frank was head of security at Sem-Con. The two of them had worked together for sixteen years, and had implemented many of the security protocols at the lab.

Michael told Frank about the situation with Dane and the urgency of getting to him as quickly as possible. Frank assured Michael that he would clear the path for a quick entry into the lab. Frank also confirmed to Michael that Dane was already there; he had checked in to the lab thirty minutes ago.

Dane's apartment was ten minutes from Sem-Con. Michael got there in five. He raced thru security and down to the lab, finding that Frank had done just as he had promised. He'd removed every possible roadblock, which made Michael's descent down to the lab as quick as he had ever experienced.

Frank met Michael at the last checkpoint and rode down with him on the elevator. When they finally got inside, Michael checked the equipment and saw that Dane had done the work to produce a new Marilyn. But Michael's worst fears were realized. Marilyn was gone, and so was Dane.

According to the computer log, she had launched ten minutes earlier. Michael frantically began the process of bringing her back. He had a bad feeling about this. Dane's note said he wanted to end his life by launching himself into space using Marilyn. It looked like he'd done exactly that, or at least attempted to.

Michael didn't even know if it was possible to bring her back, let alone Dane. They had never sent anything that heavy into space. And if he did bring her back, what condition would Dane be in when he got here? Michael pictured the worst. He imagined a lifeless lump of bloody flesh, maybe even turned inside out.

He worked frantically to bring Dane home, his hands flying over the keys, trying to retrieve the coordinates of Dane's trip. He trembled as he worked, his body shaking with anticipation. Within a matter of seconds he would know Dane's fate. He was afraid of what he would see.

Dane reached up to touch the wall of glass in front of him once again. He made a fist and began knocking on the glass. As he did, he saw winged creatures appearing out of nowhere. He stopped knocking, afraid of attracting their attention, and tried to step back away from the glass. The winged creatures continued to multiply. There were just a few at first, but then hundreds of them appeared. Some were tiny, while others were very big, like the one that had delivered the woman. Most of them were white, but some were darker, almost grey. A few of the smaller ones seemed to glow in the brilliance of the light. They flew all around the sky, flying right through the trees. Some of the creatures appeared to have human faces.

Dane watched them in awe. They didn't appear to notice him, but he was positive now that in his attempt to kill himself, he had somehow discovered Heaven.

Michael hit the final switch to bring Marilyn home, and turned toward the landing stage. Dane appeared immediately, completely wrapped in a blanket of green. He wasn't moving.

Michael ran to his side and starred. He was in an upright position and he was holding his right hand out in front of him. It was clenched in a fist. He was absolutely still.

"Dane!" Michael shouted, panicked.

Dane twitched at his name, and his hand opened slowly as if it were painful. After a moment, he looked up at Michael. Suddenly Marilyn's atmosphere disappeared, and Dane fell to his knees on the floor. He knelt over and began to cry.

Michael rushed to him and grabbed his shoulders. "My God Dane, are you alright?"

Dane rolled over and continued to cry.

"Dane, please talk to me, are you ok?"

Dane looked up at his boss. With tears still streaming from his face, he managed to form the words, "We found Heaven."

Michael let go and stepped back. "What?"

"Michael," Dane paused and wiped the tears. "I discovered Heaven."

"Dane," said Michael, "you're delusional." He ran to the intercom and called for a medical team. "I have a medical emergency in lab room four, that's lab room four. I need a medic immediately. I need transport to a hospital. Please, make it fast!" He paused, then yelled again as if no one had heard him the first time. "Get someone in here now!"

Frank was already on the phone with his security team to clear the way. He nodded to Michael, yelling into the phone, "Wave all security for these guys, we have a medical emergency. Life or death, guys, use security code Reginald, I repeat security code Reginald!"

Frank had just given an all-access pass for all medical personnel to enter the lab immediately.

Michael was more worried than ever about Dane. He could only imagine what horrors he'd just subjected himself to. He silently thanked God for bringing him back, but he added a request that God watch over him and keep him safe as well.

Michael knelt back down next to Dane. "Dane, lay down, I've got help on the way."

Dane looked at Michael and said, "Mike, I don't need help. I was face to face with the walls of Heaven. I looked through a thick wall of glass and saw Jesus. Michael, I saw angels! They brought a young woman and set her down. Jesus hugged her." Dane was talking so fast he almost ran out of breath.

"Dane, come up for air, calm down."

Dane ignored him and rambled on, his thoughts moving faster than his mouth could. "Michael, there were trees just like you said there were in your dream, lights too, just like you described. Michael, we discovered Heaven; it's out there! Michael…" Dane paused, looked at the machine that produced Marilyn. He sat up and put his hand to the metal side. "We discovered Heaven. It's real, Mike, it's really real!"

Just then the paramedics came rushing through the door and began to assess Dane's condition. He struggled against them, but then allowed them to take his vitals, his eyes glazed.

Michael got up and backed away from Dane, giving the paramedics room to attend to his friend.

One of the medics gently nudged Dane to lie down on the floor. "Lie down sir, can you tell me your name?"

"Dane!"

"Do you know where you are?"

Dane sat back up. "Yes, of course, I'm in the lab at Sem-Con!"

As Michael listened to the answers, he began to feel more assured that Dane would be alright. He seemed absolutely fine, and he was quite sure about who and where he was. Michael thought about what Dane had just told him. Was it possible? Michael was skeptical, but something inside told him not to close the door to this possibility.

Two more paramedics came through the door then, wheeling a gurney.

The first medic pushed Dane back down. "Sir, I need to start an IV! We're going to take you to the hospital for observation."

Dane looked around for Michael, who had walked back to the computer that controlled Marilyn. He was looking at the computer logs, to see if he could find out where Dane had gone. When he brought up the screen, though, it was blank – no record. He checked the log on the control panel, but it was also blank, mysteriously erased. "Damn it!" Michael slammed his fist on the desk. If Dane had erased his logs – hoping not to be traced – it would be almost impossible to repeat the journey. Michael looked around the lab and said again in total frustration, "*Damn it!*"

# Chapter 26

**Michael walked in** to Dane's hospital room, where he found his assistant sedated and resting under white sheets. He touched Dane's arm and the young man's eyes opened. "How you feeling?" he asked quietly.

"I'm ok," Dane said, looking a little confused. "Thanks."

"So you okay with being here? I read your note."

Dane closed his eyes and spoke softly. "Yeah, I don't know man." He sighed. "I don't know why I did that. I'm sorry to worry you like that."

"So are they going to let you go home?"

Dane's eyes opened and he looked at Michael despairingly. "They'll only let me go home if I have someone to stay with. I was wondering if you might like to have some company for a bit. Could I stay with you for a few days, until they give me my..." Dane paused and put his hands up and made quotes in the air, "'Unconditional release?'" He managed to smile at that, though Michael was sure it cost him dearly.

"Sure, Dane, *mi casa es su casa!*" Michael pulled a chair from under the window, dragged it next to the bed, and sat down. "We've got to talk, though, about where you went."

"You mean Heaven?"

"Yes Dane, Heaven. You know it didn't really happen, right?"

Dane sat up in his bed. "What do you mean it didn't happen? I know where I went, and it was obviously Heaven. It looked exactly like you described it – the trees, the light, the sparkles on the tree tips. Michael, the people were all young, in great shape, all really happy –"

"Dane," Michael interrupted. "I hate to burst your bubble, but you can't just go to Heaven, you have to die to get there. You didn't die, so you didn't go." Michael was very matter of fact about what he was saying. "You saw what you wanted to see. Marilyn just took what was in your head and somehow made you see a vision. You probably thought about it because of the speech I gave at Diana's funeral. It was fresh in your mind, so when your mind was stressed, that's what it brought out. Dane, haven't you ever had a dream so real that when you woke up it seemed like real life? That's what happened to you, I'm sure of it."

Dane slowly sunk back into the pillows. "Are you serious, Mike? You really believe that Marilyn did this? Let me ask you Mike, when you came into the lab, was I there? I'll answer that for you: NO! I wasn't there, because Marilyn had taken me somewhere. Somewhere that has only one explanation ... HEAVEN!" Dane was emphatic. "I went to Heaven! And another thing Michael, I don't even believe in Heaven! Well at least I didn't, but I certainly do now!"

Michael shook his head but thought to himself, *is that really even possible?* He quickly concluded, *it can't be!* "Dane you can't just start believing in Heaven because you saw it, or think you saw it. You have to believe in Jesus first, then Heaven is the consequence of your belief; it's your reward! Think about it Dane – you were on the outside of Heaven and couldn't get in, right? Well now think about this. The Bible tells a story of a poor man named Lazarus. When he died, he went to Heaven and the rich guy who wasn't very nice to Lazarus went to Hell. The rich guy in Hell could see Lazarus, and begged Jesus to let Lazarus give him some water. The point is that the rich guy could see Lazarus in Heaven, from Hell. So, I could argue that if you went anywhere, you went to Hell!"

Dane shook his head, disappointed. "Think what you want, Michael. I know what happened. I know I went to Heaven. I saw it. I know it's real!"

Michael was confused. Why would God put him in yet another woeful situation? If Dane *did* go to Heaven, or see Heaven from the outside, he would never get in if he just figured everybody gets in! Jesus is the only way into Heaven. The Bible was pretty clear about this. If Dane believed he saw Heaven, Michael would have to find a way to convince Dane that it wasn't a physical choice but a spiritual one. *This is going to be tough*, Michael thought. I'm going to need some help with this one. Michael continued his confusing train of thought. So many things didn't make sense at that moment. What if he really did find Heaven? It could very well be out there somewhere. God created the universe; couldn't He have found a spot to put heaven, somewhere safe, far enough away that no one would ever find it? *What if we were supposed to find it?* he wondered suddenly.

He turned back to his friend. With all Dane had been through, Michael knew it was going to be tough to have Dane become a believer in Jesus since he was already convinced he'd found Heaven. And even if Dane said yes to Jesus and accepted Christ, would he really do it for the right reasons?

Michael had to rely on God now, he realized. Only He knew Dane's heart. Then he thought of the bigger picture. What if Dane *did* go to Heaven, and somehow this got out? People might start believing in Heaven, but not in Jesus.

This is crazy, Michael thought. If God knows everything, past, present and future, He must know that we found Heaven. That's another reason why we probably didn't! He put a hand to his head; this was such deep philosophy that he was having trouble hanging onto it.

"Think what you want Mike, but we discovered Heaven!'" Dane was shouting. Michael could sense the urgency in his voice, and realized that he was struggling with Michael's lack of belief. He looked puzzled. "I know what you're thinking, Michael. You think that if word of this discovery gets out, it will change everything. And I do mean everything!" Dane put a heavy emphasis on his last word.

Michael sniped back, "Christianity is based on faith. But no one needs faith if they have proof!" Michael was struggling with his faith and science. The scientist in him wanted desperately to believe that Dane had somehow discovered Heaven. But the Christian wanted to keep the faith. Michael was torn. He got up and walked over to the window to look silently at the ocean in the distance. He was deep in thought, the wheels in his mind spinning. "I still think it's possible that you hallucinated the entire thing. We've never put a human being in Marilyn. How is it possible that you could breathe in that green gas? There are so many questions. You're right about one thing, though – it would change things. Maybe Marilyn's whole purpose was to make you feel better. You want to live now, right?"

"Yes, I do." Dane started to sob. "I thought I saw Diana there."

Michael stared at Dane. "WHAT?"

"There was a young woman. I didn't really make the connection, but she looked just like Diana. Michael, I want to become a Christian, so I can get in. I want to become a Christian right now, what do I have to do?"

Michael chuckled, walked back over to the chair next to the bed, and sat down. "First of all, you need to do some soul searching. You have to do it for the right reasons. I've always tried to convince people to become Christian. Shoot, I've spent my life doing that, and have shown lots of people how to do it; it's really simple. But in your case, I think you need to do some soul searching. Pray about it. I never told you this the other night, but I came to find you because I wanted to talk to you about that very thing; I wanted to talk you about becoming a Christian. I was convinced the time was right. I thought it might give you hope again. Shoot, I even thought that God was pushing me to find you, But now with this discovery, if you really found, I mean, believe you found Heaven, I don't think the time is right anymore. I don't think you would do it for the right reasons. Do me a favor Dane. Pray about it. When the time's right I'll help you, but not right now."

Michael and Dane walked into the early morning Bible study, each holding a tall latte. Michael introduced Dane to the group.

"This is my assistant from work; he's staying with me for a few days."

It was a small group this morning, only four other men. Michael sat down next to his good friend, Phil, who was dressed in jeans and a tee shirt, and laughed.

"You look like you've been out surfing already!" he muttered to his friend.

"No man, late night." Phil sounded tired. "I'm calling in sick and going back to bed the minute we're done."

The man at the end of the table laughed and added, "Phil, we'll try to keep to the schedule today!"

That was Pastor Mark, the senior pastor of the church, also a good friend of Michael's. He turned to the other men now, and began. "Shall we get started? Phil, would you lead us in prayer?"

"Guys," Michael interrupted. "Before we get started, I need to let you all know something."

Dane was nervous, thinking Michael was going to tell them about their discovery.

"I found out a couple weeks ago that Ruth has been cheating on me."

"What?" Phil sounded completely floored.

Michael lowered his head. "Yep. I'm not going to go into details, but I will say this; it's been going on for a long, long time. I'm going to file for a divorce."

Phil leaned over and put his arm around Michael. "I'll be there for you, buddy; if there's anything I can do, you let me know. But right now, how about we pray?"

"Ok," Michael whispered.

Phil bowed his head and prayed out loud. "Good morning, Lord." Phil always started his morning prayers like that. He always talked to God like he was standing with him in the room. As far as Phil was concerned, he always was! "Thank You for another beautiful morning. Lord, we are so blessed that You have made this stunning creation we call Earth just for us. I thank You for that, and for loving each of us so much and so unconditionally. I ask You, Heavenly Father, to be with our friend and Your son Mike. Comfort him, Father, and comfort his family as they go through this difficult time."

Dane shifted in his chair when he heard Phil mention Heaven. He thought back to what he had seen, and smiled.

Phil continued, "Father, lead us today in our study and help us learn from Your word and Your examples. Help us to become more like Jesus every day. Amen."

All the men in the group each added their own 'Amen.'

Pastor Mark started the discussion by bringing up a business meeting he had attended the night before. Michael didn't hear a word Pastor Mark was saying. His mind was still in the clouds. He was lost in his own thoughts, but tried to focus on what was going on around him.

"Michael." Phil looked at Michael, leaning over to look in his eyes. "You ok, man?"

"Yeah, sorry. I'm just not here this morning. You wouldn't believe the time I've had the last couple of weeks. What a nightmare. You would think God could make life a little simpler, a little easier!"

"Well I'm all for calling this thing right here and going home." Phil wasn't feeling any better, and was anxious to go home and crawl into bed.

At this point Mark spoke up. "Before you go, I have a gift for your friend. I'll be right back."

Pastor Mark got up and left the room. Michael looked at Phil, who shrugged as if to say he didn't know what Mark was doing. Within seconds, pastor Mark came back in with a brand new Bible. He handed it to Dane.

"I like to give this to anyone seeking the truth. And there are lots of comforting words in there for you in your time of need."

"Thank you," Dane said humbly.

Phil looked around the room, "Guys, I think that's enough for today. Let's get out of here."

Michael and Dane got into the car and drove back to Sem-Con. Dane sat in the passenger seat, looking at Michael with bewilderment. Finally he spoke.

"So Michael, why would God let this happen to you …

to your family? I mean, there's a lot of hurt there. Wouldn't a loving God guard you from this? Why wouldn't He keep Ruth from falling into this trap of sin?"

Michael kept his eyes on the road and sighed.

Dane realized that question was pretty harsh and offered a quick apology.

Michael smiled grimly. "It's okay Dane, I understand. And I've asked myself that question a million times. What it comes down to, I guess, is free will, and the fact that it's not about *me*! You see, when I became a Christian, I said yes to Jesus and yes to what's good for His kingdom, not necessarily what's best for me! I gave up my life, my will for His! Along with that comes some heartache. That's one of the reasons I told you to think about what you're doing; I mean like I said, it's got to be for the right reason. That's one of the things you have to consider. Anyway, for now I just have to believe that I am right where God wants me. This is something God approved when He planned my life. I don't understand it, but I'm still a fan of Jesus, and God's master plan. But believe me Dane, I'll have my long talk with Him someday! One of these days, He's going to tell me why."

Dane nodded quietly. "Michael, what do you think Heaven will be like? I mean you believe in it so much, you must have an idea, right?"

"Well Dane, I see it like this. First of all, it's hard to imagine eternity, because of how we were created, but imagine you had all the time in the world to do something, without any pressure or stress at all. Like reading a book, or even writing a book while sitting on your favorite beach. Now imagine the absolute perfect setting, like temperature, warm ocean breeze in your face, the feel of the sand under your feet. Now imagine the perfect lighting, maybe a beer in your hand."

Dane laughed. "Beer in Heaven?"

"Sure, why not? God gave us everything to make it, so why couldn't we make it in Heaven? We're the ones who screw up His creation here on Earth, by using beer to get drunk. That doesn't mean we can't enjoy it, right?

"I guess so," Dane said slowly.

"Besides, that's the product of sin and in Heaven, sin won't exist! Now picture this; you feel completely relaxed and carefree, and you feel more love than you ever thought possible. That might describe Heaven for just a few minutes. I think it's going to be so incredible. Now imagine if you were a father whose baby son was killed in a car accident or by cancer. I believe you will be able to raise that baby in Heaven, so you don't miss out on a thing! You see, with God, anything is possible! That's what we have to look forward to, Dane."

"Awesome," Dane said in amazement.

Michael walked into his house and shouted for the kids, but found the house still empty – they must not be home yet. He had just returned from his attorney's office and had his copy of divorce papers. He threw them on the kitchen table, feeling completely rejected. The woman who he'd thought he knew was someone that he'd never known at all. The sadness hit him hard, and he felt like the world was crashing down on him. He poured a glass of wine and went outside to his patio, where he sat on a chair, looking out at the ocean reminiscing. He remembered all the good times in that big house – Christmas mornings, birthday parties, watching baseball games with his kids… He thought about what he'd told Dane earlier about getting drunk, and humans screwing it all up.

"Well, forgive me Lord; I may just screw this up tonight, because I feel like shit!" he mumbled aloud.

A wave of sadness came over him like a tsunami and pushed him into an abyss of emotional darkness. The sadness kept coming, wave after wave, and he didn't think that he'd ever escape. How could he ever recover from this? He'd always considered himself one of the lucky ones. Someone who had hit life's lottery. He had a great job, a beautiful home in one of the most desired cities in the nation. A wonderful family. But now it was all coming apart.

"How could she do this?" he asked again, realizing that he was repeating himself again. "How could she possibly do this to us, my kids, and my beautiful family? How could she do this?"

He sipped the wine and contemplated his options. The divorce was really happening, but he was having second thoughts. Could he stay with Ruth? he wondered. He had been so in love with her from the first time they met. After their second date, he had come home and told his parents that he would marry her. And he did. He had never been happier. She was truly his dream girl.

But after four kids and thirty years together, in what Michael thought was a very happy marriage, it looked like she had been wasting it all away for a long time. She wasn't real, it was all make believe, all fake! This was more than a nightmare. How could this really be happening? In desperation, Michael turned to the one friend who had been there all along. He bowed his head and talked to God.

"Lord, how could this happen?" he cried out. "Help me! Free choice is one thing, but this? This is more than free choice! Couldn't You protect my family a little more, God? I mean, this is crazy. I thought You hated divorce. Isn't that what the Bible says? God hates divorce? Well, You must be getting used to it. Half the marriages today end in divorce. Thanks a lot. I thought You were better than this, God! You could have protected us, but no, You have to make your point by allowing free choice. Well, take Your free choice and stick it."

Michael got up and threw his empty wine glass over the railing to the rocks below, then walked back inside, went to his office, and opened the bottom desk drawer. He took out his pistol and walked back to his chair on the deck.

"I should be so happy," he thought. "I've been through so much. I've loved more than I ever thought possible. But it's just not fair. It's not fair to my kids. Their lives have been rocked by a very selfish person, someone I thought I knew. This *sucks!*"

He thought about the past few weeks. Ruth had told some lies about Michael to a few of their friends at church. She was trying to hang on to the friends, saying Michael was abusive, among other things. Michael knew it was in desperation to hold on to some support. Most of their friends didn't believe her, but a few did, and it hurt Michael to the core. He was watching the devil take his life apart bit by bit. It was more than he could bear.

Michael loaded two bullets in the chamber, then sat back down and turned his gaze toward the sky. "God, I've tried to live a good life, I have tried to make You proud. I've tried to make my parents proud. Isn't that what life is all about? I've always held on to what's good in this world, what's right. I describe myself as a boring middle-aged guy, but what's wrong with that? That's who I am! I love God, I love my country, and I love sticking up and fighting for what's right! And I know what's right now, and I could never stay with a woman who has done this, it's too much to carry. There are just too many things wrong here. I guess what I've figured out through all of this is that life is about loving and letting go. I'm tired of this life, Lord. I really don't want to be here anymore. It's time for me to let go. I want to go back to that place I visited in my dream, the place that Dane went. I'm so tired of fighting this God, I want to start my life with You, in Heaven."

All the wine was clouding Michael's thought process. "I know it's real now, so I have no fear. I always did, but now … now I know it's out there. I told Dane I didn't believe him, but I do. I really do. He found it didn't he? I ache to be there with You. I know I'm not supposed to play God, so I hope You can forgive me. I don't want to live anymore."

Michael closed his eyes, and breathed in the cool evening air. He held the gun in his outstretched arms and pointed it at his forehead, clumsily touching the trigger with his sweaty thumb. He opened his eyes and took a long look at the ocean, listening to the waves crashing below. He waited to hear God's voice one more time. He would give anything to hear from God again.

God knew that this was Michael's deepest need and darkest hour, but He was silent.

*Free choice*, Michael thought.

He looked at the barrel of the gun staring back at him. Strange, he thought, how such a cold, inanimate object could end his life so quickly. He whispered, "Please Lord, forgive me for this sin."

Tears formed and slowly trickled down his cheeks, and with a trembling hand, Michael squeezed the trigger.

# Chapter 27

**Marcy and Seth** were walking along the beach a few hundred yards away from Michael's house. They were neighbors of Michael and Ruth, had known them for about five years. They had both become good friends with the couple, and got together every few weeks for barbeques, wine, and cards. As they walked hand in hand on the beach, they heard a gunshot over the sounds of the ocean.

"My God, what was that?" shouted Marcy.

They looked up toward Michael's house, and saw a large plate glass window come crashing to the deck below.

"That's Michael's house!" Marcy covered her mouth in shock.

Seth started running up the beach to the stairs that led to the deck behind Michael's house. When he reached the top, he saw Michael slumped over on the deck. It looked like he had fallen forward. There were shards of glass all around him. Something had broken the window, and it now it lay in a thousand pieces all around Michael.

"Mike, Mike, are you alright?" Just then Seth saw the gun. "Oh my God!"

Marcy got to the top of the steps and saw Michael laying on the deck, Seth hunched over him.

"Seth, what happened?"

"Marcy, call 911!" Seth yelled.

Seth shook Michael and gently rolled him over. He saw the gun and imagined what could have happened, but couldn't find any blood on the man, and certainly no bullet wound.

Michael rolled his eyes suddenly and looked up at Seth.

"Michael, are you ok?"

"Yeah, I'm alright," he said.

"What the hell happened? What's with the gun?"

Michael suddenly felt very ashamed. "I thought about killing myself. Well, I guess I did more than *think* about it. I actually tried, but I guess I was shaking so badly when I pulled the trigger that I missed. When the bullet hit the window, it exploded right behind me, and I think it knocked me off my chair. I must have smacked my head."

Seth rubbed the large lump that was forming on Michael's temple. "I'd say you hit it pretty hard." Seth heard sirens in the distance, and looked back into Michael's eyes. "You're also damn lucky that this bump is the worst of your injuries."

Dane had been back in his apartment for a few days now. Michael had been gracious enough to put him up until he was officially released to be on his own. He thought now about the moments that had led to him trying to end his life, and sighed. He had come to the conclusion, thanks to long chat sessions with his therapist, that Marilyn had actually played a role in his hasty decision.

He had never really thought about the future. He'd focused too much on the past; growing up with his father largely absent, then the last year before his mom died. And then Diana's death, which Dane had mistakenly blamed himself for. He had come to the realization now, though, that he had a lot to live for, and even more to be grateful for. It took a while, and he knew there would still be dark days ahead, but Dane was beginning to feel alive again.

And part of that was due to Michael's insistence that Dane read the Bible. Dane found it very comforting, almost like getting to know a new friend. This Jesus Dane had been reading about in the Bible was a very intriguing guy. He was so full of love that Dane found it hard to comprehend. He also found it fascinating.

At first, Dane read the beginning of the New Testament. That was Michael's recommendation, as he wanted Dane to spend some time getting to know Jesus first. Then Dane wanted to know more about Heaven. He was still convinced that he had found it out there in space, but Michael said he still didn't believe.

He had asked Michael where he could read more about Heaven in the Bible and Michael had recommended reading Revelation, the last book. But Michael also warned him that it was a difficult read. It was lots of dream interpretations from one of Jesus's disciples, some guy named John, and it could be confusing. Sounded interesting to Dane, so he began reading one night while his dogs curled up at his feet on the couch. He got so into it that he read the entire chapter. But this led to many questions that needed answering. One thing Dane had learned through this whole experience was not to wait.

He learned from Michael not to wait to tell your friends that you loved them – something Dane started doing every day. The other thing he had learned was not to let questions about his Christian journey wait. Michael always said that if he had to talk, no matter what time – day or night – he would be there.

Dane was about to put that to the test. He put the Bible down, grabbed his car keys, kissed his dogs' goodbye, and headed over to Michael's. Dane was sure Michael could use someone to talk to anyway.

When Dane turned down Michael's street, he saw police cars. His heart leapt into this throat. "Oh no, what now?"

Dane got out and tried to get to the driveway, but was stopped by police tape and a cop standing guard at the entrance to the walkway.

"I'm his friend, what's going on?" he asked, worried.

All the cop would say was that there had been a shooting. Dane immediately thought the worst. He imagined that Ruth had gotten mad and decided to kill Michael. Or what if Michael had exacted revenge on Ruth for ruining their lives?

"Please sir, tell me what's going on, my boss lives here! Is he alright?"

The policeman finally sympathized with Dane. He could see the concern on the young man's face, and decided that he could give him at least some information.

"Just a minute, young man, wait right here," he said. He turned and talked to another cop, who was filling out some paperwork.

Dane looked toward the house and could see that they were about to put someone into the ambulance. He dashed forward, ducked under the tape, and ran toward the gurney. It was Michael.

Michael looked up, shocked to see Dane running toward him. "Dane, what are you doing here?"

Just then the policeman grabbed Dane's arm and started pulling him back toward the street.

"Michael," Dane said franticly, "are you okay?"

Michael yelled to the officer, "Please, give me a minute. Please, sir?"

The cop nodded in agreement, and released Dane, who ran back toward his boss.

Michael said, "I'm fine Dane, I'm just an idiot!"

"Michael," Dane said excitedly, "If you're really okay, I need to ask you a favor. I'm just so excited; finally I get it! I'm not sure if what I saw was real, but I want it … I want what you have. I want the relationship you have with Jesus! I've spent the last few days reading the Bible; I even read Revelation! Michael, I need to have that. I need to know that when I die, I'm going to go back there, to be with Diana. Please tell me what I need to do!"

Michael was stunned. It seemed like Jesus had been working on Dane's heart. He reached out and took hold of Dane's hand. The paramedics told Michael that they needed to get going, but Michael insisted. This would only take a minute.

"Please, this is really important." Michael looked at Dane, took a deep breath, and said, "Dane, it's so easy, all you need to do is ask Jesus into your heart. Close your eyes and pray with me, Dane." Dane closed his eyes. Surprisingly, so did the two paramedics standing next to Michael.

Michael said, "Dane, just repeat this prayer after me. Heavenly Father, I know I'm a sinner, and I ask Your forgiveness." Michael paused as Dane repeated his words in a whisper. Then he continued. "Lord, I want to know You and Your son Jesus. Please know that I accept Jesus as my savior, and from this day forward I'm going to do my best to follow Him. I ask Your guidance, especially in times of weakness. I thank You, God. Take me and mold me from this day forward into Your servant. I ask you these things in name of your son Jesus. Amen."

Dane said 'amen' and opened his eyes. He was surprised to see that Michael had been crying.

"Thank you Michael, I love you man."

Michael smiled, "I love you too, brother! Now go get yourself baptized and make it official"

The paramedics moved forward then to load Michael into the ambulance, and closed the doors behind him. As they started down the driveway, Dane could see Michael half sitting up, looking out the back window. Dane gave Michael a thumbs up as he rolled away.

Michael only spent one day in the hospital, mostly talking to mental health doctors and nurses. They didn't feel that he was a threat to himself anymore. Michael was good at convincing them to let him go. They let him go home almost immediately, and Michael realized that he had made a huge mistake. Through it all, God had given Michael a gripping testimony. Infidelity had taken away his life; at least that was how Michael had first looked at it. Now he saw it for what it really was: sin. Nothing more, nothing less, just a weak person who fell into a cycle of sin. Dane's conversion had helped Michael feel he had a new purpose in life. When Michael walked out of the hospital, he knew his life had meaning and that gave Michael hope again.

Jesus preached that we would have trouble in this world, but not to worry, because He had overcome the world. Michael realized that he needed to accept the things that life threw at him. Instead of complaining or getting mad at God, he was learning to see trouble as a way of sharing Jesus with a sinful world.

Waves of sadness came and went still, and Michael learned to reach out for help when the lows hit. Dane had become such a good friend through all this, since they had shared many of the same circumstances. Invariably, Dane was the one person Michael leaned on the most.

The suicide attempt was dumb, and Michael knew it. He

thought of it as a halfhearted attempt, even though he was only a few inches from ending his life. Now God had given Michael's life a new purpose, one he should have had all along. He had it five years ago after the near-death experience, but had somehow lost it. Michael vowed to never lose sight of his goal again. And that was to share Jesus Christ with the world, or at least his world, no matter how small. God said to grow where you were planted, and that was something that Michael was going to really work on.

Purpose was what Michael had asked for, and God had once again delivered, although in His own time, not Michael's. Michael had already seen God make a difference in Dane's life. He was reminded of the scripture, "And we know that in all things God works for the good of those who love him, who have been called according to his purpose."

Jesus had left the flock to find one lost sheep. Michael realized that Dane coming to know Jesus was worth his entire life, even with all the pain. Like he had told Dane time and time again, when you became a Christian, you did what was good for the kingdom of God, not necessarily what was good for you. Michael had strayed from that philosophy lately, and knew it would take some work to get back on track.

A knock on Michael's door interrupted his thoughts, and brought him back to the real world. He got up from his desk in the office, and went to open the door. He saw a man who looked vaguely familiar.

The man smiled when he saw Michael. "Do you remember me?" asked the man.

Michael struggled for a few seconds, but couldn't put his finger on who this guy was.

"Let me refresh your memory, Michael."

Michael thought, *that's strange, he obviously knows who I am!*

"I was here the night you tried to shoot yourself."

"Of course, the paramedic!"

"Yeah, that's right. I had to come by and tell you, or thank you would be more appropriate. When you led your friend to the Lord, I prayed right along with you both, and I needed that, Michael. I needed to become a Christian and I knew it. It was amazing timing, man, simply amazing. So I want to say thanks for bringing me to Jesus!" The man was smiling ear to ear. "I feel like I belong now. I needed Jesus more than you'll ever know. I see some pretty bad stuff out there, you know, on the job. And now I look for opportunities to share my faith. So God's really using you, man. Thank you."

Michael stepped out onto his front porch and hugged the man. "You're welcome," he said. "What's your name?"

"It's Jim."

"Well, it's great to have you in the family and great to meet you Jim. Thank you for coming by and letting me know. I appreciate it."

"Sure. Thanks again, maybe we can get together sometime for coffee or something and I'll tell you my story, and exactly why I really needed Jesus!" Jim turned and walked back out to his car. He smiled before opening his door, and waved.

Michael whispered, "Thank You Lord, you sure don't disappoint, do you!" And then it hit him; *One more lost sheep*, Michael thought. *Jesus saved another soul all because of my stupid suicide attempt. And that happened because of my wife's sin. One tragic event and another life completely changed, for eternity. Thank you Jesus!*

Dane hadn't been back to the Bean and Leaf since Diana's tragic death. He swallowed heavily as he opened the door for Michael, then straightened his shoulders. The two of them walked in and took their place at the back of the line.

Michael inhaled and smiled. "You're right Dane, it does smell good in here."

"I told you, Mike!"

Just then Mitch saw Dane and left his place behind the counter to walk over to the two of them. Mitch held his arms open and hugged Dane. "How you doing, man, hanging in there?"

Dane looked sad but managed to fight back tears. "I'm doing ok Mitch, and you?"

"Same old stuff around here, Dane. Saving the world, one latte at a time!" The three of them laughed. It was good to laugh again, Michael thought.

The woman in line in front of Michael turned to share in their laughter and noticed Michael's shirt. He was wearing a polo shirt with the logo of a golf course near his home. "Hey, Balboa Bay Golf Course," she said. "You play there?"

Michael was surprised and said, "Every once in a while … do you play golf?"

"Why yes," she said. "I love golf! That course is right by my house!"

"Hey, we must be neighbors, it's near my house too!"

"Well," she said, "we should get together and play there sometime. I'm not the greatest golfer in the world, but I love getting out in the beauty of nature and chasing that little white ball around!"

Michael laughed. "Me too. Yeah, that would be great. Does your husband play?"

"Oh," said the woman. "I'm not married. Are you?"

Michael knew he would get this question eventually, and it stirred all kinds of emotion in him. "I'm going through a divorce," he said. He couldn't help but sound sad.

"Well, my divorce was final a few days ago," the woman said. "So I know what you're going through. If I can be of any help, let me know. Here's my card. My name is Melissa."

She reached into her purse and pulled out a business card and handed it to Michael. "And I'm serious about golf. Let's get together and play sometime!"

"Ok, thank you. A round of golf might be just what the doctor ordered. I'll call you."

Michael was a little overwhelmed. Melissa was a beautiful blond woman, around Michael's age, with eyes the color of the Pacific Ocean on a bright sunny day. Michael thought to himself, *I can do this. I haven't dated, or even so much as looked at another woman in years, but I can do this.*

He spoke before he could change his mind. "You know what, let's just make a date right now. You have your calendar? How's Saturday, about noon? We could get a bite to eat, then hit the course!"

"Wow, you don't waste any time do you?"

Michael smiled at Melissa, then turned and winked at Dane. "I've been told that!"

Melissa smiled and said, "Sure that would be really fun. Saturday works! I guess I should know your name!"

"I'm so sorry, its Michael. Michael Owens."

"Alright Michael Owens, I'll see you this weekend."

Michael shook Melissa's hand. As he did, he felt more at ease about his life and his future than he had in months. He couldn't really explain it, but meeting Melissa, even just talking to her, felt good. As he sat down with Dane he wondered … if God really was his Heavenly Father, then He would act like a father. So maybe he sent Melissa to make Michael feel better. *If my son broke up with his girlfriend and felt lonely and betrayed, the natural reaction of any father would be to fix him up with a nice, deserving woman,* he thought. *Life is not meant to be lived alone!*

Dane looked at Michael inquisitively and said, "I have to ask Mike, because it struck me as funny when I heard it. That night I came back, I heard a guy say 'Code Reginald.' What the heck is that? It's actually bugged me ever since I heard it, but there was quite a bit more going on at the time."

Michael laughed. "There sure was. It's a really funny story. Code Reginald was named after Frank's puppy. It's a security protocol."

Dane laughed. "Seriously?" he asked.

"Yeah, the puppy, a standard poodle about ten weeks old, was sitting with Frank's little boys, ages four and six, in their bedroom. Apparently the boys had fed Reginald a bag of treats, which Reginald eagerly gobbled up. Frank happened to walk by the bedroom about the time the puppy had to go. He recognized the squatting position and the familiar arch of the puppy's back.

"Frank panicked and yelled, 'No, go potty outside, go potty outside!' He ran in, grabbed the puppy by the scruff of the neck, and ran toward the front door, the puppy dangling from Frank's fingers. It was too late. The puppy left a line of brown liquid behind; an entire bag of treats will do that to a puppy's tummy. The boys watched in horror as Frank ran toward the front door. By the time he reached the tile of the entry way, the dog was done. Frank looked back at the dark brown, stinky line he had helped create. He realized that in the chaos, he had wiped out several toys, a baseball glove, and a pair of his tennis shoes that he'd left by the door. Frank loved those shoes.

"So, the name 'Code Reginald' was born. A code meaning in a medical emergency, a path needed to be cleared!"

The two men laughed uncontrollably. Just then, Mitch

walked up to the table carrying two cups. "Here you go guys, two lattes."

"Thanks Mitch," Dane said, smiling at his friend. "Thanks for everything."

Mitch patted Dane's back. "Let me know if you need anything else, kid!"

# Chapter 28

**Michael unlocked the** front door and pushed his way inside, holding a bag of groceries. As always, Duke was there, helping open the door.

"Anybody home?" he called, not sure if any of the kids were there. No one answered. Michael put the groceries away, walked into the office, and sat down at his desk. Duke had already jumped up on the leather couch in front of him.

Michael had always wanted to write a book, and now seemed like the perfect time to start. He'd been thinking about it for several days, and had finally decided to begin. He thought, *this must be my purpose in life; that's why God let me live after the dream and why He made that bullet miss my head ... to write a book and bring hope to people; to share God's love and let them know that Heaven is real!* He turned on his computer and started writing.

"I am not a writer. I'm just a boring, middle-aged guy who has a fascination with Heaven!"

Printed in the USA
CPSIA information can be obtained
at www.ICGtesting.com
CBHW031206090224
4218CB00006B/81

9 781432 796297